MISTER DOCTOR BLO

JOHN TYNE

MISTER DOCTOR BLO

1973   HOUGHTON MIFFLIN COMPANY BOSTON

MISTER DOCTOR BLO

1

As Assistant Director of Medical Services in the Far Eastern State of Banianok I was often faced with ticklish problems that the Director did not want to deal with himself. He had been appointed when the country achieved Independence, the reasons being that he was the only native-born doctor over forty not making more in private practice than he could in government service, and that he was a second cousin of the President. He sat shivering in his office, which the air-conditioner kept at fifty-five Fahrenheit, in front of an austere and uncluttered desk the size of a snooker-table, popping different-coloured pills into his mouth every four hours or so, and left most of the work to me. This suited me very well. He spent about four months of each year attending medical congresses in various parts of the world, and another month in different Western capitals, but usually London, taking treatment for his nerves; he also had a month's leave each year; consequently he knew very little of what was going on in the Ministry of Health. He had a large, solid-gold American fountain-pen which had been presented to him by the Russian Ambassador to Cuba on the occasion of the First World Congress of Non-Aligned Heart Specialists in Havana, and with this he dutifully signed everything, or nearly everything, I laid before him.

But occasionally the system went wrong, and a problem reached him without having passed through my hands first. Which is what had happened this particular morning. I was just starting work on some written complaints by a group of Korean doctors who had recently joined the service, when I heard a scratching at the door. It opened a foot and the Director squeezed through it. He closed it behind him.

'Doctor!' he cried hoarsely, 'there is a woman outside.' Though we had been working together for five years he still addressed me as 'doctor', and I, perforce, addressed him the same way.

'What is it about?'

'Very angry, Doctor. And ... large size.' He looked upwards. If she had been standing two feet away from him and he had been looking into her eyes, that would have made her approximately six feet six.

'Is she foreign?'

'British, Doctor. Very angry; very big.'

'What is she angry about?'

'Case of assault.'

'Surely the police are the people to deal with that?'

'One of our male nurses involved. She is the sister on the leprosy ward. She assaulted the male nurse on the ward. Very bad case!'

When he said that, I thought I knew what it was all about. He was still pleading with me. I cut him short. 'All right, send her in.'

'Oh, thank you, thank you, Doctor! Please be very firm. Coming here upsetting our department, when we have so much vital work to do ...' By the time he reached the door, there was a smirk on his face. He thought that, because he was afraid of me, everybody was.

But Doreen was not.

'Oh, it's you,' she said as she came in at the door. 'I thought I was going to see the big shot.'

'I am the big shot,' I said, rising, trying to make a little joke. 'The Director's rather busy today. He asked me to see you.'

'Don't give me that shit! I know he's in there; and I know he does bugger-all all day. He's just scared, isn't he?'

'What was it about?' I asked.

'You know bloody well what it's about. It's about that hospital assistant, what's his name ... ?'

2

'Haji Ahmed,' I supplied.

'That's him—Haji Ahmed. You know all about it.'

I picked up a piece of paper that was lying on my desk. It was cheap, lined paper such as can be bought in the bazaar for sixpence a pad. It was foolscap size, but all the writing was crammed into the top eighth of the page, leaving the rest completely blank. It was addressed to the Director of Medical Services in English. (Although the country had been independent for five years English was still the official language of government correspondence.)

Dear Sir,

I have the honour to report that on 25 inst last, at 16.45 hours Sister Trimmer made the assault on me, causing me to get faeces on my hub-caps. This assault was abrupt and audacious (abruptly audacious), and hoping for you to take early action without hesitation (not overlooking possibility of dismissal).

With best wishes and hopes for satisfactory outcome, I remain,

Yours humbly,

signed, Haji Ahmed bin Deris.

Following the signature there was an indelible stamp with the government's coat of arms and 'Holder allowed to stay 7 days'. Ahmed's brother worked in the Immigration Department.

I passed it across to her. 'I don't see how you caused him to get faeces on his hub-caps.'

'His bicycle fell into the open drain in front of the hospital. That's where the drivers have their crap. I'm always telling them not to.'

'I see. I suppose he'll say you threw it there.'

'He dropped it in himself.'

'It's difficult to understand why he'd do that.'

'He says I knocked him down, then I picked up his precious bicycle and threw it in the culvert.'

'And did you?'

3

'Look at me. Do I look capable of knocking down a lout of his size? Do I?'

I looked. It was true that he was a man and she was a woman; it was true that though he was not very big he was certainly well covered; but if I were asked for a straight yes or no answer, I would have had to say yes. She was about 5ft 10in and must have weighed over 140 pounds; she had big hands and feet, and big, high shoulders. She sat back in her chair, one unshaven leg crossed over the other, a stained flip-flop dangling from the toes of her free foot. Her feet were very brown from the sun, but the callouses on her toes showed up chalky-white through the tan, and the skin over the bunion on her left foot had not gone brown but bright red. She wore no make-up; her hair was slightly longer than an urchin cut and it was pulled back in a rubber band, producing an inch-long docked pony tail. There were white, dried sweat stains under her arms.

'God, this place makes me sick. Where else in the world do you think you'd get a man bringing an unarmed assault case against a woman?' When she spoke only the right half of her mouth worked; but the other half continued to tremble with rage.

'He's not exactly bringing a case against you,' I said. 'It's just an intra-departmental complaint. The police aren't involved.'

'No doubt *that* can be arranged if necessary.'

I paused. I was not very good at this sort of thing. I said, 'I have heard that your relations with the indigenous staff are not very good.'

'Have you? Have you just? Well, isn't that brilliant! You must keep your ear very close to the ground.'

'Look, I'm not trying to lecture you, Doreen—but this sort of thing gets known.'

'I haven't made any secret of it.'

'That's the trouble. It makes it difficult for the other volunteers —the Volunteers for Peace and the Peace Corps—if one of their number is too outspoken.'

'And you know how much I care about that?' She leaned forward dangerously.

'Volunteers are in a rather ambiguous position,' I went on

4

hastily. 'They tend to become political pawns. For example, if anybody takes it into his head to attack Britain or America he can say the Peace Corps and the V.P.O.s are layabouts and should be sent home. Of course we know they're not,' I said quickly. 'But whenever they put the slightest foot out of place it always gets very much magnified.'

'I see. So for the sake of international peace I should go back to the hospital and apologize to Ahmed for taking offence. He said I smelled like a jungle pig. Maybe I do. Maybe you think so too.'

She was leaning forward right over my desk, her hands spread on my blotter. 'Sit down, Doreen,' I said. 'Tell me what happened.'

For a moment she did not move. Then she sat down. She left the damp imprint of her fingers on the blotter. Although it was only 9.00 a.m. the temperature was already in the high eighties.

'What's the use?' she said. 'You're on their side. You've got to do what they say.'

'I can't do anything for anybody unless I know what happened.'

She snarled, 'It was nothing special. It happens every day with one or other of them. They're all bloody useless from the top to the bottom. I'm the sister of the ward, he's the chief male nurse. I'm the boss. I told him to get the lavatories cleaned. He said they'd been cleaned already. I said they smelled. He said they didn't smell. He said it was myself I was smelling. So then I hit him.'

'But how did his bicycle come to be involved?'

'It was just in front of the hospital. He was just going off duty, and I'd told him to get it done three hours before.'

'Were there any people about?'

'Only about fifty.'

I breathed out slowly. 'It could look bad.'

'It would have looked a lot worse if I'd done what I felt like doing.'

'Assault is a serious matter here—more so than in England. It's not the physical injury, it's the loss of face. And he's just been on the Haj; he's just come back from Mecca—he's Haji

5

Ahmed now—quite a personage. I'm afraid it would look rather bad for you if this got out, Doreen.'

'Would it? Of course! Right! Give me a bit of paper and dictate the apology.' She clamped each hand under the opposite armpit and rocked forward then backward, her lips trembling. 'Go on. How do I start? "My very dear Haji Ahmed ..." Well, go on, what do I say next?'

Through the jalousies came the sound of cornets and drums. She looked up, we both paused, then she said:

'That'll be the Commander-in-Chief of the Army off on his latest picnic.' She clenched her teeth. 'Bastard!'

'You know him?'

'Know him? I live in the same quarters as the girl who's sleeping with him.'

'Who's that?'

She looked across at me contemptuously. 'I thought you knew everything.... Doris Krenwinckle.'

'A British girl?'

'With a name like that? No—Yank. Peace Corps. Ugly big bitch. A girl would have to be desperate to go with a little runt like him, but she's desperate all right!'

'How did it happen?'

'Who knows. One of his parties, where he invites all the Peace Corps—I suppose it happened there. God knows she's desperate, but how a girl could insult her body that way ... You know the latest thing? The silly bitch says he's going to marry her; when he gets back from this trip he's going on to buy her a ring. Poor little cow! She believes it. You'd think when she'd got to her age she'd have learned a bit of savvy. She's knocking thirty if she's a day.'

I was immediately interested. Thirty was what Doreen was 'knocking' too. I went to the balcony and pulled back the jalousie (unlike the Director I did not have air-conditioning). Medical Headquarters was a long, low building with widely overhanging roofs. We were on the first floor. The Abang Yusuf, Commander-in-Chief of the Armed Forces, was at that very moment riding by on a white horse, surrounded by his bodyguard on motor-bikes, with drawn truncheons.

'Look at the stupid big ham!' She had joined me on the balcony. 'Who's he going off to impress this time?'

He trotted off in the direction of the river. Every now and then the horse reared up and the Abang leaned forward in a western saddle it would have required a cannon-ball to dislodge him from. The crowd loved it, and there was quite a crowd because all government departments had been given official permission to see the Abang setting off for the Interior.

'Do you know what I'd like to see?' she said. 'I'd like to see the rebels give him just the biggest beating he's ever had in his life. Oh boy! I'd give something for that.'

I pulled the jalousie back across the window-space and went back to my desk. She followed me.

'Tell me something! Who is this Dr Brockley anyway?'

'Mr Dr Blo Ko Lee? Don't you know?'

'I know he's the only white man left in the Interior, and he's been there about thirty years and he's leading the rebels. But what's he *like*? Everybody talks about him, but you never run across anybody who's actually met him.'

I smiled thinly. 'He's a very straightforward old man, rather shy, very old-fashioned.'

'Why do they call him Blo Ko Lee?'

'Because they find it difficult to say Brockley. The Chinese probably found it scanned better as Blo Ko Lee, and then the other races followed suit.'

'The Chinese think a lot of him, you know. Well they all do—especially the older ones. I've heard some of them go up-river to consult him when they can't get cured down here.' (There were no roads to the Interior. The only way was by river; and to Bukit Kota, Brockley's headquarters, it took three days.) 'But why should he be starting a rebellion at his age? He must be over sixty by now.'

I paused. For a moment I debated with myself; but I knew I could not entrust Doreen with the truth. 'I don't know,' I said.

She shook her head. 'Boy, if only I thought Brockley had a

chance ... Christ! wouldn't it just shake up this shower?' She stood up and looked at her watch. 'But he hasn't. And I'm supposed to be on duty. I'd better get back. I just came down to tell you to get that little bastard Ahmed off my ward or I won't be answerable for the consequences. Right?' She started to walk towards the door but I stopped her.

'Doreen! We'll have to think carefully how to handle this.'

'I know how I'm going to handle it.'

'You're only going to make it worse.'

'Me! Me make it worse?'

'Don't you see that as far as the law of this country is concerned *you* are the one at fault. It may seem very unjust, but that's the way they'll see it. Besides, he's a native and you're a foreigner. And they're always biased against volunteers to start with.'

'That's lovely. That's wonderful, isn't it? We give up a *year* of our *life* and come here to wear ourselves out trying to teach them something, and they're biased against us to start with.'

'It may seem unfair, but that's the way it is. This is going to need very delicate handling.'

'What sort of a man are you, anyway? Can you stand up for your own race when you know they're in the right, or can't you?' She strode back towards me, her eyes blazing.

'It's a very difficult situation,' I said. 'My sympathies are with you. If only you hadn't put yourself in the wrong by hitting him.'

'What should I do? Write a memorandum every time one of these natives looks at me sideways?'

'Anything's better than hitting them. Don't you realize that? I know you don't see eye to eye with most of the native staff. You're probably right in most of what you say, but they resent being criticized by a newcomer who anyway is only earning about a quarter of what they are.'

'So because we only get three pounds a week everybody's entitled to shit on us!' Her lips trembled.

'No. But they're very much more materialistic here than you think. They want to take orders from a big man with a big

8

house and a big car. You volunteers are running round with your bicycles and flip-flops, living in servants' quarters—they think you should be taking orders from them. They resent it—very deeply—when you're put over them. If you don't use extreme tact there's bound to be trouble. Haji Ahmed's a tricky character to start with. Don't you see he's probably been trying to provoke you to hit him for weeks, and you've finally done it in front of fifty witnesses.'

'So it's my fault he said I smelled like a jungle pig? And you know he's a Moslem, so a pig's really filthy to him.' Her throat tightened. 'Oh! God!' And suddenly tears were running down her cheeks. She had the same defiant expression as before, but she could not stop the tears coming. She nodded her head angrily, shaking them away, but they came even more. Suddenly she put her hands up to her eyes; her head bent forward, then her shoulders, then her whole spine from the hips. I saw the back of her neck and the coarse ends of her hair gathered into the elastic band. 'I know I smell. It's this climate. I never stop sweating. I can't help it. It's the heat ... it's the humidity. I try to do a fair day's work, but they won't let you, they won't co-operate. God! I hate this place. I ... hate ... this ... place!'

I got up and went round the desk. I started to put my arm around her, but as my hand touched her shoulder she pulled herself violently away. 'Don't touch me! I know what you're going to do. Nothing! Just hope it blows over, and if it doesn't, land me in the dirt. "I'm sorry, Mr Haji Bloody Ahmed, Sister Trimmer shouldn't have done it, let me kiss your arse and we'll send her to another ward." Well, let me tell you—' the tears were still pouring down her cheeks—'let me tell you: I hope he won't be satisfied with a snivelling reply from you; I hope he'll make it official; I hope he'll take it right to the top; I hope he'll make the biggest stink there's ever been in this place, and then I'll have a chance to tell them all what I think of them, and get myself sent home. I can't wait. Just let him do it ... just let him do it!'

I had not sat down again. She came up to where I was standing. She stood a foot in front of me and thrust her neck forward.

She was my size, perhaps half an inch bigger, but much more solidly built. 'Look at you. Look at you in your white ducks and your nice pressed white shirt, and your "Yes, sir" and "No, sir" to these apes. Don't you ever get the desire to be a man and tell them where they get off?... No.' She shook her head violently and a couple of tears splashed on to my shirt front. 'Then you wouldn't be drawing a nice fat salary any more, would you? You'd have to go back to England and really work. Well I've warned you. You let Ahmed go ahead with that complaint and see what happens.'

She turned round and lunged from the room. She did not close the door behind her. I did not feel angry or hurt. I had passed that sort of thing long ago. I just analysed the smell she had left behind her. It was steak and kidney pudding. I reflected how much of our lives are based on arbitrary preconceptions: it was surely no more than an arbitrary preconception that steak-and-kidney-pudding smell should be so good on a steak and kidney pudding, but so unpleasant on a girl.

2

The Abang's expedition against the rebels in the Interior ended the same afternoon when his boat sank an hour up-river from Banianok. He came back to town two inches shorter because he had kicked off his built-up morocco leather boots while swimming for his life; but apart from that he was no worse for the accident.

We heard no more of the Abang for a while, but Haji Ahmed was not so easily forgotten.

The Director put his signature to a letter which said:

Dear Mr Haji Ahmed,

Thank you for your letter of the 18th September. I am very interested in what you say and I am taking appropriate action.

He hoped that Ahmed might be mollified by that and gradually forget the whole thing. But Ahmed did not. His reply came three weeks later. At the leisurely Banianok pace of doing things this was equivalent to return of post and indicated how seriously he took the matter.

Dear Dr Yusuf,

After humble greetings:

Your letter gives great hopes for me and all oppressed peoples. As you know I will always get well to my job with good difficulties or not as the case may be. Except for Sister Trimmer attacking me in areas of my body and mind (and

11

other areas), all without hint of precept or preamble. Therefore you better sack her.

Hoping (a) early satisfaction with happy issue (b) you keeping well yourself.

Yours faithfully and sincerely ...

I impressed on the Director that this was something he must handle personally, since if I were involved racial bias would be alleged. Four weeks later he had not talked to Ahmed, and the following editorial appeared in the *Banianok Herald* (the paper was printed in English):

When a Senior Hospital Assistant is attacked in the course of his lawful duties by an Overseas Volunteer bigger and stronger than himself, surely the time has come. It is well known that Volunteers are bigger and heavier than Banianok citizens because our foodstuffs and resources were exported away from us in the dark years of Colonialism to enrich Western Capitalists and fatten Western children. If our ancestors had been allowed to eat the food they grew themselves our Hospital Assistants would be as big as Volunteers and give as good as they got when attacked. But this is only the latest in a long series of adverse reports about Volunteers. We know they are immoral, insubordinate and untidy—and now we find brutality as well. Surely the time has come to stop these long-haired dissidents coming to Banianok. We sympathize with the British and American Governments, but they must not solve their problems by sending their drop-outs overseas. They must find work for them in their own countries. The British and American Governments must be informed. Meanwhile, if you see one of your countrymen being attacked by a Volunteer, go to his aid, two, three or four of you; half a dozen Banianokese with right on their side will make short work of any Volunteer.

The Director called Haji Ahmed up to see him a week later. They had a long interview, and he told me everything had been

12

satisfactorily settled. The Director left next day for the World Congress on Health and Beauty in Underdeveloped Countries, held that year in Conakry. A week later another letter arrived from Haji Ahmed.

Dear Doctor,

After sincere and humble greetings of my heart:

Further to our happy conversations, here is the business card of my brother, hoping you fix him up nicely on the Medical Register.

Re: Sister Trimmer. Surely, Doctor, you are right to show the sorrow and mercy, and I will follow because you are my Good Head and merciful to all peoples. (Who will not follow such a leader?)

Wishing you speedy actions to register my brother so that he may realize at last his good dreams to serve the people as always.

Attached to the letter was a printed card:

Health is Wealth
P. Waheed.
Qualified Muscles Massage Man.
(London Returned)
When you are tired and sick you can
have the services of the undersigned
Success only guaranteed   Prices Moderate

Haji Ahmed had obviously told the Director he could see his way of dropping his complaint if his brother were put on the Medical Register; the Director had obviously allowed him to think he would do this. P. Waheed had applied before, along with other massage men and herb-sellers, and had been refused. (When doctors were brought in from Korea and the Philippines to replace the departing British there were puzzled editorials in the paper asking why we imported doctors when we had plenty of good doctors of our own who were not allowed to practise.)

I told one of the clerks to send Haji Ahmed a note saying the Director was away and would not be back for three months, and sat back to wait for the next blistering editorial in the paper. It looked as though we would have to transfer Doreen, and if she refused to go we would have to send her back to England. I set aside an evening to walk round and see her at home and persuade her to accept a transfer.

The editorial never came, but on the day I decided to go round and see Doreen another letter came from Haji Ahmed. It was very long. In it he apologized for any misapprehensions he might have laboured under concerning Sister Trimmer's character. He described it as a privilege to work under her and learn from her, he looked forward to doing so for a long time to come. He emphasized his gratefulness to the British Government for sending out personnel of her calibre. He concluded by expressing regret at the antipathy that was felt towards volunteers in certain quarters and said he had already dedicated himself to working untiringly to change it. If only all the volunteers were of Sister Trimmer's quality how easy his task would be.

I did not stop to wonder what had caused his change of heart. Things like that happened all the time in Banianok. One learned not to be curious.

My reason for going to see Doreen had thus been disposed of; but I decided to go all the same.

3

I lived in a large house on a hill to which I was not entitled
by my rank. It was in the shadow of the Portuguese fort and
said to be haunted. The Director of Medical Services, whose
entitlement it was, would not live there, and neither would any
of the other senior Banianokese government servants, so it had
fallen to me. I left it just before six that evening and walked
down the gravel track past the fort. It was at that hour when the
hard heat of the day gives way to the soft, sticky heat of the
night; the temperatures were still in the eighties, but up on
the hill I caught whatever breeze was going. Down in the bazaar
the air did not move. That was where Doreen lived. I stopped
for a moment, as I always did when I passed the fort, and
tried to imagine 150 years of Portuguese rule. For 150 years the
Portuguese had ruled the island, a tiny outpost of an empire that
had stretched from Muscat to Maçao, and the fort, now little
more than a heap of rubble, was all that remained. The Portuguese empire had died of luxury and surfeit, and almost
everything they had conquered and built had fallen to the Dutch.
I walked past the Dutch Governor's mansion, a rambling, gabled
building about two hundred yards along the hill which was
now the Ministry of Agriculture. The Dutch had had 150 years
too, and then had come the British for their 150 years. As I
emerged from the road behind the Dutch Governor's mansion,
there on the opposite side of the river was a sight that always
gave me a tug of nostalgia for London and the sunset over St
Pancras Station. It was the British Government House, built in

15

a material costly in Asia and unique in Banianok to this one building—red brick.

I came off the high ground. As I passed the new Presidential Palace, a long, low, flat-roofed building festooned with coloured light-bulbs, I noticed that the neon sign flashing on and off over the entrance was showing 'Presidential Pal' instead of 'Presidential Palace', as it usually did. The loudspeaker projecting from the topmost minaret of the mosque beside the palace crackled into its pre-recorded exhortation of the faithful to prayer, and I knew it was sunset. Then I was in the bazaar. I threaded my way through the narrow streets, all with the names still up in English. From Bath and Wells Avenue I turned into Victoria Road, which was about twenty feet across, and then cut off down Albert Lane towards the river. Every shop was open —they had hours of business to do yet—and people were eating, sleeping, fighting and playing mah-jong under the glare of the naked electric light-bulbs. I stopped at a coffee-shop and ordered what the Chinese call a Copi-O: coffee essence without condensed milk, with an inch of sugar sitting in the bottom. While I sipped my coffee I watched a noisy mah-jong game in progress between four elderly Chinese squatting cross-legged on tiny stools. I waited in vain for one of them to fall off. As I left a little boy dashed out shrieking in Cantonese the equivalent of 'red-haired devil' which is the customary Chinese description for a European, and soon half a dozen ten-year-olds were following me in silence, nudging each other urgently. I passed a Malay satay-seller, singeing morsels of beef over a charcoal grill, and stopped for a moment to sniff. I half turned and my escort disappeared in terror. Three dogs snarled in an open drain over a prize of chicken's entrails; two Foochow women fought on the floor of a shop while the elderly Towkay, in steel-rimmed glasses, did his accounts in the corner. When I closed my eyes I took in that special smell compounded of satay, cured fish, curry powder, limes, soy sauce and sewage, which is the same for every bazaar from Mandalay to Maçao.

I cut off down Lady Pauline Jones Lane, and close to the wharves where the lights were dim and the water snakes came

16

up on to the damp earth, I arrived at Doreen's quarters. She lived in one of a row of cottages put up by the colonial government for government ferrymen and their families. They were built on stilts and consisted of two rooms and one outside tap. The lavatory was called a dry lavatory, but when the river flooded, as it did quite often, the lavatory was flooded too, and its contents mixed with whatever else might be floating in the water. The cottages were designated Class Four because under the British everything had to have a class, and Class Four was the lowest class there was.

I heard her feet padding rapidly across the bare wooden floor after I knocked. The door was thrown open and she almost fell into my arms.

'Oh! It's you.' Her smile disappeared and she walked back into the centre of the room.

'Were you expecting somebody?' I closed the door.

'My boy-friend. He should be here pretty soon. I'll have to throw you out when he comes. He doesn't like company.'

'That's all right.'

She looked at her watch. 'Well, you can sit down till then. If you want a coffee you'll have to make it yourself. I've got to finish this.... Well, go on then. There's a tin in the kitchen.'

'It's all right. I had a coffee in the bazaar.'

She had one foot up on a small table in front of her chair. Brow furrowed, lips pursed, she applied scarlet varnish to the last three nails. Then she stood up and shuffled around on her heels.

'I've got to give them five minutes to dry.' She stopped for a moment. 'How do I look?'

She was wearing a bright green-and-yellow sarong, and a brown baju—the dress of the Malay women of the Indonesian Archipelago. The sarong is loose; the baju—the bodice—is always tight. It clings to their slim shoulders and delicate breasts and curves in to a tiny waist. The brassière, usually black, is always visible beneath it. Doreen was not wearing a brassière. The lace of her baju stretched firm across her strong Anglo-Saxon shoulders and her substantial waist. The sarong was not

17

quite long enough for her, and her sturdy bristle-haired calves protruded from it like a man's below his dressing-gown when he has not got his pyjama trousers on. Her hair was lifted up in a chignon which emphasized the muscularity of her neck, and over one ear she had contrived a sprig of bougainvillaea. She evoked the image of a saucy transvestist fancy-dress competitor at Butlin's. And the lipstick and mascara reinforced it: surely only a man would wear so much. I had never seen her with make-up before.

'Well—how do I look?'

'Very nice,' I said calmly.

'Dead right,' she said. 'And so I should. Do you know how much this thing cost me?' She plucked at her sarong. 'One hundred rupiahs. It's silk. The best.... You like this nail varnish?' She raised her sarong to her knees.

'Very nice,' I repeated.

'Charles of the Ritz. Most expensive you can get.... I suppose you're wondering why I haven't shaved my legs?'

Happily she did not give me time to answer.

'The answer is my boy-friend likes them like that. All right, so where does it say everybody's got to be the same? Just because all the silly bitches in England shave their legs why do I have to?'

'Quite!' I said hastily.

'The Malay women don't have any hairs on their legs; they're smooth-skinned, like babies. But that's not what he wants.'

'Who is he?' I said.

'You'd like to know, wouldn't you? Well, stick around. You'll find out when he gets here. Be prepared for a surprise. And don't forget to stand up pretty quickly. He likes respect.'

'Actually I came round to tell you that Haji Ahmed has withdrawn his complaint against you,' I said.

She burst into laughter, but there was no mirth in it. It ceased as suddenly as it had begun. 'Tell me something I don't know. I knew that a week ago.'

'A week ago? But I only got the letter this morning.'

'And I knew it was on the way. How do you think he changed

18

his mind? Because he suddenly discovered I was good news? Uh-huh! My boy-friend sent one of his men. He passed on the word, and Haji Ahmed just did the necessary. Just like that.'

'He certainly did.'

She laughed, mirthlessly again. 'He knows what's good for him.... Sorry your journey was wasted if that was what you came to tell me. Funny though, isn't it; you and that Director—you couldn't do a thing about it and you're supposed to be the obstinate bastard's bosses, but Yusuf just drops a word—one word—and Haji Ahmed's shitting his pants.'

'Yusuf?' I said. 'You mean Abang Yusuf—the Commander-in-Chief of the Armed Forces?'

'Right first time.'

Perhaps I took a slight malicious pleasure in asking, 'But what happened to Doris Krenwickle?'

It went right over her head. 'Doris Krenwickle? That *child*? It says in the records she was sent home by the Peace Corps. But you know what really happened? Yusuf got tired of her pestering him. He got on to the Peace Corps Director, Mike McBerski—he's a personal friend—and got her shipped out. Oh! but she was desperate, Jim. Just because he'd shown her a little kindness now and then she was making out they were engaged or something.... Women—they're his trouble. He's too much of a gentleman. He treats them all as though they were made of porcelain, and then what do they do? They try to take advantage of him. But that's not going to happen to me, Jim. All right, he's tied up in a very unhappy situation at home, he can't get a divorce just now, but that's not going to come between me and him.'

'You mean you're thinking of getting married?'

My astonishment pleased her. Without a word she held out her left hand. On the fourth finger was a diamond-and-sapphire ring. 'Valued at five hundred pounds, thanks very much.' This time she did not laugh.

'But when?'

'As soon as his divorce comes through.'

'But I thought Moslems could divorce their women on the spot.'

'You'd like him to do that, wouldn't you?' Her lips tightened. 'You'd like that. That would be good, wouldn't it? Then you could turn round and say what a barbarian he is. But he's cleverer than the lot of you. Everybody thinks he's arrogant and cocky and rides rough-shod over people—' Her expression softened momentarily. 'So he does, the bastard—but women, he loves them, all of them; he treats them as though they're precious things, he likes to take care of them. A woman knows when she's with a man like that. It's not a thing you'd understand, Jim. I'm not trying to be nasty; you just wouldn't. . . . So he can't get rid of his wife just like that. He's got to give her time. Though he's not *in* love with her any more he still cares for her. He told me I'm the first real woman he's ever had, but that's not going to make him desert her just like that. You see—' she pushed her face towards mine—'that's something you people just don't understand; he's a gentleman.'

'But what happens when . . .' I did not finish. I had been going to say 'when another woman comes along', but even as I began I realized the pointlessness of it.

But Doreen realized. 'You think he's going to be hanging his fancy out all over town. Uh-huh! Not with this girl. Because she's not going to be so stupid as to let him. That's where women make me sick—letting themselves go as soon as they're married; then the silly bitches come snivelling round because their man's buggered off with someone else. *Well not this girl!* Besides—' her face softened into an almost maternal smile— 'there are little tricks I can do for him that he won't get anywhere else, the randy bastard. . . . So if you're worried for my future—don't bother!'

'Does the High Commission know?'

'How should I know? The High Commission can take a running jump. Listen, if he wanted to he could get the High Commission closed down tomorrow.'

Her chignon started to come apart, she went over to the mirror to pin it up again. 'Look, Jim,' she said, speaking into the mirror,

'I know you're a good doctor, and conscientious. You spend all your time in that brown building hunched over your desk. You carry the Medical Department single-handed. Great! If that's what you want, great! But in my book life's for living. Don't you ever wonder what it's all about, stuck down there in Medical Headquarters?'

She turned round and scrutinized me. Then she slowly shook her head. 'No, you don't, do you? Who do you know in this town, anyway? All right, you're Number Two in the Medical Department, but do you know any of the people who really count? No! Just a few throw-outs from U.K. Well not for this girl, thank you very much. If I wanted to go round with a bunch of alcoholics, misfits and superannuated queens I'd have stayed in U.K. I came out to get away from that drab existence. I came for life, excitement, and that's what I'm going to get, so you and the High Commission and the British Government for that matter can take a running jump!'

'Your contract will be up in two months,' I said.

'I've extended it.'

'Did Volunteers for Peace agree?'

'It doesn't matter a damn whether they agree or not.'

I started another sentence. 'As a matter of fact they didn't agree,' she interrupted. 'That little squit down there—Ernest Haukbeck—what a name, for Christ's sake! Racist bastard! "It's not him being coloured that worries us, Doreen dear, it's the fact that he's married." He didn't fool me. So I said, "Well, quite frankly, Ernie, you and V.P.O. can get stuffed." Listen, if those bastards knew anything about Moslem law at all they'd know that under their law he's entitled to four wives. But he only has one.'

'At a time,' I qualified. 'I understand he's on number four at the moment.'

Doreen strode back from the mirror. 'She can't give him a son. She had two daughters and she said, "Right Jack, that's it." Do you realize they haven't been man and wife for nearly a year? Do you realize what that can do to a man? Yusuf's a hundred per cent male. He's a hundred per cent full-blooded man. Can

21

you imagine what a situation like that can do to a man?' She looked me up and down slowly, then she shook her head meaningfully.

She felt a wisp of hair from her chignon against the side of her neck. She put up her hand to tuck it back into shape, then she changed her mind: 'Ah! shit!' she muttered, and with hooked fingers she tore it loose, scattering pins on the floor. She started back to the mirror. She stopped halfway. 'Listen, Jim, you're not a bad fellow; I'd like to help you; so I'll tell you something else between you and me: if you want to save yourself a lot of trouble you'd better get your pal Dr Brockley out of the Interior.'

'He's not my pal.'

'He's in your department. He's under your control.'

'I wish he were. He does what he likes.'

'Exactly. He thinks he's still back in the old colonial days. Well, Yusuf's pretty sick of it. He's going up there to get him out.'

'But why? For what reason?'

'Isn't leading a rebellion a good enough reason?'

'Brockley's not leading any rebellion.'

'Are you calling Yusuf a liar?'

'I'm saying Brockley's not involved in any rebellion. The opposite in fact. He's the only man with sufficient prestige to *keep* the peace in the Interior.'

She pushed the palm of her hand at me. 'All right, I don't know all the ins and outs of the situation. I'm just trying to give you some friendly advice. Don't stand in his way, Jim. He's a gentleman as I said, but cross him and he's ruthless. He's a man, Jim; he knows what he wants and he gets it. Brockley's going out one way or the other, so he'd better get used to it—and you too, Jim—because you don't stand up to a man like Yusuf for very long—'

With a little strangled shriek she cried, 'That's him!' Her face changed in her happiness: for a moment she looked radiant, almost pretty. She said rapidly, 'I'll just introduce you to say hello, then you'll have to go.' She dashed to the mirror and

22

sucked her lips together to spread her lipstick. She had heard the car long before I had; now there was the blare of a klaxon and the shriek of tyres skidding to a halt. She scraped her hair forward over the side of her face, and punched the folds of her sarong flat; then she dashed for the door tugging at her nipples through the lace of her baju. She threw it open, and I saw two soldiers standing almost to attention beside a big black Mercedes, each with a gun bulging on his hip. The Abang came bounding up the wooden steps.

The thing that always struck people first about the Abang was his vitality—a rare enough quality in that climate for any race, but more or less unknown among Malays. You got the impression of compressed energy, of barely controlled violence in everything he did.

Then there was the matter of his American accent....

I was introduced as Dr Reed. 'I'm happy to know you, Doctor.' He clamped my hand into one of his, and then slapped the other on top. 'Doreen has told me about you and the wonderful work you're doing for us poor people here.'

I shook my head modestly. It is the custom in the Archipelago to make out that your efforts are as nothing.

The skin around his eyes crinkled into an expression of strained sincerity. 'But why haven't you been to see me, Doc?—Please?'

The reason I had not been to see him was that I had not been invited, and the reason I had not been invited was that he had never heard of me till that moment. But it was not a question that demanded an answer. In fact it was not a question at all, but a statement, a polite expression of pleasure at having made my acquaintance.

'And how are you liking life in Banianok, Doctor?'

I told him I liked it.

He obviously thought I had only recently arrived. 'You're joining a great bunch of guys and a great tradition of great doctors sent to us by our good friends the British. You know Dr Brockley, of course—a very great doctor, and a very beautiful person.' He was still holding my hand. He pulled it

23

closer. 'Tell you something, Doc—Dr Brockley was the first hero I ever had. When I was a kid and he was running the Resistance against the Japs. All that time ago—nearly thirty years. He was a great man then, Doc, a great man.' He raised his head suddenly and blinked away a tear from each eye. 'It's sad when things have to change....'

Doreen's scarlet nail tapped the door just above the knob. He glanced at the noise, and as quickly as his tears had come they were gone. 'Well, you know how it is, Doc....' He looked at me very seriously, and suddenly the top two buttons of his tunic had popped open. He put his arm around me and started to move me towards the door, which Doreen opened like a bullfighter performing a delicate pass. 'And please, Doc, don't ignore us simple folk. We're only simple folk—can't offer you anything fancy—but if you get away from all that work of yours any night, come in and see us. Appreciate it, Doc.'

Doreen said coldly, 'Goodnight. Thank you very much. Goodnight.'

The Abang wheeled me round. 'And don't forget, Doc, if ever you want anything done, anybody gives you any trouble ... I'm not General McArthur, but I draw a little water in this town.' He patted his revolver holster affectionately, and another couple of buttons popped open. 'Tell you the truth, Doc, I may be having a little bit of trouble myself next month or so. Maybe going up-river. Little bit of trouble up there; headhunters been on the rampage. Maybe we got a communist situation. Got to take a look-see, maybe take a few heads myself. I might be calling on you for some medical advice—keep it to yourself, Doc.'

'What's the use of having mosquito-wire on the windows if you're going to stand here all night with the bloody door open?' Doreen rasped.

'O.K., Doc.' The Abang motioned me out. 'I'll take care of this sassy chick. I'm going to chastise her good—now.' He reached behind him and sank his hand into her bottom.

'Hey, that hurt, you sadistic bastard!' She laughed breathlessly, then smacked her balled-up fist into his stomach. He

24

grunted. She made a grab for his hand and bit into it. He tore the baju from her shoulders in one movement.

I let myself out. A second later the bolt slammed in the door. There was a shuffling sound and then a muffled crash. As I walked away I heard one of the soldiers by the car groaning 'Hai! hai! hai!' in an agony of hopeless desire. Then the light went out.

4

There are three reasons why important personages go abroad from Banianok. They are 'medical check-up', 'further studies', and 'conference'. When I read in the *Herald* two days later that the Abang had left for the Philippines 'on conference' I was delighted. It was well known in Banianok that he had a profound affection for the Philippines, and he never lost an opportunity for a long visit. He had been at the famous Hickory Stick Military Academy during the American colonial period, and it was there that he had developed his American accent, his interest in big breasts, and the slang of the late 1940s.

I looked forward to a prolonged absence and settled back into the untroubled monotony of my medical routine.

Two weeks later I was called to the laboratory to see a slide of an infection that was causing considerable inconvenience to a very important personage. As I entered, the assistant said to me in awe, 'Very strong, Doctor. Penicillin-resistant plus plus,' and when I looked down the microscope I saw Gram-negative extracellular cocci nestling in pairs all over the slide and I knew we were dealing with a case of gonorrhoea.

Though we were a sequestered community in Banianok, well away from the main shipping lanes of Asia, gonorrhoea was not so exceptional that it required my presence in the laboratory— even if it was resistant to penicillin. It was just that it was part of the social ethic of Banianok that important matters concerning important personages should be dealt with only by persons of equivalent distinction.

26

The door opened and the Abang was shown in. 'Jesus, Doc—the most expensive doctor in Manila—a Harvard man—and he can't cure me of a simple dose I got in his own goddam town. What is it, Doc? It's bad?'

'I didn't know you were back,' I said.

'I just came off the plane. Come on, Doc—tell me the truth.'

'What treatment did you have in Manila?' I asked.

'Penicillin. Injections. Painful—and no goddam result at all.'

'It must be penicillin-resistant, as Mr Seifu said.' I nodded at the laboratory assistant, and the Abang looked at him too, distractedly. He looked at him again, and then made a movement with his left hand as though brushing crumbs off a table. Mr Seifu vanished.

'Have you had it before?'

The Abang smiled modestly. 'I'm a soldier, Doc.'

'We'd better give you some tetracyclines.'

'That's injections?' he started suspiciously.

'You take them by mouth.'

He straightened up. 'Great, Doc, great!' A spasm of pain suddenly stiffened his face. His hands went down to his lower abdomen. 'You got a comfort station here?'

When he came back he began a dissertation on political corruption in Manila. This is a subject of perennial interest, but the only evidence he seemed to have was that he had contracted his present infection from the wife of a high official in the Finance Ministry. When he left the second time for the lavatory I had occasion to move his swagger-stick and gloves to get at my prescription pad, and I noticed that he had a book lying between them. I had never thought of the Abang as a man who read books.

His second absence from the room was more prolonged than the other had been. I was interested to see what sort of thing he read. I picked up the book and saw that it was called *A Walk in the Sun* by Major-General Sir Charles Wheeler. Military —I lost interest. But as I dropped it back on the bench it fell open where the dust-flap had been inserted, and, as sometimes happens, one word in the flurry of print as I closed the book

27

jumped from the page and hooked itself into my mind. The word was 'Brockley'.

I opened it again. It was on page 154.

Another character in the best tradition was Arthur 'Ulu' Brockley, who, when the Japs arrived, decided to do a little soldiering on his own. Disappearing into the Interior with his gun and blowpipe, and precious little else, he organized the Dayaks of the Interior for guerilla war against the invaders to such effect that he was able to present the Australians with one hundred prisoners when they arrived, and was the only Englishman on the island to remain at large throughout the occupation. Had it not been that he disobeyed orders in the first place in not remaining at his post to greet the invaders, and that he had allowed the plucky little chaps under his command to resume their age-old practice of lopping the heads off their prisoners, he would have been eligible for the highest honours. An effort was made by disgruntled senior officers, both civil and military, who at this distance in time may remain nameless, to have 'Ulu' indicted for atrocities, but as he said, it was impossible for him to stop his people killing the Japs, particularly when they saw what the Japs did to the Chinese in their midst, and the fact that he had managed to muster one hundred prisoners at the end of the war, at considerable risk to himself, showed that he personally had tried to minimize the killing. In the end he got off with a censure, but the black mark he incurred in refusing to surrender to the Japs followed him throughout his subsequent colonial service career, and he was never promoted beyond General Duties Medical Officer (Class III). Had he been a professional soldier I am certain he would have ended his career at the highest level.

Meanwhile, back in Calcutta, Dickie Mountbatten and I . . .

The book must have been still in my hand as the Abang came back into the room. Perhaps passing urine had been more painful this time. A hurt, petulant frown appeared on his face. He seemed to know instinctively which page I had been on.

'What you reading that shit for?' he cried. 'Wheeler, Charles Wheeler—who the hell's ever heard of him? I never heard of him. Just something I picked up to read in the plane.'

Before I could reply he snarled, 'Building up old Doc Brockley into some sort of superman, something. Well, he's no superman, Mr Dr Blo. My law-and-order boys are going to show just how much a superman he is—in just about a week from now.'

He stamped over to the window. When he turned round his expression had completely changed. He smiled almost shyly. 'Doc, I wanted to ask you could I take Doreen along on the trip for—uh!—medicinal reasons?' He winked. 'You fix that?'

'That would be a matter for the Director,' I said coldly.

'Raschid?' he said contemptuously. 'That fink? No, I'm asking you, Doc. Far as I'm concerned you're the boss. Tell you the truth, Doc—there's just something about this girl I just got to get out of my system. I think I can say I've just about screwed my way around this wonderful world of ours, but I never had a girl like this Doreen. You can talk about the Mexicans, the Parisians, the niggers ... no sir, give me a British girl every time. Gentle, wistful, refined—to start with. But get her going, just get her going, and oh mister!' He tapped the side of his nose with his forefinger and then touched it to his lips.

I realized it would be churlish of me to take offence; he was paying Doreen, and through her British womanhood, the highest compliment he knew.

The hand that had touched his lips clasped my wrist. 'O.K., Doc, I can tell Doreen it's all fixed? ... And please, Doc—' suddenly he looked very sincere—'don't worry about that little thing I picked up in Manila. As my old Superintendent at Hickory Stick, General Linus R. Pyle, said to me: "Always be a gentleman, Bill." My friends—my real friends, Doc—call me Bill. Like you to do the same.'

It was not clear exactly how he intended to ensure that he did not pass the infection to Doreen, and I was reluctant to question him in detail. I resolved that my treatment must be thorough.

'Good, General, now if you'll just lower your trousers ...'

5

The Editor of the *Tribune* gave the Abang a heartening send-off
—in English, of course:

> When colonialist remnants start to re-assert themselves
> again only six years after Independence, then surely the time
> has come. The Commander-in-Chief of the Banianok Defence
> Force thinks so too. Today he sets off into the Interior with
> five hundred men to settle a very nasty situation. Rebellion
> has broken out among the up-river savages, headed by a
> well-known Colonialist-Imperialist element who should be
> saving lives instead of putting them in jeopardy.
>
> Well, he has been warned. The Defence Force are on their
> way. If he is wise he will pack his bags and try to make
> reparation to the Banianok women he has debauched so
> shamelessly over the years. And then get back where he came
> from. If he does not—Banianok justice has a short answer to
> people like him.
>
> Good luck, Abang Yusuf, beloved commander! All decent
> people are behind you!!!

He had got the wrong end of the stick about debauchery. That
was a Korean doctor at the other end of the island. The story had
come to light about the same time, so there was an excuse for
the confusion. And nobody likes to offend the Koreans.

The Chinese, who are the usual targets of communal strife
in South-East Asia, were so delighted that the Dayaks were
being picked on for a change that several groups demonstrated

outside the Presidential Palace in support of the Abang and his Malay troops. As I walked past at lunchtime I was tripped over accidentally by a youth who had been fighting another over a banner. They both immediately stopped fighting and helped me, with many apologies, to my feet. There were two banners lying on the ground. One said 'Peace, Democracy, Liberty'; the other 'Bring Him Back in a Basket'. It appeared they both wanted to carry the second.

As they unnecessarily brushed imaginary dust from my shirt I pointed to the second banner, now propped against a bush, and asked, 'Who?'

'Pardon, sir?' they said politely.

'Who does this refer to?'

'Peace and Freedom, sir. Like Democracy.'

'All working together.'

'But who do you want brought back in a basket?'

'Democracy Number One.'

'Abang Yusuf Number One.'

'Imperialism Number Ten.'

'Communism Number Ten.'

'Savages Number Ten. Kill! Kill! Kill! Excuse me, sir, must go now to present loyal petition of support.'

This time the Abang's boat did not sink. He disappeared into the roadless Interior, and we settled down to wait for news. Ten days later Brockley's son arrived in the country.

I was sitting in my yellow-walled office with the jalousies drawn against the heat of the day, which had already started to build up though it was not yet nine o'clock. I was going through some monthly reports from the outstations, the creaking ceiling-fan ploughing its way laboriously through the thick air above me, a cup of thinly scented China tea at my elbow. Oddly enough I was quite content.

Then the door opened and the Director squeezed through.

'Doctor!' he gasped. 'Man outside!'

I looked up. 'Local or foreign?'

'British, Doctor. Also very large size.' He looked up to a height of about seven feet, and then from side to side, indicating a breadth of about a yard.

'What does he want?'

'Looking for Dr Blo Ko Lee,' he cried agitatedly. He put his hands up flat in front of him. 'I have nothing to do. Abang Yusuf want to go up bring Blo Ko Lee back in a basket. O.K. Not me. Blo Ko Lee—Abang, very nice men, same-same, no trouble. Doctor, I got terrible pain my bloody inside.'

He squeezed both fists piteously into his abdomen, signifying the torments of curry and nervous indigestion, and I said:

'Send him in. I'll see him.'

The Director seemed doomed to have fierce-looking young English people calling on him and upsetting his stomach. But in Graham's case it was only the appearance, I think, that was fierce. Of course he needed a bath, a change of clothes, a haircut and a radical pruning of his beard so that he could at least take nourishment without leaving evidence in the tangle of hair around his mouth. He looked frightening rather than fierce. He needed his back straightening fifteen degrees, a few buttons of his shirt doing up, and the straps of his open-toed floppy sandals tightening. He also had rather a plump bottom. He jogged one of my childhood ambitions, which had been to be a P.T. instructor.

He came through the door with his hand already outstretched, and when he reached the desk he said in a very soft voice, 'Hallo!' He looked through me with the sort of mystic adoration one sees on the faces of lovers and the more tedious type of saint. 'My name's Graham Brockley. I'm a Volunteer for Peace.'

I felt a faint tightening of something in my stomach that could have been the same symptom as the Director's.

'Happy to meet you,' I said guardedly.

'I'm looking for a job,' he said confidingly. 'They told me you were the man to see.'

'Aren't volunteers assigned jobs by the V.P.O. Director in town?' I realized I didn't sound very welcoming, so I contrived a smile for a moment or so.

'Yes. But I want to work for the Medical Department.'

'I see. You're specially trained for something medical, are you?'

'I did Sociology at Hull for two years.'

Sociology! My heart sank.

'Teaching sounds just the thing for you,' I said rapidly. 'I'll just let the Education Department know you're here.'

I made a grab for the phone, but in spite of his appearance his reflexes were very fast. He had stopped me before I was halfway there. 'No, that's not what I want at all . . . I really want to work with my father.'

'Your father?'

Though he had introduced himself as Graham Brockley I had just accepted it as another surname—like Smith or Brown.

'You mean you're Brockley's son?'

He gave me three long, slow nods, and then smiled a private smile that was something between him and an invisible third party who was sitting on my right. My shock clearly tickled him.

'I thought they might let me go up and help out with the cholera epidemic. I've had the injections.'

I did not immediately catch on to what he was talking about. 'Cholera epidemic? What cholera epidemic?'

'Well, the cholera epidemic here, of course.'

'But there's no cholera epidemic here.'

He looked at me with forbearance. Most volunteers start their work abroad with the conviction that the British remnants of the colonial régimes that they find there are complete halfwits, and that only natives can be expected to have any intelligence.

'I wouldn't have read it in the *Straits Times* if it hadn't been true, would I?' he said kindly—and slowly.

'What did it say?'

'I can't remember the exact wording—it was only a four-line report: cholera epidemic; Interior sealed off; nobody allowed in or out. Like that.'

I forgot my stomach.

'When was this?' I said urgently.

34

'Well—ten days ago. It was complete chance I happened to see it.'

Ten days ago! That would be just when the Abang's expedition was leaving for the Interior. I cut him short: 'Excuse me a moment. Just stay here. I'll be back in a moment.'

I went through to the Director's office.

As usual he was teetering on the brink of pneumonia through keeping the air-conditioner down to fifty-five degrees, and he was sneezing vigorously as I went in. His face was down near the surface of his desk, buried in a huge paper handkerchief. He did not raise it.

'He's gone, Doctor?'

'No, he's still there.'

'It's trouble?'

'It's Brockley's son,' I said.

'Oh my God! Better calling policeman right away!' Still not raising his head, he reached for his red telephone, and then, remembering the red one was not connected, moved on to the ordinary black one.

I released it quietly from his hand and replaced it on the receiver. 'There's no need,' I said. 'He's just looking for a job. He wants to go and work for his father. He tells me something which may surprise you.'

The Director shook his head, open-mouthed.

'He tells me there's a cholera epidemic in the Interior.'

The Director obviously did not know whether to look astounded or to nod his agreement. He moved his head around like a boxer rolling with a punch in slow motion.

I went on, 'He tells me it was reported in the *Straits Times* ten days ago—about the time the Abang was leaving for the Interior.'

We sat and looked at each other. I said slowly, 'There isn't really an epidemic in the Interior, is there?'

'Oh, no!' He shook his head rapidly. 'No, no! No epidemic.'

'And yet there was one reported.'

He shrugged ingratiatingly. 'Mistake maybe.'

'Has it occurred to you that a cholera scare could provide a very good cover for quite a lot of deaths up there in the Interior?'

Unfortunately the Director had never got to know me. He did not know when I was happy or when I was angry; he did not know when I was being absolutely serious and when I was being ironic. But he was always anxious to please.

'Exactly, my Doctor,' he squeaked excitedly. 'Just what the Abang said. No more bloody trouble from bloody fucken Nayans. Plenty trouble this time last time; but no more fucken trouble next time!'

When I got back to my office Graham had turned the ceiling fan up so that it was beating as fast as it would go. One of the first mistakes new arrivals make is to turn everything cold up to its highest—fan, air-conditioner, cold tap. When they have to go out into the open air they have the feeling of having been prodded into a blast furnace.

'I have to go down to the Port Health Office,' I said. 'I'll walk as far as the Rest House with you.'

When we were downstairs and into the street I said, 'It seems there *is* a little trouble up-river. And your father may be involved.'

'My father? I don't understand.'

'Well, it seems that the government has decided to build a road across the island, passing, of course, right through the Interior, which is your father's territory—and he objects.'

'He objects? No, not Dad! He really loves these people.' Graham looked at me tolerantly, giving me to understand that if I thought about it a little more carefully I would see that I must be mistaken.

'I think he wants to protect the Nayans,' I said carefully. 'They are the most primitive tribe of the Interior. Unfortunately they killed a couple of surveyors, and the Army has gone up to ... er—pacify them.'

'Well I know Dad will help all he can. I know he wouldn't be involved in any trouble because he just loves these people. You know, he always had very bad reports in the old colonial days because of the way he used to stick up for the natives.'

36

'Unfortunately it's not quite as simple as it sounds. You see—there is no real intention to build the road.'

Sweat was beginning to run down Graham's temple and into his beard, and he started to itch at a barricade of small pustules where the hairline met the skin of his neck. He started to lose his seraphic smile and take on one of irritation; and the irritation, it was clear, was with me—and the heat.

I hurried him on down Freedom Street. 'Five million rupiahs was voted to a Road Fund. Curiously, it was put in the jurisdiction of the Army, not the Public Works Department....'

'Well?'

'It's all disappeared,' I said simply.

'But that's impossible!'

'Yes,' I agreed; but we did not mean the same thing. 'They were too greedy. They were bound to be found out. If they'd been content with fifteen or twenty per cent, which is usual, they'd have been all right. But 600,000 U.S. dollars was bound to be missed.'

'They never told us about anything like this in London,' he muttered, shaking sweat from his eyes.

I pressed on stolidly: 'Luckily for the Army two of their surveyors were killed.'

'*Luckily?*' he cried.

'They reported it as a company—ambushed by the Nayans. All sorts of people found the notion of a Nayan uprising extraordinarily convenient. Speeches were made, feelings were whipped up, and finally the *Banianok Tribune* demanded that the Army return in strength to avenge the dead soldiers and pacify the Interior. When they come back from doing that the five million rupiahs will have been written off.'

'But I just can't believe—'

Graham got no further. Across the padang in front of Government House came a group of Chinese youths. Round the side of the building were three or four older Chinese urging them to make more noise. They came across the padang baying and chattering and waving banners. One of the banners said, 'God bless. We will never forget wonderful army'; another, 'Victory on correct principles'.

We stopped and watched them shuffle by. A maiden in the middle danced along with a light balsa-wood and cartridge-paper placard on which was inscribed 'He has interfered with womens'.

'He has interfered with women's what?' Graham said to me. The girl heard him.

'He has interfered with womens,' she repeated.

'Who?'

'He has interfered with womens—no mercy!'

'Who are they talking about?' Graham turned back to me.

'I haven't the slightest idea,' I lied.

A little boy at the back romped along trying to hold up the front page of that day's *Banianok Herald* like a placard. I stopped him.

It was the lead story, under a banner headline:

FURTHER TRIUMPHS FOR DEMOCRACY

From the steaming jungle hell of the Interior the word is that the end is in sight for the counter-democratic Neo-Colonialist agencies that have festered there for so long. General Abang Yusuf and his men are proving that correct principles, modern weapons and thorough training are more than a match for the unarmed savages of the Interior. Over one hundred of the ill-advised tools of Neo-Colonialist counter-revolutionary subversion have perished.

And there will be more!

God speed Abang Yusuf, Saviour of his People, and Patron of Freedom!!

6

Most people's notion of the jungle is shaped by the films they have seen in which William Holden or Errol Flynn hack their way, step by step, through a wall of eye-level greenery, with pythons uncoiling at intervals along the way, tarantulas hopping from log to log, and poisoned snakes planted under carpets of autumn leaves by bad natives, discovered in the nick of time by good natives. The reality is at the same time better and worse. Primary jungle—and eighty per cent of Banianok is primary jungle—is jungle that has never been cleared or planted. The trees rise sometimes eighty feet before a single branch appears, and at one hundred feet their foliage interlocks, cutting off what is above from what is below. Above the foliage is the brilliant tropical sun; below is eternal twilight. The things that grow best on the floor of the jungle are ferns and mosses. There is little else because everything else needs the sun. There is always a path; even in completely uninhabited jungle there is a path used by the animals. So it is never necessary to use a cutting instrument. You can step off the path with no hindrance if you wish; but you do not. The jungle stretches away from you, tree after tree exactly the same as the one before it and the one after; there is no perspective: one bit of jungle is exactly the same as every other bit. There is only one colour—green. The air never moves. That is why a slender dart five inches long can travel one hundred yards to a destination no bigger than a man's head. In an English meadow it would be cut down by the slightest puff of wind. You long for that puff of wind, and for a glance of the sun.

The inhabitants of the jungle are reticent—the humans and the animals. A species of the largest python known to man lurks in the far Interior of Banianok, but usually it slithers away when people approach. Wild boar crash into the twilight when they are disturbed. The orang-utan—literally, jungle-man—swings away chattering long before you get to him, and the rarest animal of all, the beautiful white rhinoceros, is so shy that it was declared extinct in Banianok in 1959, and since then has only been seen by, among outsiders, Brockley and myself. They are there, but you cannot see them. Most of them you cannot even hear. Most of their business is conducted in silence. Only the birds, five hundred species of them, mostly beautifully coloured, welcome the opportunity to show off.

People stay out of the jungle if they can. The Chinese in the towns, the Malays by the sea; the Dayaks always in sight of a river. In Banianok only the Nayans are completely at home in the jungle—the Nayans and Brockley. Think of yourself going into the jungle. Not as a friend of Brockley's, escorted everywhere by marvelling savages, but as an interloper, an armed outsider, unwanted and feared. Within fifty yards of you are a dozen Nayans, but you cannot see them. At any moment the darts could come—one for each man. There is something awesome about the tiny effort that is required to use a blowpipe. A gun makes an explosion; firing an arrow requires the bowstring to be drawn back taut; but with a blowpipe a little inflation of the cheeks, a sharp puff, no more, and a man can be lying on the jungle floor with minutes left to live. Every half-hour or so you have to stop, light cigarettes, take off your boots and socks and burn the engorged leeches of your feet and ankles. They could get you then, when you are completely defenceless, and that is when you expect it most. But they don't. Then comes the fever; first the insidious feeling of more than usual weariness, then the headache building up, first just like a hangover headache, but then more, and then more, until it feels as though it is being pressed between two massive rocks, and you find yourself on the jungle floor vomiting, the sweat running in rills into every channel and orifice of your body. Now they could get you. But

40

they don't. Day after day, weaker every day with fever, you slog on, but they will not show themselves. But you know they are there because at night, in camp, while you sleep, things are moved—plates, clothes, water-bags, ammunition. No matter how many guards are posted they get in, and out, unseen. When you go to sleep at night you dread waking up and seeing the subtle changes in the camp. There is a sound like a man calling mockingly. It is only a hornbill ... but perhaps it was a man. A sergeant tears his pistol off his hip and blazes away into the jungle in the direction it came from. For a moment there is silence. Then it comes again. He stands there with his pistol empty, then hurls it on to the ground and starts to sob.

At last the time comes when he can stand it no longer....

It was six o'clock three weeks later, and I was drinking my tea. I was busy as usual, artificially busy with a report I could have left to the Head of Malaria Eradication, working with all the louvres open, the sun dipping into the trees across the river immediately in front of me. Since I was not expecting anybody I had changed into a sarong, and I sweated gently into it as the hard, sunny heat of the day changed into the soft, oppressive heat of the night. My dour steward came round the corner from the kitchen, trod across the floor with unaccustomed stealth until he was right beside me, and then said directly into my ear, 'There are some men to see the lord.'

I looked up at him irritably. 'At the back door?' We spoke in Malay.

He whispered. 'Yes, lord, serious matter.'

'Who are they?'

He looked round, out of the door he had just come through; then he looked out over the verandah directly in front of him. 'Soldiers,' he whispered hoarsely. It was the first time I had seen his expression anything but exhausted.

'How many?'

'Not many.'

The immediate thought passed through my head that they had come to arrest me and that in the truly gentlemanly Malay

41

fashion they were waiting at the back door until I could see them.

'What do they want?'

'Serious matter for the lord.'

'Well, what is it?'

'Sick. Big sick.'

'All of them?'

He gave a long, serious nod.

'Well, tell them to go to the hospital.'

'Off duty.'

'But there's always somebody on duty at the hospital.'

'Soldiers off duty, lord.'

'Well, they can still go to the hospital.'

'Doctor ...' He leaned over and whispered, 'Worse than off duty. Cannot go to hospital. In danger of arresting because too long off duty.'

I got up in exasperation and followed him to the kitchen. There were four sitting and three lying on the concrete flags outside the back door. They had the hot, dry, flushed, staring look of men who have been suffering from high fever. It did not take me long to discover what 'worse than off duty' meant. They had been in the force the Abang had taken up-river six weeks before and they had come back before him. They were deserters.

From the snatches of what they painfully told me and my servant I started to piece together what had gone on up there, and as they spoke a new enemy emerged, one they had not thought of—more taciturn than Brockley, more savage than the Nayans.

7

I continued to get deserters in ones and twos, dribs and drabs. Their story was always the same and they were always found to be suffering from malaria.

Then one evening at nine o'clock my telephone jangled and I was speaking to the most important deserter of all.

'Jim?'

There was no mistaking that Wolverhampton accent.

'Doreen!'

'Jim, I've got to see you.'

'I'm looking forward to seeing you too, Doreen.'

'I'm not talking about social life,' she gulped. 'I've got to see you medically. Do you keep any medicines at your place?'

'Some.'

'Can I come round now? I've got this rash and it's driving me mad.'

'Yes, of course. But what's been going on? When did you get back?'

'I got back today. I was going to wait till the morning, but I couldn't, Jim. I can't stop scratching. I can't sit still, I haven't slept for a week.'

'I'll come and pick you up,' I said.

'No, don't. I'll come on my bicycle. It'll be quicker.'

'Will you be all right?'

'These local dwarfs don't bother me,' she snarled.

'All right. I'll expect you any minute.'

I tried to continue with the monthly reports I had been going through, but I could not. I closed them up and started to walk about the room.

I heard the soft rustle of soft slippers on the gravel outside. I walked out on to the verandah, and there was Graham hesitating on the bottom step.

'Oh! ... hullo, James. I wanted to talk to you about Dad. I can't get a job. Whenever it comes out who I am nobody wants me. I've been sitting here two weeks and nobody'll take me on.'

'Well, if you want to hear some news of your father,' I said kindly, 'come in. There's a volunteer coming round who has just got back from the Interior.'

'Thanks!' he mumbled. 'I just can't believe the things they're saying about him.'

I sat him down and gave him a bottle of beer. He took a deep gulp, then put his glass down and asked for a cigarette. I brought a pack from the store-room. He opened the pack and took two out. One he put in his mouth, the other in the outside breast pocket of his shirt. He did not put the pack in his pocket, but kept it on the arm-rest of his chair where he could not forget it when he left. (Volunteers earned so little that they had no objection to their better-paid countrymen supplying the little luxuries they could not afford themselves.)

He took a deep, prolonged drag—obviously the first of the day—and then let it out languorously on a breath that seemed to last half a minute.

For a moment there was complete silence and peace, then there was a shriek of tyres. A high-powered car was coming up the path to my house in low gear; finally there was the sound of the gravel grinding into the earth as it skidded to a halt. I always told the hospital driver not to do that; it ruined the path, and when the rain came it stood in large pools where the cars had been. But this was not the hospital driver. I heard the doors of the car closing—not the tinny bang of a Land-Rover, but the discreet clunk of a solid, expensive car door. There was only one car in Banianok that was driven like that and made a sound like that. So *he* must be back too. 'Well,

44

it looks as though you're going to have the opportunity of meeting the Abang Yusuf,' I said.

We heard the sound of boots on the verandah steps—more than one pair. Then we heard more on the back steps, leading up to the kitchen. There were shouts from the direction of the servants' quarters, then a giant spotlight from the car flooded the garden.

'What's going on?' said Graham.

'The Abang's team hamming it up as usual,' I replied in a bored voice. 'This must be a formal visit.'

'Does this happen often?'

'Normally his visits are informal,' I said. 'His myrmidons stay in the car and their guns stay in their holsters.'

'You mean they have guns?' Graham sat up straight in his chair.

But then the Abang ruined the whole effect, as he always managed to do somehow or another. This time he did it by knocking. I shouted 'Come in' and he burst through the door, a thug on either side with his hand on his holster. But it was too late for him to be menacing; he shouldn't have forgotten not to knock; details like that make all the difference.

'Doc,' he said sternly, 'I got information Doreen's here.'

'No,' I said. 'But she's coming over. She should be here any minute.'

He looked round in sharp, darting glances. 'I want to see her.' He seemed very agitated.

'Well, she'll be here soon. Why don't you sit down and wait? Perhaps my servant could entertain your two assistants,' I said pointedly.

'What are you doing in here? Get out!' he bellowed in Malay at his two thugs.

They left. I was in the act of introducing Graham to the Abang, when there was a scream of pain from outside the house. It was a man's scream. Two seconds later Doreen was frog-marched into the house by the two soldiers. One of them had blood beginning to ooze from four parallel scratch-marks down his left cheek.

45

I was about to tell the Abang that I couldn't have his men in the house—not that I was hurt or angry, but I knew if I did not he would lose any respect he might have for me—but I did not get the chance; Doreen was ahead of me.

'Your little boys shape up pretty well against women, don't they?' she snarled at the Abang. 'Pity they couldn't do the same thing to the men in the Interior!' She shook the soldiers off, or they allowed themselves to be shaken off. The one who had been scratched immediately put his hand to his cheek.

'Get out!' the Abang roared at them. 'And stay out!'

Doreen's eyes darted round the room. She was quivering with rage. She looked at Graham, then at me, then jerked her head at him. 'Who's this?'

'This is Graham Brockley—Dr Brockley's son.'

Her expression changed. She strode over to him. Graham shrank back in his chair, but she pulled him to his feet. She stuck her face into his. 'I want to shake your hand. I want to shake your hand and tell you you ought to be proud of that father of yours—the only real man in the whole country.' She was pumping Graham's hand every word or so, but she was not looking at him; she was looking at the Abang, rage dancing in her eyes. 'The only man I ever heard of who could take on an army and rout them! Ask him!' She pointed at the Abang. 'Mind you, maybe it's not such a fantastic achievement when you think what sort of army—a thousand overfed, overdressed little brown bullies.'

At the word 'brown' Graham withdrew his hand, and looked fearfully at the Abang. That came under racial prejudice. Perhaps Doreen thought she had gone too far as well. Suddenly there was silence.

I broke it by saying, 'What exactly did happen in the Interior? We've had very conflicting reports down here.' I addressed myself to the Abang, but it was Doreen who replied:

'Just to put it in a nutshell, when we got to Bukit Kota Brockley had disappeared up-river leaving a message to say he had a whooping-cough epidemic to sort out up there. Nobody believed that, but what could we do about it? So we wandered

46

around the jungle for a bit like Boy Scouts looking for a good turn, but whenever we came to a Dayak long-house our brave boys wouldn't go in. That terrified the Dayaks, naturally. Went to Penghara Ngang's long-house and they brought out some of their Japanese heads; couple of dozen of our boys took a boat and deserted the very next day. So we thought this isn't very good, better go up and bash the Nayans instead. So off we set for the mountains—never saw one in two weeks. Then our boys started coming down with fevers because the medical set-up was so lousy. So then another fifty deserted.'

I was just going to ask about the reports of the Nayans killed, but I did not get the chance.

'All right, you bitch!' the Abang shouted. He bellowed for his men and two of them ran in with a small tin trunk that looked like a medicine-chest. They put it on the floor.

'Open it!' he roared.

They pulled back the lid. Inside were rolls of dressings, tins, bottles, and packets of instruments that one expects to see in a medicine-chest. There was also a very curious aroma that I could not identify for the moment, except that it was not appropriate to a medicine-chest.

The Abang took out two tins. He held them up. 'Seen these before?'

I recognized them immediately. They were aluminium tins in which tablets are packed in bulk by the manufacturers. Each would hold a thousand tablets.

'You know what the fever was all my boys got? I just got the diagnosis—malaria. You know what it says on this tin? Aspirin. You know what it says on this tin?' He pulled forward the other tin. 'Paludrine! And you know what's in this tin, and you know what's in *this* tin?' He put his hand on the other tin. 'I just got it from the laboratory.' He looked at Graham, then me, and finally at Doreen. He thrust his face down at hers. 'You know, don't you, you bitch?' he shrieked at the top of his voice. 'We got aspirin in the Paludrine tin, and Paludrine in the aspirin tin. And why? Because you changed them.'

But it was obvious that she hadn't. I could see her looking

at him in blank astonishment. 'What are you talking about, you bloody fool?'

'You know what I'm talking about, you bitch! So we have a row, so you decide you're going to ruin the whole expedition. So what's a nice easy way to do it? Give my boys malaria.'

She tried to laugh, but it came out as a snarl. 'You poor slob! When did the soldiers start going down with the fever? On the Friday. And when did we have our row? On the Wednesday night. And how long does it take between getting bitten by a mosquito and getting malaria?' She shrieked, 'Ten days!'

She turned on me and her fingers sank painfully into the muscle of my upper arm.

'Ten days!' she bellowed. It was a command and a question in one.

I confirmed it.

'Ten days!' She was back at the Abang. 'So your precious pills had been changed at least a week before we had our row!'

'Ten days ... ?' The Abang looked at me interrogatively.
'At least ten days,' I said.
'But who ... ?'
'When did we start finding that the Nayans had been in the camp at night while we were asleep?'

'Shut up, you bitch!'

'They're all going to find out sooner or later.' She looked at us triumphantly. 'He posted guards at night, such marvellous guards. But the Nayans got into the camp at night and moved everything round just to show us they'd been there. Otherwise we'd never have known. The guards never saw them once. And when did that start? The third night after we left Bukit Kota, when we really got deep into the jungle. And how long did it go on for? A week! Those tins could have been changed any one of those nights.'

'But those savages wouldn't have known anything about that. They don't even know what malaria is.'

'Well, who else would have done it—your own medical orderly?'

'But they can't read! They wouldn't even be able to read the labels on the tins. They wouldn't have the first idea what they were looking for.'

I was sniffing over the open chest. The strange aroma I knew was familiar, but I could not put a name to it. As I bent closer I saw some brown flakes caught on one of the rolls of cotton-wool. I picked one off. There were some more on the bottom of the chest. I raised it to my eyes, then to my nostrils.

I noticed they were all watching me. 'What's that?' the Abang cried irritably.

'I don't know.'

He saw me smelling the flake. He leaned over me and smelled it too. 'Tobacco!' he snarled. 'So what?'

That was it! I had not been able to identify it because it was so mild—it hardly smelt like tobacco at all—and because I did not associate it with medicine-chests. But I knew it! It was Brockley's No. 14 Mixture, three pounds of which arrived every three months, and which it was my job to trans-ship on to the up-river launch for him, just as I did with his shirts and socks from Gieves, and his *Times* and *Illustrated London News*.

'So who did it then—if she didn't?' The Abang faced Graham and me and the soldiers.

I had the answer. And yet it seemed so preposterous I could hardly believe it myself. I knew Brockley was exceptionally fit, and I judged that the Nayans would be quite capable of getting in and out of the Abang's camp unseen. But surely not Brockley at the age of sixty-two? Surely that was beyond even his jungle-craft. And yet there was the evidence of the tobacco. It was as mild but as idiosyncratic as a Lapsang Souchong tea; it was a chance in millions that anybody else on the island smoked the same mixture. And as I examined the chest again I picked up a film of ash on my finger—the tobacco could only have come from Brockley's lighted pipe.

Doreen lunged across the room and scrabbled in the chest. She came up with a cloud of flakes of tobacco and a film of ash.

'Who smokes?' she cried excitedly.

'What do you mean—who smokes?'

She jerked her head at him. 'Do you smoke? Does your medical orderly smoke? Do any of your men smoke?'

'You know it's forbidden under Islam.'

'Yes—like drinking,' she sneered.

He took it, his face distorted with rage. 'Nobody in my army smokes.'

'Who else smokes up-river?'

'How do I know? The Dayaks smoke.'

'But *not* English tobacco? Can't you see it, you bloody fool? It's staring you in the face. Can't you see it? Oh, boy! that old man's made such a mug of you. Brockley, of course!'

Everybody stared at her silently.

'It's impossible!' the Abang shouted. 'Impossible! How could a man of sixty-two get past my guards?'

'Your guards!' Doreen sneered. 'Your guards! All right, how else could it have happened?'

There was silence. The Abang slapped his open hand against his cheek twice or thrice. 'All right, why didn't you or me get it?' he cried.

'Because you had to have special sugar-coated Resochin for your delicate tummy.'

There was silence again. It seemed to be unanswerable.

Then Graham shuddered. 'But it's awful—awful.'

'Why?' Doreen turned on him. 'What's Brockley supposed to do? This ape decides to go up there with a thousand men for a little quiet Nayan-bashing—what's Brockley supposed to do? Sit there and take it? No! He fights back with the weapons he's got. Pretty-boy here has all the latest machine-guns. How many machine-guns has Brockley got? None! So he fights back with the weapons he has got.'

'Germ warfare,' Graham breathed.

'Ah! for Christ's sake!' She turned away contemptuously. 'Did you say you were his son? You ought to be proud of him, not arse-licking this ape here.'

'Shut up! Shut up! Shut up!' the Abang shouted.

50

One of his men burst in breathlessly through the door. Then he stopped, hand on holster, watching them. Doreen and the Abang were both on their feet, leaning forward from the waist, quivering with hate.

'Something I forgot,' she rasped and, tearing the diamond-and-sapphire ring off her engagement finger, she flung it in his face as hard as she could. His hands went up to his face for an automatic second, and when he separated them there was blood running down the depression between his nose and his eye. It ran into the corner of his mouth. He tasted it and started to spit convulsively. 'Jesus! That's my blood! She's killed me. Oh, Jesus!' He staggered to a chair. I noted that even in his extremity, when I should have expected him to invoke Allah in his native tongue, he groaned in American.

Doreen was still standing, weight balanced on both feet, panting. He continued to groan: 'Jesus! Help me. Oh, God! Oh, God!'

His soldier started across the room to aid him, then obviously decided he would not know what to do when he got there, and just stopped halfway. While I was preparing a pressure-dressing from two handkerchiefs the groaning stopped, the Abang went from his normal rich brown colour to a jaundiced grey, moved forward on his seat, and crumpled to the floor.

'The great general! Faints at the sight of a little blood!' said Doreen. She looked at him contemptuously, then flicked his head over with one of her massive, corn-palisaded feet. 'Well, you're a doctor,' she said carelessly. 'Better do something.'

'Get some water and some cotton-wool,' I said.

Graham, who had sat silent and petrified in his chair all this time, jumped up to help. While I was bathing his forehead the Abang awoke. I kept one hand on his chest. Graham, breathing over my shoulder, said sympathetically, 'Easy, General! You fainted.'

He lay back and closed his eyes. 'How bad is it?'

'It's a clean cut,' I said. 'It looks a lot worse than it is, but it'll need a couple of stitches. We'd better get you to the hospital.'

'Stitches!' He fainted again, and lay still and silent.

'Bring your friend in,' I said to the soldier in Malay.

He hurried out. A minute later he was back with the other soldier.

There is always something very chastening about the sight of a lot of blood. They trod quickly and nervously across the room, not raising their eyes from the floor. They lifted the Abang with Graham's help, then supported him out to the Mercedes.

I went back into the house to get the Abang's medicine-chest, and Graham followed me. Doreen was still standing there, but her lips were trembling. When she saw Graham her eyes closed momentarily, then she said politely:

'Do you mind buggering off now? I've got something personal to discuss.' Her tone was cursive, but her voice sounded as though it was about to crack. I nodded at Graham urgently and motioned to him to go.

He looked at Doreen with awe, then picked up the medicine-chest. 'I'll go down to the hospital with the general—see if there's anything I can do.' He stopped as he passed the packet of cigarettes. 'Mind if I take one for the morning?' I pressed the whole packet on him and swept him out to the Mercedes.

'To the hospital,' I said to the driver in Malay. 'I'll telephone the doctor on duty; he'll be expecting you.'

When I got back inside Doreen was sitting with her hands squeezed between her knees. I went straight to the telephone. When I came back she said, 'What an insulting little rat—', but before she could finish her bravado cracked. This time it was not as it had been in my office at Medical Headquarters— trying to stop herself, clenching her teeth, defiantly pretending that she wasn't really crying at all; this time she gave way completely. Her shoulders hunched, her back bent forward, her legs were folded beneath her. She toppled sideways, and lay sobbing on the sofa. Then she started rubbing the insides of her thighs—first the left with her left hand, then the right one. She rubbed harder, both hands together. A frightening hissing noise came from her throat. Her fingers bent and she was scouring her nails into the flesh.

52

'It's awful!' she whispered. 'I can't stop. I can't stop scratching. I haven't slept for a week!'

'What is it? A rash?'

'That's what started it all,' she sobbed. 'He said I was unclean; said I'd have to sleep away from him. He said all w-white girls were d-dirty. What am I going to do? It's spreading. It's getting more every day. It's right down my legs now, and up over my stomach.'

I patted her on the shoulder. It was strange touching a woman's flesh after all this time. 'It's probably ringworm. I'm sure I'll have something for it. And some sleeping-tablets as well, so you can sleep.'

'I'll show you—please tell me the truth.' Before I could say anything she had undone the buttons at the side of her pants and pushed them down to her knees and pulled her blouse up to her chest. It was ringworm all right, spreading outwards from between her legs, a huge fiery-red area streaked with blood where her scratching nails had broken the skin, and pus where the breaks had become infected.

'All right,' I said. 'You can dress up. Yes, it's ringworm.'

'But how did I get it?'

'We whites all tend to get it. Because we're so much hairier than the local people. We have the hair to protect us from cold in our northern climates, but here it just makes a warm, damp, incubation medium for the growth of fungi and suchlike.'

'Oh this bloody country! But can you cure it?'

'Yes. I'll give you some tablets and some cream.'

'Give me something to sleep, Jim. Please.'

'Of course.'

While we had been talking—me talking, she whispering—she had stopped sobbing. 'Thank God! Thank God! Six weeks. I'm finished in six weeks, and then I'm on the first plane out. Oh, England! Civilization! How do you people stick this place? How do you do it? The heat, the filth, the squalor, the corruption ...' She was weeping again. She dragged herself up on to the chair, and I watched her cry herself to silence and some kind of temporary repose. I saw her, hefty, broad-shouldered, sweating

53

into her constricting Western clothes, itching once again at her thighs without even knowing she was doing it. She must have thought it would be so easy and so exciting to be the Abang's odalisque and go off into the jungle with him to fight the savages. But of course it was not. She should never have come. They should never have sent her. For a moment I saw in her all those unhappy Europeans who over the last three hundred years have thought that the East would solve their problems for them. It never does.

8

The Abang was not going to take his defeat lying down. In fact
he was not going to take it as a defeat at all. Three days later
it was announced in the *Tribune*, and transmitted thence to the
world's press, that two hundred Nayans had been killed. The
Army Information Officer later explained to me that he had
published a bulletin stating that there had been two hundred
'casualties' (all Army casualties, though that had not been
included in the bulletin) and that he had included deserters as
casualties; it made for tidier statistics. For one reason or another
nobody got round to explaining the error to the press agencies,
so the official story remained that two hundred Nayans had been
killed, which was regarded as a very satisfactory result all round.

My Director was very relieved. He was convinced that if the
Army had failed against Brockley, he, as Brockley's Head of
Department, would have been blamed.

'Mission completely successful, Doctor!' he cried delightedly
when I next saw him.

'You mean they got Brockley?' I said ironically.

His smile slipped. He looked at me reproachfully. 'That was
not the object of the mission,' he said. 'The object was to subdue
the Nayans, and that is what has been done. Do you know how
many killed, Doctor? Over one hundred.'

He picked up my expression of stony non-enthusiasm and
changed his own.

'Very sad, of course,' he said hastily; and then more defiantly,
'But they should do as they are told.'

'Surely Brockley didn't stand by and allow one hundred

55

Nayans to get killed,' I said evenly.

'He couldn't stop it,' Raschid cried eagerly. 'Nobody can tell the Army what to do. Even Dr Brockley can't tell the Army what to do.' There was a lilt in his voice, as though Brockley had been a giant force of evil and the Army the David who had taken him on and beaten him. 'Dr Brockley has realized that he must do what he is told. There will be no more trouble from Dr Brockley or the Nayans. And next year the road to Serenpahit will be commenced—probably.' He sat back in his big chair. 'It is a terrible thing, Doctor, when audacious minority people try to obstruct the workings of democracy. They will always ultimately be crushed. Do you know, Doctor, that Nayan obstruction and attacks on that road cost the country 400,000.'

Of course I did not need to ask what currency. Manipulation of their overseas bank accounts had habituated the new élite to thinking in U.S. dollars.

I looked at him ironically. Then I realized it was a waste of time and stood up. It would all pass over his head because he wouldn't even know there had been any fraud on the road. He was too little a man to know; his department was not necessary to Them and neither was his influence. So he would never be admitted to the inner circle of big embezzlement. They surmised that he would be satisfied with his trips to conferences overseas four or five times a year; and They were right. He would never know the really big money.

Of the 350 Army casualties, 90 spent varying periods in hospital recovering from malaria; 150 reported back for duty over the next few weeks; 80 were subsequently found to be living with their wives and children; and 30 were never heard of again.

For the moment the Abang wanted nothing more to do with the Interior. He wanted to re-train his men, reorganize his private life, and learn to drive the two new transport helicopters that had been delivered just before the last expedition.

The Medical Department had never got round to finding Graham a job, so the Abang had taken him on to his staff for 'liaison work'. He seemed to spend most of the day sleeping, and his duties began in the evening. They consisted of providing young British and American volunteers of both sexes for parties at the Abang's residence. They seemed to happen every night, but there was nothing immoral about them, or not usually; it was just that the Abang liked to be surrounded by young people, especially Western young people, most of all American young people. Graham still talked of wanting to go up-river to his father, but as the months went by he talked about it less and less. He must have felt very fulfilled bringing the races together as he was doing in Banianok, and it apparently did not offend his radical principles to be brought home in a black Mercedes after a night of drinking and dancing.

The Abang and Graham were happy; the Director was happy because he had not been blamed for Brockley's misdemeanours; presumably Brockley was happy, alone, undisturbed in the Interior without his road. Everything seemed to settle down. Then something happened to stir it all up again. It was one of those haphazard, unforeseeable and completely unnecessary occurrences. When you look back on them you see that they could have been avoided in a hundred ways; and, perhaps because none of these hundred ways presented itself, the only possible explanation seems to be that it was 'inevitable'.

9

One evening, about four months after the Abang had got back from the Interior, the Chinese launch from up-river puttered in to the wharf, paid the customary bribe to dock in the space reserved for the President's launch—which had sunk two years before—and out piled the usual assembly of Chinese, Malays, Dayaks, chickens, pigs and children. When they had all gone away, and only the captain of the boat and his family were left on board, they discovered, crouching behind a stack of petrol drums, a strange figure unfamiliar even to men who had been as far up-river as Bukit Kota and as far across the sea as Hong Kong. Beneath him was a pool of liquid faeces streaked with blood. He had amoebic dysentery, though they did not know it, and though they did not know it either, and neither did anybody else for twenty-four hours, he was a Nayan. They shouted at him because he had shat on the wharf, instead of over the side of the wharf, as he was supposed to; then they kicked him on the bottom because it was exposed; then they hit him over the head with a stick, but not very hard, because he obviously had not understood a word they had said and he looked so funny trying; then they pushed him out through one of the many holes in the port fence, where he was last seen wiping with some plantain leaves the stuff that had still been running down his legs when they had evicted him.

He then disappeared.

Later that evening a nearly naked man with a large stick was seen skirting the bazaar area, and a couple of hours after that a mother reported that her five-year-old daughter had disappeared. The daughter was later found with her grand-mother, but by then word had spread of the stranger's presence in town, and with it hysteria. Doors were bolted that had not been closed for years, he was spotted in half a dozen parts of the town simultaneously, and when the cinema came out, Chinese and Malay youths, fresh from the slaughter of a Japanese-made Western, united for once to search the streets. But they did not find him.

I went to bed unaware of what was happening. Next morning I walked down to my office at seven o'clock as usual, and at seven-thirty I received an urgent message to go down to the police station. I went immediately. When I arrived there were so many people crowded round the door that I had difficulty forcing my way in. When I finally got inside I was conducted to the charge room, and there on the floor was a man covered with blood, unconscious, lying in his own dirt.

The inspector did not stand up as I came in. 'This man needs medical attention,' he said.

I went down on one knee and rolled the man over gently. 'What's happened to him?' I asked.

'This is the man who has been making terror in the town. We have apprehended him.'

'But how did he get these injuries?'

'He was trespassing and stealing.'

'In my house,' a woman cried in Malay, 'sitting on the floor, drinking the water—and—' She pointed, but could not describe the stuff that was trickling down his legs. By now it was chiefly blood.

'He tried to escape,' the inspector said. 'Luckily brave children pursued him all the way here. When I went out he was in the corner of the courtyard behind the bicycles, and the children were stoning him.'

'He's very sick,' I said. 'He obviously has dysentery.' I pointed at the bloodstained excrement on his legs, and the inspector peered politely over my finger.

'Treat him, please.'

'He'll have to come to the hospital.'

59

'Treat him here, please. Very dangerous man.'

'He doesn't look very dangerous now, does he?'

He was a small man, a bit under five feet (though that is not small in Banianok); he had been powerfully built, but now he was wasted away. I plucked at his skin and it stood up in folds where I left it. I had never seen a man so dehydrated. He was wearing nothing but a bangsal, and a belt made of tree-bark. Tucked into a compartment of the belt at one side I saw a piece of paper. I pulled it out and smoothed the folds.

To the Doctor, Banianok.

Dear Colleague,

Dr Brockley asked us to bring Galag down to his hospital in Bukit Kota, but due to change of plan we cannot do this. So we are putting him on the Chinese launch to Banianok. Hoping that you will be able to help him.

Sincerely,

E. Bones M.B. (Doctor)

Banianok Evangelical Mission.

P.S. We think he has dysentery, and we would treat him ourselves, but we have no facilities for treating Nayans.

I handed the note to the policeman. 'Evidence, Inspector,' I said ironically.

Of course, I should have realized; the pudding-basin haircut with the long hank of hair at the back tied up to his neck in a knot, the paleness of the face, the pathetic plait of beads around his head. Some of the very oldest Dayaks have still never worn trousers, but only the Nayans still have bark belts.

'He's a Nayan,' I said. Involuntarily everybody shrank back. Even the commissioner began to look serious.

'Savage man,' he said. 'Native.'

'He's come down for treatment,' I said. 'It's all a mistake. He was meant to go to Bukit Kota.'

'But Nayan dangerous, savage people. Kill all civilized people. Must be locked up.'

60

'Do you think he's going to kill anybody in this condition?' I asked.

But the inspector had the answer to logical enquiry. 'You ask me, Doctor? You are the doctor. The doctor does not know, how can I know?' There were approving murmurs from the crowd.

'All right—he's *not* going to kill anybody. I'll guarantee it. But if he's not treated *in hospital, today,* he's going to die. Send him to the hospital immediately. If you're not happy about letting him out of your custody you can put a guard on him.'

'Ah! The doctor wants to take the police into hospital to guard sick criminals. But why doesn't the doctor come here with medicine? The place for criminal is in prison, not in hospital.'

Again there was a rumble of approval from the crowd. But having, as it were, won his case, he was prepared to be magnanimous.

'The doctor—' he addressed the crowd—'is an honourable man. He says the criminal will not be any more criminal because he is sick. The doctor is an honourable man and we know he speaks the truth at all times. So let the criminal go to hospital. But let him not commit any more crimes.' He sat down to a swell of approval that was almost applause.

'Let's have a stretcher,' I said to one of his juniors standing by.

'Regret no stretcher available.' The inspector's features composed themselves happily.

I picked the man up in my arms. He did not weigh any more than five stone. The crowd shrank away from me as I walked to the door. At the door an old woman dashed up and spat at him. Most of it landed in his face, but some of it landed on my shirt. With tears in her eyes she begged my forgiveness and assured me that none of it had been intended for me. As I put him on the back seat of the Land-Rover he came round. He opened his eyes and stared at me in terror. He babbled at me, clinging on to me; I could not understand his language. But three words, that came over and over again, I did understand. He lapsed back into unconsciousness, but the three words echoed as I drove to the hospital—*Blo ... Ko ... Lee ...*

I undertook the treatment of the Nayan personally. The details of the treatment are not sufficiently technical to be of interest to a non-medical person, but he lay in a child's cot, delirious, with a policeman beside him night and day for five days; he could not eat or drink during this time, and we had to put fluid into his veins. I saw him two or three times a day, but I could not be there all the time. I noticed that whenever I went there was always a crowd around his bed, sometimes in animated discussion, sometimes silently studying him. One of the difficulties of doctoring primitive people is that the presence of their relations is almost as necessary to them as drugs. If you do not allow the relations, you will often not get the patient; for that reason the hospital was always full of people. But I gradually came to realize that the people around the Nayan were not the relations of other patients, as I had thought, but complete outsiders, and when I asked one of the Chinese nurses what they were all doing there, she giggled happily and said, 'Coming to see the savage, sir.' I cleared them all out, but when I returned a few hours later there were just as many. I tried cajoling them, being humorous, getting angry, but whatever I did there was a fresh crowd of people there each time I arrived, which politely parted to allow me near the sick man, and patiently shuffled away when I bellowed at them. The other doctors lost no time in bringing their friends and relations along to view the Nayan, and when I saw the few English people in the town filing hesitantly in to inspect the curiosity I lost hope of ever controlling the crowds.

Seven days after he had arrived, when he was beginning to do well, an urgent signal arrived from Brockley. It said: 'Have you got a sick Nayan called Galag?' I signalled back: 'Yes.'

His reply came within six hours. 'Do not let him go. I am coming. Please isolate. Do not—repeat, do not—allow other people near him.'

I was astonished that he should make a special journey all the way down to Banianok just to collect this one man. (It would be his first time out of the Interior for seven years.) I was also disquieted by that terse instruction 'Isolate him'. The punctilious Brockley would not have presumed to give another doctor instructions. I knew this did not mean isolate him medically, it meant isolate him socially. I began to wonder for the first time whether everybody else was right, that he had gone jungle-happy, that there was something obsessive and unnatural in his devotion to the Nayans, and in his desire to maintain them in their primeval state.

Partly because of this suspicion, partly because Galag suddenly started to have a totally unexpected social success, I relaxed my efforts to keep people away from him. He began to sit up, to take liquids, then soft foods. The population seemed to have forgiven him for being a savage. In fact, seeing him sitting there so helpless in his cot, with the sides up, they had probably developed the sort of affection for him that they might for a dangerous animal they had tamed. There were some people who, metaphorically speaking, wanted to put their fingers through the bars, but most people were content to stand around in a half-circle a discreet foot or so away from the cot, saying in Malay and Cantonese things like 'You are the ugliest little savage I have ever seen', and roaring with good-natured laughter when he shyly nodded and smiled his agreement. (Of course he could not speak Malay, Cantonese, English, or even the Dayak language, but only his own.) When he saw me his face lit up and he grunted in his queer, guttural voice, 'Blo Ko Lee! Blo Ko Lee?' sometimes as an exclamation, sometimes as a question, and I tried to let him know by sign language, pointing far away, squinting into the distance and saying 'Blo Ko Lee', then bringing my arm in a big sweep and pointing to him, that Blo Ko Lee was coming for him. This was something else to add to the crowd's good-natured amusement.

The Director of Medical Services now learned of the signals I had received from Brockley, and asked me into his office. He was not happy.

'I understand you have received signals from Dr Brockley,' he said. He had copies of them on his desk. He picked them up and scanned them sadly. 'But why does he send them to you

63

straight? Why does he not send them through me? I am the head of the department; he should send them through me, like that. Is that correct procedure?'

'I think he regards this as almost a personal matter,' I said soothingly. 'You know how he feels about Nayans.'

'No, it is not personal matter. It is because he doesn't respect me.'

'I'm sure he does.'

'No, excuse me, *not* respect me. *Never* respected me. I am just a coolie to him.' His eyes blinked furiously, and his wet little mouth puckered.

'He speaks very highly of you,' I said untruthfully.

'No, no, I know. I respect him, but he—' he pointed a finger at me—'he does not respect me. Treat me very bad.' The accusing finger, left in mid-air, trembled, drooped, and fell back on to the desk.

I thought I ought to comfort him, but I could think of nothing else to say.

He spoke himself: 'Is he coming down here?'

'He's coming to collect his Nayan.'

'Just coming to collect his Nayan. Not telling anyone, not asking permission from anyone. Is that correct procedure? He should ask permission. Like that. From me. I am the boss. And why must he come for Nayan? Does he come when a Dayak is sick? We are giving medical service in the Interior for *all* the savages, not just the Nayans.' He trembled with righteous indignation. 'Well, he is not my responsibility any more,' he went on thankfully. 'The Abang has asked me to tell him if ever Doctor comes down-river. I will have to let him know when Doctor arrives.'

A suspicion went through my mind; more than a suspicion, a certainty. 'Why does he want to know?' I asked.

'Because he says Doctor is making trouble in the Interior. But impossible to make him come down-river. So if himself comes maybe stop him going back. Tell him contract finished, go back to England.'

'But he hates England. He hasn't even got a home there any more. It would kill him.'

'Very sorry.'

'Besides, if they send Brockley away who would go and take his job?'

He shrugged his shoulders. 'One of our own doctors. Why not?'

'You know they'd resign rather than go in there.'

He shrugged again.

'But it's an important point.'

'Ugh! Savage people!' he muttered. 'They don't want doctors anyway. Don't want houses, cars, trousers or transistors. Too proud! How can we help them? Many nice people dying of diseases down here. First look after own people.'

I sent a signal to warn Brockley not to come. But five hours later the message came back from the transmitting station: the line was dead.

The next day something happened that made it even more vital that he shouldn't come.

I was having my dinner when I received an ambiguous message that the Nayan was causing some disturbance at the hospital. It did not sound very serious, but it was always a pleasure to get away from Ahmed's revolting chicken curry, so I looked at him very seriously, made a dash for the car and drove off to the hospital.

When I got there I found a Malay woman of middle age shrieking on the floor. She was covered from head to foot in blood. I did not at first realize that she was lying on top of a boy of about eighteen, trying to breathe into his mouth. The blood was coming from him. A bowie-type knife was being passed from hand to hand. The boy was dead. Galag was gone.

I asked what had happened, and everybody babbled at once. It took me about ten minutes to establish that the boy lying on the floor had come in as a visitor with a couple of other Malay boys and two Chinese boys. One of the Chinese boys had produced a knife and said, for a joke, that he was going to give the Nayan a haircut. (His mane of hair, hanging down his back, fascinated everyone in Banianok.) Galag, terrified, had wrested the knife away from the youth and, as the youth backed away hastily, had plunged it into the chest of the boy who had been standing next to him. He had then jumped out of his cot and dashed from the hospital.

He was never seen again in Banianok. The police, who arrived within the hour, searched the town but refused to go farther since, as they told me, Nayans had the power to make themselves invisible in the jungle, and pursuit was therefore not only difficult but pointless.

Galag had got away, but Brockley was still coming—paddling now directly into a trap. I telegraphed every hour on the hour until midnight. At midnight the faintest sound of a voice crackled through the static, as though from the bottom of the sea. It was impossible for us to converse. I shouted, 'Dr Brockley! Dr Brockley!' and coming back, just audibly, I heard 'Gone ... a-way! Gone ... a-way!'

'When?' I shouted. 'When?'

'Banianok!' came the rustle from the other end of the earth. 'Banianok!'

10

There had been a slight falling-out between the Abang and the Editor of the *Herald* over the latter's acceptance of the Lenin Prize for Underdeveloped Journalism. This was reflected in the editorial the next day:

When the forces of disruptive and divisive savagery come to the very gates of our capital city—then surely the time has come. Today a martyr of the fight for civilization and revolutionary Socialism lies in state in the hospital refrigerator. His killer goes free.

WHY?

Several months ago a force of the crack blue berets under their beloved commander, Abang Yusuf, went into the Interior to purge these elements from our polity. Perhaps the task we gave them was too great. But if our beloved Commander-in-Chief cannot do it—WHO CAN? We must be sure that our children can play, and our wives go about their duties safe from fear that adventurist-speculative stone-age cliques are lurking around our very capital, with their hideous weapons of destruction. As is well known, blow-pipes and poisoned darts are forbidden under the Geneva Convention, but the London-orientated agency of the Neo-Colonialist conspiracy who is backing these evil savages cares nothing for the Geneva Convention. Let us not forget the atrocities committed against the Japanese by this same agency in 1942. Yesterday the Japanese! Tomorrow our wives and children ... ?

MR PRESIDENT—ACTION PLEASE!

It wasn't long before the Abang was on the telephone to me. 'Doc!' he said tersely. 'I'm in trouble. You seen the press this morning? I had the President on the line too. The heat's on, Doc. I got to get Brockley out of that Interior or my credibility is going to be figure zero. You know where he is now?'

I was certain the Director must have informed him that Brockley was on his way. 'I have no more idea than you have,' I said carefully.

'Listen, Doc—I got an idea. You come round later, spill a brew with Graham and me, and maybe chew it over?'

I paused. 'What does it involve?'

'I'll tell you all that when you get here. Just tell me one thing, Doc—isn't this about time for your annual inspection of the out-stations?'

'The Director's annual inspection,' I corrected him.

'Yeah—that fink Raschid. Never been more than ten miles up-river in his life. The word I got is that you do it every year and you're due out next week. Right?'

'I shall have to check with the Director before I tell you the exact date.'

He laughed shortly. But it was not a happy laugh. He sounded, for once, near the end of his tether. 'Well, you might as well tell me now, Doc. You won't be consulting Raschid for a month or two. Rings me up and tells me he's got something I got to know. Two hours later he's flown out to Singapore.'

'To Singapore?' I gasped. 'When?'

'Last night about eighteen-hundred. Busted his ulcer—according to him.'

'But I didn't know a thing about this,' I said.

'Well, he wouldn't tell you, Doc, would he? You're about the one guy in the country could prove he hadn't got an ulcer.... Tell me, Doc—does a guy with a busted ulcer sit in Singapore airport for three hours and then get on a plane for London ...? I'll see you in a couple, three hours, Doc. I think you're going to like my proposition.'

So Raschid had not told him! After five years dedicated to avoiding decisions the iron had eaten so far into his soul that he had been incapable of initiating even so modest a piece of action as Brockley's apprehension in Banianok. Or could it be that he could not, when it came down to it, traduce his old master? It was pleasant to believe so, but it involved great intellectual effort. I did not pursue it.

As the Abang had said, I was leaving for my inspection of the out-stations the next week. Mohammed, my boatman, had been preparing the stores for the past fortnight.

I went straight down to the wharf, where I knew he would be. I found him with the boat drawn up on the jetty, bottom upwards. He was squatting contentedly behind a bucket of pitch, pipe in mouth, stirring slowly with a piece of wood and contemplating the freshly caulked beams he was about to cover.

Mohammed was one of those natives often described in colonial memoirs as 'one of the good old type'. I sometimes worried that I identified myself with all that was most reactionary in colonialism by liking him so much. He was not interested in politics, transistor radios or blue jeans. He went to the mosque regularly and would never touch pork which is forbidden under Islam; he enjoyed smoking a pipe and drinking beer and whisky, which are also forbidden under Islam. He would invite me to his house for his son's wedding, but would consider it improper if I should invite him to mine. He despised equally his own new leaders, with their mohair suits, dark glasses and gold watches, and the new imperialists with their beards, beads and flip-flops. His only ambition was to go to Mecca. He never smiled. I hardly ever said a word to him and he hardly ever said a word to me. We got on perfectly. He stood up, of course, as I stepped on to the wharf.

'Good evening, Mohammed,' I said.

'Good evening, *tuan*.' We spoke in Malay as Mohammed did not speak any English.

'Dr Brockley is coming down-river today,' I said.

He nodded slowly. 'Blo Ko Lee.'

'He is coming for the Nayan,' I said. 'But the Nayan has

gone.' Mohammed had heard about the Nayan of course. Everybody had.

He nodded again gravely. I had the impression he knew exactly what was in my mind.

'Brockley should not come into town,' I said, trying to keep my voice as even as possible. 'I want you to go up-river and meet him. I want you to give him this letter and tell him to go back. Tell him the Nayan is gone, and we will be with him in Bukit Kota in ten days.'

Mohammed's expression did not change. He put out his hand. I put the letter into it. I said, 'You know Brockley, don't you?'

Mohammed nodded again expressionlessly. 'Not more than thirty years.'

That was all.

The first thing the Abang did was show me his scar. He still had a turban-like bandage over it which he doffed for my inspection.

'You like it, Doc?'

'It's healed very well.'

'The young doc who did it—Junaidi—nice kid. I'm going to see if we can't get him over to the Army. We need a doctor of our own, and somebody who knows what he's doing surgery-wise'd be a real asset.'

He put his bandage back on and pulled it down comfortably over one eye. I recognized it easily as local work—beautifully done, but quite unnecessary. A clerk in the government service would have had a piece of sticking-plaster over his stitches; somebody related to the doctor's wife would have a bandage right round the head; the Abang had to have a creation all of his own. A coolie would have no dressing at all, and his wound, exposed to the fresh air, would have healed the quickest of all.

'Anyway, sit down, Doc, I tell you about my new idea. Drink? Scotch, rye, vermouth?'

Graham brought the Abang a rye, and me a scotch, without asking either of us. But I knew the Abang never drank his rye, so I would not have to drink my scotch.

'This is the idea, Doc, and it's a winner. You take Graham up with you next week and Graham talks to the old man—as his son—his only son—and tells him it's the best thing for everybody he hands in his checks and goes back to England.'

'He may listen to me,' Graham said, softly but fervently. 'I know he loves this country and these people. When he realizes the suffering he's caused I think he'll accept that the time has come. I think so.'

'And if he doesn't—?' I began.

The Abang leaned forward eagerly, breathing all over me. 'We got something else up our sleeve—severance pay!'

'Severance pay?' I repeated.

'Severance pay. To get him started in his new life. Nobody's going to pass up that sort of deal.'

'How much did you have in mind?' I asked.

'Hundred thousand? Hundred and fifty. Maybe two hundred. It's negotiable, Doc.'

Once again I did not need to ask what currency.

'Do you really think Brockley's going to respond?' I asked, astonished.

The Abang leaned right forward, elbows on his knees. 'He's got to, Doc. It's his last chance.'

He almost whispered it, his head only a few inches from my own. The door opened quietly, and glancing up over his shoulder, I saw Doreen. She looked as menacing as ever. She put her finger to her lips and crept with long tip-toe strides to the Abang. I was mesmerized. Remembering the circumstances in which I had last seen them, the thought crossed my mind that perhaps there was going to be a murder. And while I was trying to decide whether that would be good or bad, she reached him, and her hands were around his neck squeezing. His lips split and his tongue popped out. His hands clawed up at hers and he finally jerked himself free.

'Jesus, you want to kill me?'

'One of these days.' She bent down and bit his cheek affectionately. 'Give me a drink, will you?'

She flopped into one of the long bamboo chairs, and Graham jumped up to get her a drink. He poured a double gin, then added half a mug of white vermouth and finally shovelled in half a dozen olives. He gave it to her. She took a deep gulp, coughed contentedly, and put it down.

'O.K., Doc? It's fixed? Gra, you think you can handle your old man?'

'I'll do my damnedest, Bill.'

'You're not talking about Brockley again, are you?' Doreen enquired idly, dropping a handful of nuts into her mouth from a height of about six inches. 'Don't you ever get tired of talking about him? Come on, I want to have some fun.'

The door opened and in walked one of the Abang's junior servants. He was holding a large silver tray on which was a bulky letter. He carried the tray first to the Abang, then to Doreen. He was smiling very happily. Doreen reached up and took the letter, then slowly picked it open. A small leather bag fell on to the floor and about a dozen little black pebbles scattered. Doreen ignored them; the servant immediately fell on his knees and started scrabbling around under her chair to collect them again. She smoothed out the letter. It took her only about five seconds to read it. Then she started laughing. 'Well, what do you know? Talk of the devil! You'd better ask him in for a drink.' She passed the letter over to the Abang. He and I read it together.

Dear Miss Trimmer,

I am in town on medical busines, and remembering that you said, when you were in the Interior recently, that you would like some monkey gall-stones as souvenirs of Banianok, I have given myself the pleasure of obtaining some for you.

Trusting that you are keeping well, and with my very best wishes,

Arthur Brockley.

'What? He's outside?' I had expected the Abang to leap to his feet with the joy of the chase, and immediately order

Brockley's arrest. But I did not know him as well as I had thought. It was just at times like this that the Abang really made himself insufferable, that he infuriated you by doing something so generous or gentle that you found yourself liking him, try as you might not to.

He faltered, shrank back in his chair. 'No ... we can't do it like this....' He put his hands up to his head. 'Jesus, what a stupid thing to do, to come right here!' He looked at his servant desperately. 'He's outside?'

The servant beamed happily, and then to Doreen in English he said excitedly, 'Very nice stones; very good price for old Chinese man.' Monkey gall-stones, like powdered rhinoceros-horn, were valued by the Chinese as an aphrodisiac.

The Abang smacked his forehead. 'What can I do? I got to take him in.' He turned to Graham. 'Gra boy, you're not going to like this.'

I looked at Graham too. Did he realize he was going to meet his father for the first time in seven years—but that his father was going to be a prisoner? Apparently he did not. He looked up at the Abang adoringly. As usual he did not appear to have the first idea what was going on.

Then we heard through the window, but coming from somewhere around the side of the building, a voice raised in song. The song was 'Nearer my God to Thee'. The tone was one of rather deperate serenity, the accent recognizably from South Wales; the voice was familiar, but it was not Brockley's.

The Abang covered his face wearily. 'O.K. Let's have him.'

His servant dashed out. There was a grunt as though the singer had been prodded in the back with something certainly no softer than a rifle butt; then 'Carry me over to Jordan' started a semitone higher and in much more urgent tempo. The door opened and a gaunt little man was propelled through it. He seemed dwarfed by a pair of huge grey flannel trousers.

'He came from Blo Ko Lee,' one of the bodyguard said. 'Maybe coming to assassinate the General-Highness.'

'All right—where is he?' the Abang said to Dr Eric Bones. Bones's eyes glazed. He stared unseeing at the Abang, then he cried: 'For fifteen years I fought the corruption and licence, drinking and smoking, of the imperialists. But I never endured brutality such as this.' He spoke in Malay. The Abang took that, quite correctly, to signify that Bones thought of him as a native.

'All right—we know you're working for him. Where is he?' the Abang roared in English.

Bones folded his hands serenely in front of him and closed his eyes for a good five seconds. Then he said, in a voice of great gentleness, 'I did not have to come here today ...'

'And you won't be leaving either unless you give us some straight answers. Now where's Brockley? And where did you get that letter?'

'It was given me by a Malay boatman of the Medical Department. I knew that this was the place it should be brought because it is common knowledge that Miss Trimmer is always here. I did not have to deliver it personally. I could have sent one of our deacons. But I came myself—as I am—to plead with her—' He turned to Doreen and took a couple of steps towards her. '—to plead with her to end the state of concubinage into which she has fallen, and to walk again in the paths of—'

'Cheeky bastard!' Doreen observed dispassionately.

'Wait a minute! Just who the hell are you?' the Abang roared.

The noise died away, there was a moment of silence, then Bones said, 'Doctor Eric Bones, Banianok Evangelical Mission.'

'Bones!' Doreen jumped up. 'He was the one who caused all the trouble in the first place.'

The Abang leaned forward. 'You! So you're the one? You're the bungler who brought the Nayan down to town.'

Bones looked for a moment as though he were considering the indictment. Then he put it to one side and returned to his real purpose. This time he addressed the Abang. 'Our God, though you do not know it, is your God too. It cannot be His will that you should turn your face from Him and your wife—'

'Ah! Shut up!' Doreen said contemptuously. 'You know you were supposed to take him to Bukit Kota. Brockley told you never on any account to bring Nayans down here.'

74

'God does not always let us do what we want,' Bones said patiently.

'You know that little savage turned out to be a murderer—he did a murder?' the Abang cried.

'It has not yet pleased God to lead the Nayans to Him,' Bones replied with composure. He kept closing the discussion in a way that, if he had been an Oxford Union debater, would have excited envy.

But the Abang did not envy it; it made him angry. 'You know what?' he cried. 'I think you're a bit too smart. I think you're trying to make a fool out of me and my friends.'

It was interesting to see how even now, five years after Independence, the new authorities followed so much that had been laid down under the British. The Abang would never have hectored any other white man like this. This was the sort of intimidation he reserved for his own people. But missionaries had always been different under the British, a menace or an entertainment according to your viewpoint, but never part of the Raj, always outsiders—as, indeed, they wished to be. And it was as such that the Abang bullied Bones.

'Right—where is Brockley?'

'I had not seen Dr Brockley for many weeks until today when I met him about five miles up-river. His boat was pulled in to the bank, as was that of the government boatman I mentioned earlier. He set off again up-river and the boatman asked me to deliver this package to Miss Trimmer.'

'What's that?' the Abang shrieked. 'Not only you bring that murderer down to town, you come in here insulting me and my girl—but you let Brockley get away as well!'

He picked up the full bottle of Old Crow. For a second it looked as though he was going to throw it at Bones, and Bones ducked accordingly, but at the last moment his aim changed, and it shattered against a nude study on the wall that he had cut out of his favourite American periodical.

Bones's eyes opened, then slowly his head turned to follow the trajectory. Of course he saw bare-breasted native women every day; but not white women, and never in a bubble bath. He looked back at the Abang, and then turned again to the picture, and then again.

He went very pale. He managed to start the first verse of 'Christians Up and Smite Them', then his knees gave way beneath him and he crumpled to the floor unconscious.

11

Mohammed knew the river as well as the patch of water beneath his own house. He had been born on it, in one of those Malay houses built out over the water on stilts; he had grown up on it and worked on it as a boatman all his life. He was the Malay boatman Bones had mentioned, of course. I never taxed him about the letter, and he never spoke of it to me. I would not have expected him to. He had spent thirty years in the Medical Department; and he knew the first rule of the British Civil Service: never know more than you ought to, and if you do, never tell anybody. As far as he was concerned, and as far as I was concerned, it had never happened.

Now he pulled his hat down over his eyes, adjusted his pipe, and eased himself back against the oilskin padding he had rigged up between the side of the boat and the tiller; then he let the forty-horse-power motor go, and we were roaring upstream at twenty miles an hour. If we could have gone to Bukit Kota by plane the distance would have been eighty miles and we could have done it in perhaps half an hour; by the river, looping backwards and forwards across the coastal plain of the country, it was 250 and took two and a half days. There was, of course, no road. We were on the only pathway into the Interior. Here, only twenty miles from the sea, the river was a fat, brown, sluggish flow, sliding between mangrove swamps 400 yards apart. But soon it would narrow, sixty miles inland it would be a faster flow between stricter banks. Two days inland, gravel banks would begin to appear. The day after that—a day's travel above Bukit Kota—we would come to the rapids. We would have to ship our engine and haul the boat up over them. Then we would put the engine back into the water and drive on to the next rapids. Soon we would find the bed of the river was so uneven and so shallow that we would not risk our propeller in it. We would leave our engine and our prahu at a long-house and change to smaller flat-bottomed boats which we would pole up-stream as though we were punting on the Thames. Ultimately the water would become so shallow and the rapids so frequent as to be more or less continuous, and we would leave the boats altogether, take our gear on our backs and labour up-river on foot, up to our knees in water but still in the river because it was still the best pathway through the jungle.

At that point we would still be a day away from the area where the Nayans roamed.

Mohammed liked to arrive at Brockley's H.Q. at mid-morning when everybody on shore would be tired from the day's first labours and ready for distraction. He liked a good audience—he had a flair for arriving.

As we came round the final bend the prahu cut close to the bank, almost under the branches of the nipah palms, and then Mohammed swept wide, out into the middle of the water and straight ahead up-river as though we were going to pass Bukit Kota completely. At the last moment he turned the boat for a dramatic ride-in, and fifty yards from the jetty he cut his engine and sat back calmly as though he were the chief passenger. I looked at his face; not a muscle flickered.

When we were still ten yards out hands reached for our rope, but Mohammed appeared not to see them. Finally he threw it, like a Roman emperor tossing coins to the crowd; the boat bumped against the soggy plank of the jetty, and everybody was reaching down to help us out.

Each jabbered in his own language, some proudly trying out what they knew of English: 'Hallo, sir!' 'Thank you very much.' 'Sorry sir, welcome!' 'Hyde Park Corner, Piccadilly Circus.' One or two children cried out, 'Give me money now', but when

Graham turned his bearded visage on them they scattered in terror.

At the top of the steps stood a small, round-shouldered half-caste of about retiring age, wearing very clean long white trousers and a white shirt, and not concerning himself at all with ropes or luggage. He advanced with a charming smile as we were hauled on to the jetty and, taking my hand, he said in a high, piping voice, 'Welcome, sir, welcome! Mr Brockley, I presume.'

'No, this is Mr Brockley.' I indicated Graham, who was coming up the stairs behind me.

'This,' he whispered. 'This is Doctor's son?'

I ignored the implied reproach in his voice. 'You must be Mr Chumley, of course, Dr Brockley's assistant. You were on leave last time I came, but I've heard all about you.'

His face crinkled and his head wagged ingratiatingly. 'Thank you, sir; thank you very much.'

I took hold of Graham's arm. 'Graham, this is Mr Chumley.'

'Pronounced Chumley,' Mr Chumley said, extending his hand. 'I am happy to know you, sir,' he said with a worried frown.

Then he cleared Graham from his mind and launched into a speech of greeting:

'Welcome, sirs, very welcome! Dr Brockley is unfortunately unable to meet you; performing vital operation, appendix case, enough said. He begs that you will proceed to the Residency where all things are in preparation and he will join you soonest. I should like to conduct you personally, gentlemen, but pressure of work renders this almost impossible. So please to follow *my* assistant.' He turned from us with a bow and an ingratiating smile and started shrieking at the men who were standing around as though he had a mutiny on his hands. They picked up our bags.

'It's all right,' called Graham. 'I'll carry my own.'

'Oh no, please, sir! These lazy coolies will do it.'

Graham hoisted his bag on to his shoulder.

'Give them your bag,' I said in an undertone.

'I'm quite able to carry it myself.'

One of the boys started to take it off him.

'It's all right. I don't need you to carry it.' But of course the boy knew no English and did not understand.

A second boy who did understand English bashed the first boy over the head and wrestled him to the ground.

'Thank you,' said Graham.

But the boy immediately grabbed the bag out of Graham's hands, slung it on to his own shoulders and said, 'O.K. Number one boy; let's go.'

The hospital was exactly opposite the jetty, about thirty yards from it. Brockley's house was on the hill behind it at a height of about four hundred feet. A winding track led up to it.

'I suppose it's nice the way they're so keen to carry the bags, isn't it?' Graham said as he puffed along beside me.

'What they get for a tip will be the equivalent of a day's wages —if they had a job,' I said.

'You mean—' he stopped—'they want a tip?'

'Of course.'

'But I haven't got any money.'

I shrugged. 'I'll pay.'

It was ironic and sad that the volunteers should have sacrificed so much to come out to work for the natives, and that the chief reason those very natives despised them was that first among the things they had sacrificed was the wherewithal to give tips.

12

We were greeted at the house by Wee Kit Chong, Brockley's cook, immaculate in white smock and white trousers. (It was beginning to strike me that up here, two and a half days farther from civilization than Banianok, the people surrounding Brockley looked a good deal smarter than most in the capital itself.) Wee Kit Chong did not speak any English and I could not speak Cantonese, of course, but we conversed easily in Malay. Graham was by this time looking even more hot and dishevelled. When I introduced him as Brockley's son, Kit Chong, though enthusiastic, was visibly shocked. He led us to our rooms, where our bags were dropped, then we went out on to the verandah to drink lime juice and water in tall glasses. The sun was now directly overhead and it was very hot, but whatever breeze was going we caught up on the hill. We looked out over the jungle stretching as far as we could see, which was twenty miles in every direction, uniform, featureless, broken only by the river which glinted silver in the reflection of the clouds above. To me it was very mysterious, and perhaps I confused mystery with beauty.

We saw Brockley coming a good twenty minutes before he arrived. He left the back door of the hospital, a tiny white figure who started the long trudge up the hill. The path wound in and out of little groves of trees around the side of the hill, and he disappeared and reappeared through them, all the time getting bigger and bigger, as we watched lazily over the verandah rail.

'That must be a hell of a sweat twice a day,' I said, 'for a man of sixty-two.'

'What's that he's got with him?' Graham said. 'Some sort of animal?'

'That's Briok—his Nayan boy.' As Brockley trudged upwards, pipe clenched between his teeth, leaning forward into the gradient, hands together behind his back, Briok capered around him laughing, turning somersaults, tripping over his blowpipe, occasionally falling into step to perform a parody of the old man's walk.

'Who's he?'

'You know Briok,' I said. 'I told you about him in Banianok. He's the mongol.'

'No, you didn't tell me about him,' he said. 'What's a mongol, anyway?'

'You remember when you came and told me you'd heard from some of the other volunteers that your father was a homo-sexual and had a stable of native boys ...'

Graham flushed. 'Yes, I remember now,' he mumbled. 'Those silly buggers—always getting the wrong end of the stick.'

'As always the myth wasn't completely made up; there was some tenuous connection with fact. He had a stable of one—a mental defective Nayan he brought down to Bukit Kota to save him from being left out in the jungle by his own people to die.'

'How long has he had him?'

'Briok was about two when the Nayans realized he was never going to grow up. As far as anybody can remember he's been down here with Brockley ever since.'

Graham's eyes clouded. Natives with Boston accents and inter-national venereal disease, driving around in black Mercedes, he took in his stride; but this sort of relationship was something he had not been prepared for.

By now I had the binoculars on Brockley. As I watched him trudge up the hill he seemed just the same as when I had seen him two years before. His bald head and his face glowed a blotchy red as they always did when he was out in the sun—after thirty-five years he had still not managed to get an even brown tan. There had been a few streaks of grey in the fringe of hair around the back of his scalp from ear to ear; now it was completely white. If anything he had lost weight: the skin of his throat was deeply scored by creases, with no underlying fat to smooth them out; but his stringy calves were as strong as ever, and his step did not falter.

I asked the imaginary journalist at my elbow if this was the monster who held the Interior in a state of terror, for whom no sadistic or lascivious pleasure was beyond relish? Surely not in those trousers! He was wearing what the *Tribune* had called his uniform of colonial oppression: white shirt, long white stockings with a pipe tucked in one garter, and huge brown brogues, completed by white shorts, loose at the waist and flapping down almost to his knees.

And yet he did not look either the part of His Majesty's representative. He was so small—no more than five feet six or seven—and thin, and round-shouldered. As he stopped halfway and looked up at us, there was an expression almost of agitation on his face—so different from those imperial proconsuls with their straight backs, plump figures and air of gracious condescension. Then he pushed his neck forward again and thrust himself into the final part of the climb.

At last we could hear the crunch of the old man's ridiculous brogues on the gravel, and the high cackle of Briok's private laughter. Graham, in his cane chair with his lime juice beside him, craned to see his father coming. Seven years, he told me, it had been since they had met. His father reached the bottom step of the verandah, and I stood up. But for some reason Graham did not. Maybe it was something in the ethos of his generation or his group that would not let him treat such an important meeting in a ceremonial way.

'Hallo, Dad!' he said from his chair. 'You're looking well.'

But Brockley was more than a match for him in manufacturing anticlimax. He extended his hand and said:

'Oh, hallo! Rather warm, isn't it?'

Graham flushed a deep red; he must have realized he had done something stupid, but he could not bring himself to correct it. He remained seated.

'I see you've both got drinks,' Brockley said. He gave an

order in the jerky sing-song of Cantonese to Wee Kit Chong, who had appeared as soon as he had reached the top of the hill and was standing by looking very troubled. Briok was given a slice of paw-paw and Brockley was handed a small whisky and water.

'Well, how are things in the metropolis?' he said to Graham. 'How did you like Banianok?'

'I like it. Very interesting.'

'Yes. Bit noisy, isn't it? Bit too much like Singapore or London.... How is everybody? How is the Abang?'

Graham shrugged. 'How should I know?'

'I understood you were a friend of his.'

Graham looked at his father and then at me, open-mouthed. I had told him his father's sources of information were quite beyond the Intelligence services of the Army.

'We had him up here a month or two ago. I don't think he'd realized what a difficult place the Interior can be unless you have good friends.' A suggestion of a smile crinkled the skin round his eyes for a second, but it was only a second. 'I'm afraid he's not the man his father was. Shall we go into lunch?'

After lunch—Wee Kit Chong served a Chinese mee, boar-meat and an ice-cream flavoured with durian fruit that tasted like frozen egg and bacon—we sat on the verandah and drank coffee. Brockley had no more whisky. Graham seemed disappointed. He seemed to expect that his father would go through the afternoon with the bottle at his elbow.

Brockley studiously avoided discussing family matters with his son, probably thinking it would be discourteous to me; nothing in the conversation during their first hour together would have revealed that they were father and son. It was typical of him to observe such punctilio. Not that it would have mattered—conversation would have been as stilted whatever we were talking about. We talked haltingly of medical matters, the plans of the Administration in Banianok, the international situation, with which he was remarkably *au fait* (I saw a neat pile of *The Times* air-mail editions on a cane chair beside the long bamboo one which was obviously where he habitually sat to read them). Graham said very little. He followed the conversation with his eyes, backwards and forwards from his father to me, according to who was speaking.

At one-fifteen the old man got up. 'I hope you will make yourselves at home until I come back,' he said stiltedly. 'You can bathe in the river from our jetty if you wish, or some of the trees behind us here on the hill have some very interesting orchids. There are newspapers, magazines and books in the sitting-room.'

'Where are you going?' said Graham. This time he stood up.

'I have to go to work at one-thirty. I'll be back about five o'clock.'

'But aren't the government hours seven to one-thirty?'

'We work the old colonial hours here: eight to twelve and one-thirty to four-thirty. People are more efficient if they have a break in the middle.'

'But how can you have different hours to what the government lays down? You're a government department, aren't you?'

'We do what we like up here.' Again the skin round his eyes crinkled. For the space of about a second and a half he was almost smiling.

'But surely you have to do what headquarters tells you?'

'Damned silly of them to change it in the first place! Political decision. Thought it would be a good idea to change a bit of the colonial organization to emphasize they were independent. And the coolies welcomed it because they thought they would be working fewer hours. Ridiculous system! People just go home and sleep the day away or drink themselves stupid, then wake up about six looking for trouble. I must go.' There was no change of intonation between his denunciation of the government's working hours and his valediction. In fact it was not until he had finished that we realized he had changed the subject.

'Hold on.' Graham ran after him. 'I'd quite like to see round your hospital.'

'It will be a pleasure to show you,' his father said formally.

'Now?'

'Not now.'

'If you haven't got much to do ...?'

'Perhaps tomorrow would be more convenient, when you've had an opportunity to rest and—' he paused a second '—get cleaned up from your journey.'

Graham flushed immediately. 'How do you mean—get cleaned up?'

'Have a shave; change your clothes.'

'But I haven't got any other clothes.'

'I see.' Brockley looked him up and down—sandals, jeans, stained shirt hanging open with St Christopher medal showing, red beard, red, sweating face, cascade of copper-coloured hair. It seemed to go on for about two minutes, but in reality it took no longer than a second. 'You might find clothes similar to mine rather cooler. Perhaps I can ask Wee to lay you out a set.'

'That won't be necessary.'

'No trouble. I've got dozens.' He turned and walked solidly down the verandah steps. We watched him down the path. He stopped about two hundred yards down and pulled the pipe from his sock, and tobacco pouch from the breast-pocket of his shirt. When he had got the pipe going he went on down the path and we saw him turn in at the back door of the hospital. I looked at my watch. It was exactly one-thirty. I thought as I watched him idly that something was missing, but I could not say what it was. When I went out into the garden I realized. There was Briok lying face-down on the grass asleep in the shade of the jacaranda, one hand outflung, still clutching his blowpipe. Later he woke up, rubbed his eyes, grinned at us, giggled privately and set off at a trot down the path to the hospital, still clutching his blowpipe, stopping every now and then to put it to his lips as though he were shooting birds and wild boar as his people did.

I looked at the piles of *Country Life*, *Field* and *Illustrated London News* at the bottom of the bookshelf, and the latest copy of each laid out on a bamboo occasional table, and wondered idly whether I wanted to look at them, go out for a walk, or just continue wondering. I had worked hard for the last year.

86

It was pleasant to do nothing.

But Graham was up on his feet. 'Have you noticed something about this room?' he said.

'What is it?'

'Look around. Something that makes it different from any other European's house in the country.'

I started to look around, but Graham could not wait. 'There is nothing in this room apart from the bamboo chairs to suggest that it isn't a sitting-room slap in the middle of England.'

I had noticed that the decoration of the room was sparse, but I had not put my finger on that one essential point: there was nothing of the East in it. The man who had spent thirty-five years in Banianok, was the best-known man in it still, even at the coast; who had entered more deeply into the life and the culture of the country, to the extent of speaking seven of its languages and being acknowledged in anthropological circles as the world's expert on the Nayans, had nothing of the country in his own house. There were no ornaments. There were three picture-frames. They were hung on two walls, the other two walls being completely taken up by window spaces. I walked round the room studying them. One was a pencil drawing of the Governor's Residence in Banianok. It was signed 'M. Brockley'.

'My mother,' Graham said softly. 'She was quite good at drawing.' He looked at it, rapt, for several seconds. 'Fancy him still having it up on the wall!'

It was an indifferent drawing such as you will see in a hundred dining-rooms, but he seemed to be unable to stop looking at it. At last he pulled himself back brusquely to the present. He took me by the elbow. 'Here are the choice pieces. Look at these,' he said accusingly.

There were two photographs, one above the other, beside the verandah door. One was Trinity College 1st Eleven, 1925, the other was Trinity College 1st Eleven, 1926. Eleven tight-lipped young men stared out of each, wearing huge, baggy white flannels all with knife-edge partings to their hair (mostly slightly to the left side of the middle) and the hair flattened, gleaming, against their scalps in a way no one has seen since the war.

Where, now, were those young men who had thought so much of themselves forty years ago? I looked at the names; I had never heard of any of them. But wherever they were their insolent stares must have disappeared by now, and surely none of them was in such singular circumstances as their captain for 1926.

'I hate those old team photographs,' Graham grimaced. 'They're so ...'

'What is it exactly that you dislike about them?' I asked idly.

'They're just so ... ugh!'

'You mean the illusion of self-assurance they emanate?'

'Yes! The—I mean—just the whole bit.'

'The waste of so many gifted young men spending so much of their youth in pursuit of fours and sixes.'

'Check! I mean what gave them the right ... just standing there looking so bloody ... I mean—'

'The rentier class idling on the cricket square while stunted men worked their lungs out thousands of feet below the ground.'

'Right!' Graham cried. 'You know exactly what I mean, Jim. You agree!'

'Not necessarily,' I said. 'But I'm always ready to hear a well-put argument.'

I picked up a copy of *Country Life* and he wandered away. When he was safely out of the room I put it down and closed my eyes. I was not really asleep. Then I heard him calling agitatedly, 'James! James!' and I dashed in the direction from which the voice had come. He was standing in Brockley's bedroom, gazing at a large framed photograph of a beautiful young woman.

'You know who that is?'

I had never seen her, but I knew who it must be. I said, 'Your mother.'

He nodded slowly. 'She was beautiful—then—wasn't she?'

She was beautiful in the way women were expected to be beautiful in the 'thirties—swan-like neck, oval face, high forehead, slim nose absolutely straight, with slightly flared nostrils, but not a hint of retroussé at the bridge, or snub at the tip. Her hair was

88

marcelled, and a single long string of beads fell almost to her lap. The dole queues must have been forming all over Europe, but there was a delicious air about her of never having done a stroke of work in her life, of never having missed a bath, or an extra blanket at night. How beautifully she fitted her period! Today she would probably not have received a second glance.

'She left here in 1941 and he's still got her picture over his bed,' Graham murmured. 'Honestly—that breaks me up.'

'Why did she leave?' I asked.

'She was leaving anyway. Couldn't stand it. But then word came that the Japs were coming, so they sent *all* the women and children. She met someone else in London during the war.... You know how it goes.'

I had the impression it hurt him to say that.

'And he had her picture up all these years!' He looked at me. 'I thought he hated her. I really thought he hated her. And he must have wanted her all the time!'

I turned away. It was like turning out the pockets of a dead man. 'Come on—' I started to walk back to the sitting-room. As I reached the verandah I heard a sound that was as foreign to Bukit Kota as the shunting of railway engines—a bugle call. I looked out over the rail, at the ground sloping away at a forty-five-degree gradient to the hospital four hundred feet below. There was an explosive sound behind me and Wee Kit Chong launched himself from the house.

'Number six call, Doctor!' he shouted to me in Malay. 'Emergency call!'

I watched him all the way down, wondering whether I should be with him. Alternately running and walking it took him ten minutes.

As he reached the hospital I saw Brockley come out and talk to him, then Wee jumped on a bicycle and pedalled away towards the bazaar. Brockley turned his back to the hospital and started the long trudge up the hill. I wondered whether he was coming to fetch me to give an anaesthetic for an emergency operation, and whether I should be going to meet him. Then he stopped for a moment and looked up. I waved. He waved me back and

89

set off once more up the hill. By the time he reached the top Graham was with me on the verandah. As he came up the last thirty yards I could see he was panting and the sweat was running off him.

'What is it, Dad?' Graham called. 'What's happened?'

'White men!' Brockley gasped as he pushed past us. 'In town. Two of them.'

Graham beamed. 'Great! You must get lonely up here all on your own.'

'Big one and a small one—' Brockley muttered, scrabbling for his field-glasses in the drawer. 'Middle-aged, cameras ... How do these people get up here?' He trained the glasses on them. 'They're crossing the padang now.... Ah! there's Mr Chumley and Kit Chong. They'll soon find out what they're up to.'

'Oh, good! Will they be inviting them up?' Graham asked innocently.

Brockley lowered the binoculars about a foot in front of his chest. 'No, they will not.'

He raised the binoculars again. Then he passed them to me. 'Here, Reed, have a look and see if you recognize them.'

'I'm afraid they've disappeared into one of the shop-houses,' I said, when I had focused. 'But I can see Mr Chumley. He's talking to a group of Chinese outside the shop.'

He walked back from the verandah. 'Well, we'd better leave it to him.' He turned round. 'Damn these people! How do they get up here? Why can't they leave us alone? There's nothing up here for them.'

'But why shouldn't people come, Dad?' Graham exclaimed good-naturedly. 'They're probably rich American tourists; bring some money into the place, open it up.'

'We don't want visitors up here,' Brockley said coldly, 'and we certainly don't want to be "opened up".' He supplied the inverted commas himself.

'You mean *you* don't, Dad,' Graham chuckled. 'But if you gave the natives a chance they'd probably jump at it.'

'We do not intend to give them the chance.'

90

'But, Dad, you don't mean we; you mean you. Who is we?'

'I'm referring to the government of this country.'

'But you're wrong, Dad. I don't think you really know what the government wants.... I'm not knocking you, Dad.' He fanned his hands flat in front of him. 'You're entitled to your point of view, but it's not the same as the government's; in fact it's the complete opposite. And that's one of the reasons I'm here. The government asked me to come up and talk to you.'

'Oh?' Brockley looked astonished. 'What about?'

'Sit down, Dad,' he said kindly. 'It may not be pleasant. Let's get the tea in. Kit Chong!'

In Banianok it is important to remember never to order other people's servants around; but Graham did not know that.

Kit Chong's wife brought the tea in.

'Now, Dad, you know what I'm doing in Banianok?'

'I'm afraid I don't.'

'You don't? God! Well, why do you think I'm here?'

'I have no idea.'

'I'm a volunteer. I'm working for the Volunteers for Peace.'

'I see.'

'You know who they are, of course.'

'No, I'm afraid not.'

'Dad, please sit down—I'm trying to talk to you about a pretty serious matter.' Brockley was still shuffling around the window with his binoculars.

'There they are! They've come out of the shop-houses. They're walking back across the padang. Quick, Reed! See if you recognize them.'

I walked over and took the binoculars. 'No! I've never seen them before. They look like tourists to me. They've both got multi-coloured shirts; they're wearing flip-flops; they've both got cameras.'

'It's revolting, isn't it? Why do they have to look so disreputable. It gives white people such a bad name. We need to keep standards even higher now there are so few of us left.'

'*Few* of us?' Graham laughed. 'There aren't any of us left—apart from you, of course.'

91

Brockley turned back to me. 'I wonder what they want? How long will they stay?'

'There isn't anywhere for them to stay, is there?' I said.

'The rest-house hasn't functioned for four years. You wouldn't think they could stay anywhere, but they do. You may not believe this—' he lowered his voice and looked at me carefully— 'but some of them stay at the Chinese shop-houses.'

I did not reply. Graham called, 'Well, what on earth's wrong with that?' There was a hint of exasperation in his voice now.

The old man closed his eyes. 'It just isn't done.'

'By who?'

'It isn't done by white people. If we lower ourselves to that sort of familiarity what sort of position will we be in?'

'Dad, can't you get it into your head that we have no sort of position any more anyway? It doesn't matter any more what we do. We're out—finished. We can only come here as visitors and helpers—or tourists.'

'We do not want tourists coming in here with their so-called civilization,' Brockley said coldly. 'Keep your tourists down at the coast. We do not want transistor radios, blue jeans or venereal disease.'

Graham laughed, but his laugh was a little shrill. 'Really, Dad, I think you ought to be out of your jungle for a while. Your ideas of Western civilization seem to be a bit limited.'

'I've nothing against Western civilization. We happen to have something here that works better. But your friend the Abang doesn't agree. He wants to smash it up. We have peace here; we have enough to eat; everybody is happy, everybody lives contentedly together—we have none of the communal strife you have down in the capital. But Yusuf wants to smash it up ... smash it up,' he repeated, staring at his son, his face as usual expressionless, but his lower lip trembling.

'Father—let's be rational. He's only trying to build a road.'

'We don't want a road. We don't even need it. We've never needed one till now.'

'But don't you see that's what they said when the steam engine was invented?'

92

I was in a difficult position. I gave my allegiance to that vague concept 'progress', so I should have been in favour of the road, but I also knew, which Graham did not, that there was no real intention to build the road and that it was just a convenient way of diverting public money to private bank accounts.

Neither of them had mentioned the most concrete argument: 'I understand the World Bank has refused funds for the road,' I said.

'World Bank? More interfering busybodies?' Brockley growled.

'They say the road is impractical. Too expensive to build and too expensive to maintain, and not enough traffic to justify it. So they've refused the government's request for a loan.'

Brockley grunted. 'Oh! I see.' But then, accusingly, 'But they're still building it.'

'But out of their own money. Partly development and partly the defence vote.'

'Defence!' he exploded. 'What on earth has it got to do with defence?'

'With all due respect, Father,' Graham said, 'you might expect the Abang to know more about that than you.'

'That young man is a fool. I saw him grow up. He never had any fibre. Not like his father. His father was a man of great character, but Yusuf has always been a Westernized corner-boy. Then he went to the Philippines and the Americans completed his degradation. I will *not* have him coming here with his thugs upsetting my boys. I will *not* have it. I have taken steps. I will take further steps if necessary.' He trembled with agitation. Then suddenly he flushed bright red and stamped away to change.

'You don't think he could be insane, do you?' Graham whispered to me.

13

Brockley came back half an hour later, freshly shaven and dressed for evening—in starched white shirt with long sleeves, black trousers, black patent-leather shoes and a Sixty Club tie. He sat down and called for the drinks tray.

We heard the slow crunching of feet on the gravel outside, then the hollow, reverberating sound as they ascended the wooden stairs to the verandah. There was a knock at the door; it opened, and a head appeared around it. The head was Caucasian. It had that peculiar shapelessness that is only seen on Americans, and then only on Americans with very short haircuts. It was a broad face, of apparently uniform consistency, with a broken nose and large flat ears. The scalp was covered by a two-day growth of grey bristles which were prolonged, at the front, into a peak about half an inch long. The expression was intelligent or, at least, apprehensive. 'Pardon me,' the man said but did not withdraw.

Brockley stood up. 'Please come in,' he said diffidently.

The man entered, and behind him another, smaller man who looked roughly the same, except that his hair was the palest blond and he had no eyebrows.

'How do you do, sir! I am the Area Director of the Peace Corps—Mike McBerski is my name—and this is Mr Bunk Wankel of the Central Intelligence Agency.'

The smaller man stepped forward. He inclined his head formally. 'Gentlemen!'

'We're very happy to know you gentlemen.'

'Yes, quite,' Brockley said agitatedly. 'Please sit down. What can I do for you?'

94

'Well, sir, we just arrived in Bukit Kota this afternoon to conduct a survey of the Volunteer Employment potential of this sector of this country.'

'I see. Most kind. But quite unnecessary. Situation quite under control.'

'Oh?' He looked disappointed.

'Yes. What a pity, what a pity!' Brockley said briskly to hide his agitation. 'Will you have a drink?'

They looked at each other, then the big man said, 'Well, I don't know whether that's wise....'

'I think it'd do you good, Mike,' the smaller man said, and then looked at Brockley. 'I understand you're a doctor, sir.'

'That's right.'

'Well we'd like to ask your advice, Doctor, if we may.'

'One of the reasons we came up here—apart from the anticipated pleasure of making your acquaintance—was to consult you professionally. You see—'

'We've got problem bowels.'

Brockley's face, as usual, dazzled by its impassivity.

The little man looked round at each of us in turn. 'Mike and I have the most God-awful bowels!' Then, presumably because I looked the most sympathetic, he singled me out. 'Mike's got piles too.'

'Yes, I've got piles too. I'm worse off than Bunk. And when I get this diarrhoea on top of it, why it's—'

'Murder!' said Bunk.

'Murder!' Mike agreed.

'And since we've been on this river—'

'The last four days. Well, excuse me, but long strings of *something* we've been getting in it. Semi-liquid with these strings, and oh! about seven or eight times a day, Bunk?'

'I've been seven or eight times a day, Mike, but you've been worse.'

'Well, maybe I have. Come to think of it, that's right. Anyway, Doctor, the situation is: eight to ten times a day, with these long strings of matter in it, and both of us exactly the same.'

Bunk leaned forward in his chair and said urgently, 'Can you tell me where the comfort station is, Doctor?'

Brockley fluttered his hand in the direction of the lavatory, and Bunk blundered away. Mike looked at us all meaningfully in turn.

'Kit Chong,' Brockley shouted in Malay. 'Let's have some drinks out here.' But of course Kit Chong was still in the bazaar finding out about Bunk and Mike. (I had always thought he was not very efficient.) I got up and went to get the drinks myself.

When I got back Brockley was saying, 'Perhaps I'll be able to find something for it.'

'Well, Doctor, we'd surely be very obliged. We've tried everything in the Peace Corps kit, but ...' he shook his head once to the right and once to the left.

Brockley looked round rapidly like a wild animal in a trap, then he said rapidly, 'Er—yes, but you didn't tell me what you would like to drink.'

'Well, if you really think I ought to, Doctor—I'll have a weak scotch and Coke if I might.'

'I ... beg your pardon.'

'Coke. Coca-Cola.'

'Is that a cocktail?'

'No, it's the largest-selling soft drink in the world,' said Graham woodenly; then, standing up, he went over to the American. 'Graham Brockley. We haven't been introduced,' he said, looking coldly at his father. There was another round of 'I'm happy to know you' etc. and then I, perforce, went over and did the same thing.

'It doesn't look as though he's got any Coke,' Graham said to the American.

'I'm afraid we have no stock of that beverage,' Brockley said gravely. 'Could I perhaps get you a brandy and orange squash, or something of that nature?'

'Maybe I'd better just have some milk, Doctor.'

Bunk came back into the room. He shook his head meaningfully at Mike. 'No change,' he said. He sat down.

'The doctor thinks he may be able to help us,' Mike said.

'Did you give him the samples?'

'Not yet.' Mike turned to Brockley. 'No doubt you'd like to see some samples, Doctor?'

'No, I don't think that will be necessary,' Brockley said hastily.

'We got them with us, doc. It's no trouble.'

'No, no!' Brockley's voice rose a tone. 'I've got just the thing for you. I'll go and get them.' And he scurried from the room.

He came back with some pills that looked like Suphaguanidine, the usual treatment. 'Here! Take these. Two every four hours.'

'And you're sure you don't want the samples, Doctor?'

'No. Thank you very much, no.'

'My physician back home told me there are one hundred and forty-three known causes of, excuse me, diarrhoea.'

'Yes! Quite! Very many,' Brockley muttered meaninglessly.

'What do you think could have done it, Doctor? Ever since we got on to this river three days ago it's been this way.'

There was silence for a moment. Then Graham said, 'What about the Abang's cholera scare?'

'Ah yes—the Abang's cholera scare,' Brockley said contemptuously. He tried to laugh but he only managed a grimace.

Bunk leaned forward. 'What was that?'

'The Abang's cholera scare?' Brockley snuffled. This time he did manage a laugh.

Mike and Bunk looked at each other rapidly. 'But the Abang never told us anything about cholera.'

'He doesn't always remember.'

'But that's serious business, Doctor. I mean that's people's lives.'

'How long's it been going on?'

'Well, about five months ago the Abang decided—' He stopped. He looked at me and suddenly he seemed to realize the potential of the cholera scare. He turned back to Bunk and Mike, his eyes narrowed. 'Five months ago an outbreak of cholera was declared in this province,' he said seriously.

'But why weren't we told?' Mike wailed.

'It was reported in the *Straits Times.*'

'But nobody told us. The Abang—a very dear friend—how could he have forgotten to tell us a thing like that?'

'I understand he's a very busy man.'

'But how could he forget a thing like cholera? Forty-eight hours isn't it, Doctor?'

'I beg your pardon.'

'Till you're dead. Forty-eight hours.'

'Oh, yes! In a serious case. Forty-eight hours. Quite correct. A dreadful end.'

'We should never have been allowed up here.'

'No.'

'How bad has it been, Doctor?' Mike leaned forward.

Brockley paused. 'Not as bad as initial reports suggested,' he said, scrupulously avoiding untruth. He permitted himself an expressionless glance in my direction. He seemed to be enjoying himself a little more now.

'What should we do, Doctor?' Bunk said calmly.

'I think you would be better to return to the coast as soon as possible in the circumstances. Perhaps we could make arrangements for a boat.'

'That's very kind of you, Doctor.'

'Not at all.'

'But what about you fellows?' Mike asked.

Brockley shrugged. 'Don't worry about us.'

'Are you the only medical team up here?'

'That's right.'

'And you've been handling this thing single-handed?'

Brockley lowered his head modestly. 'We're doing what we can.' He shouted for Kit Chong. Kit Chong puffed in, having just returned from his mission. Brockley spoke to him in the rapid sing-song of Cantonese, and he scurried away again. 'I've told my man to arrange a boat for you immediately.'

'Thank you, Doctor.'

'It should be waiting at the wharf in about half an hour. Please don't give the driver more than a hundred and fifty rupiahs.'

'One-fifty? But that's ridiculous. We paid five hundred coming up.'

'A hundred and fifty rupiahs is the price. Please don't exceed it.'

Brockley seemed to have recovered from his initial nervousness. 'And if you do see the Abang,' he said blandly, 'I would be grateful if you'd give him our best wishes.'

'Oh certainly, Doctor. We surely will.'

'And do remind him to enforce his closure of the Interior to travellers. You might have caught something serious,' he said, sounding now almost avuncular.

'Yes sir!'

'And do get an expert to look at your bowels very soon.'

'We will.'

'They have some very good specialists in Singapore.'

'Manila's our Area H.Q.'

'Manila,' he beamed. 'Even better!' Manila was even farther away than Singapore.

'Well, Doctor, thank you for everything!'

'Such a pity our acquaintance was so short,' Brockley said happily.

We shook hands all round and Brockley escorted them along the verandah to the steps. We heard more goodbyes outside, and then the crunch of their boots on the gravel gradually fading away into silence. We expected Brockley to come in from the verandah, but there was not a sound from outside. I looked out of the door and saw him standing with his back to me, his hands clutching the verandah rail, his shoulders shaking noiselessly.

'Are you all right, Brockley?' I said sharply.

He turned round and came towards me. There were tears streaming down his cheeks and his mouth was distorted into a rictus of what could have been pain or laughter, but not a sound came from his lips. He fell into his own chair, with the piles of *The Times* and *Country Life* beside it.

'So there is a cholera scare?' Graham said eagerly.

His father's only reply was to sink his head into the crook of his arm; his shoulders continued shaking.

'It's true about there being cholera up here?' Graham repeated.

Brockley choked and rubbed his fists in his eyes. 'No. It's complete rubbish,' he gasped. 'But they fell for it hook, line and sinker. Oh dear!'

'But it must be true. The Abang wouldn't say so if it—'

'I'm the only one who knows what is going on in this province. I know there's no cholera.'

Graham stood up. 'So why did you tell them there was?'

Brockley pulled a huge, dazzling white handkerchief from his pocket, and started scrubbing his face. 'Excuse me, old thing, I didn't tell them. *You* did!'

'I was only quoting the Abang.'

'Of course. That's the cream of the joke; s-so was I.' And his head fell back against the back of the chair, his handkerchief over his face. I discovered a very odd feeling: I had got so used to Brockley not laughing over the past five years, that when he did for once, and with such abandon, it seemed faintly improper.

'You mean you deliberately allowed those people to believe something that was absolutely untrue? Just so that you could get rid of them? People who only wanted to help, to build, to make something of the place? So you could go on playing the tin God up here? I didn't realize till now. You're sick, that's what you are. You're sick!' He tramped to the window and back, and then back to the window. 'I'm going straight down there to tell them.'

'My dear old thing, I'm sorry to say they won't b-believe you.'

'They'll believe me.'

'Apart from calling the Abang a liar and making a complete fool of yourself for having been taken in in the first place, you've got to remember something else: the Americans are a brave people but two things terrify them—unboiled water and loose bowels. The question of cholera has been raised. They will not rest now until they have seen their doctor and he has assured them they have not got it. They will no doubt have to undergo exhaustive medical investigations—you know how thorough the Americans are; they will have to have their samples checked. Oh dear—those samples!' And he collapsed again.

100

Graham stared at him for a few moments, then he broke away and dashed from the house.

I stood up. As I did so Brockley fell back into his chair. 'No, let him go,' he said. He closed his eyes. Two seconds before he had been laughing with almost hysterical hilarity. Now he looked old and weary.

He opened his eyes again. 'What happened down there in Banianok, Reed? To Galag, I mean.'

I told him in a few words how his Nayan had come, how he had been treated, what he had finally done.

His face remained expressionless. He said heavily: 'The Banianok Evangelical Mission.... I asked them never under any circumstances to take anybody to Banianok Town. And then to take a Nayan!'

'I got a note from their doctor—Bones. They hadn't intended to, but they had a change of plan at the last minute.'

I had no idea why I defended Bones. But Brockley did not seem to mind. 'They always change their plans. They never know what they're doing from day to day. Gave themselves straight up when the Japs came. Whole lot of them died of dysentery within three months. No guts!'

He leaned forward in his chair with his back very straight, and said calmly and slowly, 'This was rather important, you see, Reed—Galag was the very first Nayan who had ever ventured down-river for treatment.' His hands were folded in each other; each syllable had the same weight, he spoke in a monotone as though he feared that, if he let himself go, the words would come out faster and faster until he was panting and incoherent. 'Twenty-five years I begged them to come down to Bukit Kota for treatment. They were afraid. They wouldn't come. Finally Galag came. Now he's dead. It's important.'

'Is it absolutely certain he'll be dead?' I said.

'Nobody could cross two hundred and fifty miles of jungle without even a blowpipe. Even Nayan jungle-craft isn't equal to that. No, he'll be dead all right,' the old man said calmly. 'I'll have to go to them, Reed. They're going to be very frightened and distressed. They're going to need me. I'll leave

101

tomorrow. I think ... I'd like you to come along—if you have the time.'

'What about Graham?' I said.

The two vertical grooves between his eyebrows drew together, as though he had difficulty recalling who Graham was.

'Hasn't he left with the Americans?' he muttered.

'Perhaps.'

But he had not. An hour later he returned.

'They didn't waste any time,' he said, quite brightly. 'They'd gone when I got there.'

Brockley was sipping a malt whisky, I a glass of fresh lime juice. 'I'm sorry I flew off the handle a bit, Dad, I—'

But apologies, confessions, anything like that, frightened Brockley. The old man jerked his head rapidly. 'You must have a drink before dinner. Sherry? Gin? Do you take malt whisky?'

14

The mechanical regularity of the life I led in Banianok had made me so habituated to wakening at six that I was unable to prevent myself from doing the same thing in Bukit Kota. By five past six I was wide awake. The sky had made its transition from gunmetal to violet-grey and was just turning to pale blue. It was the fifteen minutes when it is no longer night, but not yet day; you do not need a light to see everything, but nothing that you see seems real. I pulled up the sarong in which I slept and walked out on to the verandah to look at the mist rising off the river, and was struck, as I always was, by how cold it could be in the early morning exactly on the Equator, only a few hundred feet above sea-level.

I walked to the edge of the verandah and looked down, my hands on the railings, at the almost sheer drop to the river below.

'He could still be alive, Reed.'

I whirled round, my heart thumping, and there was Brockley, sitting in a bamboo chair just inside the doorway. He was also wearing only a sarong. In the half-light he looked very old and frail.

I felt that reflex, physical anger that comes when one is startled. But in the next few seconds it drained away.

'A distance of two hundred and fifty miles through completely hostile jungle?' I said as gently as I could. 'You admitted yourself last night ...'

'I know. It sounds impossible.' His voice was thick. 'But you don't know the Nayans as I do—the jungle-craft. You know, when the Abang and his men were up there they got in and out of his camp every night. They could have killed every one of them in absolute silence. They brought me out that big medicine-chest, so I could change the malaria pills—without disturbing a soul.'

So I had been right! He did not seem to realize that I was not supposed to know it had happened. Perhaps he thought of me as an accomplice.

'There's a chance. Oh! it's only about one in a hundred. But if anybody can do it Galag is the man. There's a chance. There's a chance, Reed. If he's made it he'll be there already. They'll be waiting for me. I'll have a lot of explaining to do—but it'll be all right.'

There was a long pause. I shivered with the cold. 'And if he's not there?'

'They won't see me. They won't receive me. It was I who begged them for twenty-five years to send their sick down-river. For twenty-five years, Reed. And when they finally did ... He's got to get back. Savages aren't like civilized people. You only get one chance. They don't forgive you your mistakes.'

He stood up, still in the shadows. 'But there is a chance. Don't you think so? What do you think?'

He looked at me intently, willing me to say Galag was still alive. I remained silent. When he had stood up the top half of his body remained in the shadow, but his legs were clearly visible. One side of his sarong had become hooked up around his thigh. I saw the division on his skin below the knee where the top of his long white socks normally reached. Above it was a hard brown knee, below it a thin white leg with stringy calf muscles and a knotted concourse of varicose veins showing clear and blue through the skin.

'They're my boys, Reed,' he pleaded.

Round the corner of the house Briok jigged, rubbing sleep from his eyes. The first rays of the sun slanted over the top of the jungle. It was day. Brockley shambled away to the wash-house. As he moved out into the light he put his hand over his mouth and made a noise as though politely clearing his

104

throat, and kept it there as he scurried across the floor. He had no teeth in.

There were eight of us: Brockley, myself, Graham; Law Kiat How, Brockley's Chinese dresser, a young man in his twenties; Domeng, Brockley's cook; Nasir, his driver; and Mohammed, my driver from Banianok, all three Malays, old men with scores of grandchildren between them who had been in the government service almost as long as Brockley had. Briok was the eighth. There were two boats. Graham was in the same boat with me, with Mohammed and Law Kiat How the dresser; the rest were in the other boat.

We could all have gone in the same large boat, but it would only have taken us one day up-river. The next day the river would become tòo shallow to use an outboard engine on anything but the shallowest draught of boat. The day after we would come to the rapids; the smaller the boat the easier it would be to pull up over the rapids. Above the first couple of rapids we would be able to use the engine for short periods, but then we would have to go into the jungle and cut poles and punt our way up-river. Ultimately the water would become so shallow that we would have to leave the boats and walk—still along the river-bed. The smaller the boats the farther we could get before we had to leave them.

Briok danced around with his blowpipe, singing to himself and getting in everybody's way. When we were all ready to go, Brockley called him and rolled on to him over his head a large, heavy, navy sweater with a polo neck. It came to just below his knees. Brockley got into the boat and Briok jumped in and settled himself alongside the old man.

Nasir called out 'Ready to go' in Malay. Brockley produced two hats. One, a broad-brimmed triangular palm hat such as the Chinese wear to protect themselves from the sun in their pepper plantations, he jammed on to Briok's head. The other was an English boater, yellow and frayed. The ribbon had obviously been washed many times. I had to study it closely to make out the yellow, green and red stripe of his college colours.

He put it on, gave the crown a gentle tap, folded his arms in front of him, stretched out his legs, and away we went.

It was bitterly cold on the river just after six o'clock in the morning. I noticed Graham looking a little apprehensively at everybody else in their thick sweaters; he had refused Brockley's offer of one the night before. Then the chick-chacks had grated in the bedroom, and the ceiling-fan full on could not stop the sweat from soaking into our clothes, and Graham had laughed, 'Sweaters? On the Equator?'

Of course it was not cold by English standards, but we were only wearing one layer of clothing in preparation for the heat of the day which would be building up by eight o'clock. We saw the mist lying on the river as the light strengthened, and when we started to slice through it at twenty-five miles an hour the wind tugged its way into his thin shirt as he sat beside me hugging his chest and trying to slide himself below the side of the boat. When I offered him my oilskin he jerked his head in curt refusal; but when Law Kiat How offered him his oilskin he relented and, thanking him graciously, slipped it on.

Before nine, when we had been on the river less than three hours, we were pulling off our sweaters and Brockley was cautiously removing his boater to give his scalp a little sun. Now we should rely on the twenty-five-m.p.h. breeze created by the speed of the boat to cool us. But it could only cool us a little. Sweat started to appear in beads on lips and foreheads. Some of it evaporated, but where the beads became confluent they ran in sudden spurting rills down the sides of our faces to necks and chests, and the breeze could not do much to evaporate the dampness that had begun to accumulate in shirts and trousers. I thought of Doreen and her ringworm. Had the fungus already settled on our damp, hairy, Northern skins?

We were just leaving the mangrove swamp of the coastal plain and coming into the evergreen rain forest proper of the higher ground. The river was still about a hundred yards wide and we kept to the middle of it as much as we could. But when we pulled closer to the side to avoid floating debris or to round a bend we could see the thick black slime under the mangroves,

106

and their trunks standing out of it like the limbs of petrified ballet-dancers—ballet-dancers and hunchbacks. Every now and then there was a tributary and a tunnel over which the twisted trunks intertwined at a height of about six feet. Where did they lead? What menace could be hidden in them? What perfect places they would have been for ambushes by tiny prahus! How impossible it would be to give pursuit up those little creeks! I found myself thinking of the Japanese, and then of the Abang and his troops, pushing apprehensively upstream, wondering when they would come to something resembling solid ground, something that could be turned into a defendable position.

'Are there crocodiles?' Graham asked Law Kiat How, peering into the eternal twilight between the mangrove trunks, as we came particularly close to avoid a whole tree that floated downstream towards us.

'Before, very big, and Blo Ko Lee used to shoot. Now not so big. But crocodile is not very interesting subject, sir. I would like to ask you some questions on the subject of British Constitution.'

'You don't want to know anything about the British Constitution, Kiat How. Your own constitution is much more important.'

'Sorry sir, not so important. I am studying British Constitution for Cambridge Certificate.'

'But why—why *British* Constitution?'

'More easy examination, sir. After passing British Constitution, English Language, Mechanical Drawing, Tropical Hygiene and Geography I have opportunity to better myself and get higher-paid job—or office boy American Oil Company, or senior Government Hygienist.'

'Oh! Well, I'll try to answer your questions. But one thing, Kiat How—please don't call me sir. I'd be very pleased if you'd call me Graham.'

'Yes sir, very happy. Now on subject of Defences of the Realm Act, 1911 ...'

The two boats drove up-river, sometimes separated by a hundred yards, sometimes by as much as half a mile. Whenever Brockley's boat came near the bank Briok raised his blowpipe, four feet long, to his lips and shot at imaginary birds and animals.

I wondered if he knew what he was doing; I also wondered who had taught him to do it. He would have been only a baby when he left his own people, and nobody down in Bukit Kota used a blowpipe. It must have been Brockley, with his obsession for keeping everything just the way it was; Briok was a Nayan, so he should have a blowpipe—even though he would never be able to use it.

Leaning out to shoot a large branch of a tree, complete with foliage, that drifted by, he dropped his weapon in the water. Brockley's boat turned in a wide arc to retrieve it, but we, coming up behind, picked it up first. As the boats came together and we handed it back, Brockley called out cheerfully, 'Fine morning! We usually stop for lunch about twelve, if that's convenient to everyone.' And then he was away again.

'He's in a good humour,' Graham cried gaily as we waited, allowing the other boat to get clear of us. 'But he'd better watch his dress. He'll have the Colonial Secretary after him.'

Brockley had left his whites in Bukit Kota. He was wearing a grey bush-shirt, open at the neck, with pockets absolutely everywhere, brown shorts, very thick but short brown stockings, and white tennis-shoes. With his Trinity boater on his head he looked an extraordinary sight. But the most extraordinary thing of all was that, looking at him sitting there erect in his seat, his arms folded in front of him, boater tipped slightly forward and to the left, one could not imagine him wearing anything else to go up-river. He looked perfectly correct. This was obviously his equivalent to a tweed suit for the country in England. And just as the tweed suit, though only for country wear, would have been as impeccably tailored as his herring-bone for town, his bush-shirt was just as starched and creased as his whites had been in Bukit Kota, his tennis-shoes as immaculately blancoed.

When we halted for lunch on a gravel bank by the river he leaped out of the boat and strode around the tiny little ten-yard-square peninsula, stopping now and then to take deep, grateful
108

breaths, as though he had just come from Wigan or Burnley.

'Aah! it's good to get away from the hurly-burly, isn't it, Reed?'

Domeng and Nasir brought out the sticks they had carried from Bukit Kota and started to lay out a fire; Mohammed went off to collect fresh sticks to dry over this fire so that they could be used to start our next one; Graham and Law Kiat How sat on two stones in the shade of an entayut tree, discoursing inaudibly with heads together; Briok splashed in the shallow water round the boats. Brockley stood looking at them all, boater tipped back, his hands on his buttocks: 'It's always good to get out of town....' He beamed at them all impartially; by 'town' he meant not London, not Singapore, not even Banianok. The hurly-burly from which he sought surcease was the hurly-burly of Bukit Kota.

We had lunch—chicken and boiled rice—which everyone ate with relish except Graham and myself. We sat on flat stones in a circle with the rice-pot in the middle for anybody who should want second helpings. Brockley was served first, then I, then Graham. Conversation was largely in Malay because Nasir, Domeng and Mohammed could not speak English. Law Kiat How was the only Banianokese who spoke English, and Graham was the only Englishman who did not speak Malay; luckily they seemed to have a lot to say to each other. But they did not talk much over lunch because Brockley was busy chaffing Nasir, Domeng and Mohammed. In Bukit Kota he would never have dreamed of asking them to his house, and they would have been shocked to receive an invitation. I do not think he would have served Malay chicken and rice at his table either. Only three hours away from Bukit Kota the eating arrangements, like the food and dress regulations, were quite different.

We butted on up-stream. Now the river was becoming narrower and the flow perceptibly faster. During the afternoon we left the mangrove swamps for good, and entered the true evergreen rain forest. Now there was scarcely thirty yards of water on either side of us; the black slime of the mangrove swamp had become firm ground, but it would offer little more

109

in the way of comfort to invaders coming up the river as we were doing. The vegetation grew to the very edge of the water; the huge evergreens—belian, rangau, jonking—ranged upwards and outwards over the river. Now and then we would see a few feet of bare bank where the wild animals came to drink; apart from that the featureless forest receded from the river, mile after mile the same—eternal twilight cut off for ever from the sun by the interlacing foliage of those stupendous trees. Mile after mile we did not see more than twenty square yards at a time where a platoon could pitch a tent. The Abang had had five hundred men.

As I pictured the Abang and his men searching for a place where they could be safe and together, I thought of that other fugitive—Galag—flitting alone through the same twilight and going to the same place.

15

As we got into the boats an hour after dawn next day Brockley
murmured to me: 'It won't be possible to avoid the Dayaks, I'm
afraid. We'll be spending the night at Penghara Ngang's long-
house. It wouldn't be possible for me to go up-river without
seeing him. He and I were very closely associated at one
time.'

It was well known that Brockley never spoke about his three
years in the jungle during the war. That was the nearest he was
ever to come to it with me.

The sun was settling into the topmost branches of the forest
when we came to Penghara Ngang's. They must have heard the
noise of our engines a long way off because, when we rounded
the final bend, there were children racing up and down the bank,
bare-breasted women standing in groups, each of them with a
baby at her hip, heavily tattooed men standing in other groups.
And as we came into the bank we saw the Penghara himself
struggling down the notched log that was the staircase from the
long-house to the ground.

Nasir put the nose of the boat at the bank, aiming for a spot
about twenty yards above the landing-place, cut the engine forty
yards from the bank and, with his customary panache, steered
it into the end with the merest bump against the black earth of
the bank. The children fell, splashing, into the water, giggling
'Blo Ko Lee, Blo Ko Lee,' and Briok, hearing the familiar name,
chanted it too. The Penghara was still struggling towards the
bank. The two young men on either side of him kept trying to

pick him up bodily, and it would not have been difficult for he could not have weighed more than six stone; but he kept knocking them on the head with a heavy stone he carried, and when they put him down he tottered a few more steps towards the river until they tried to hoist him again. This was the legendary Wild Man who was almost as well known by report in Banianok as Brockley himself. Even in 1942 he had been old by native standards. Now, as far as anybody could remember, he was about eighty. He looked like a plucked chicken. He wore nothing but the native bangsal, disdaining the trousers and shirts the young men were now affecting. He was very thin, and his skin hung in little corrugations from its natural creases; his back was bent in a rigid arc that would never now straighten again; round the borders of his scalp there were just a few wisps of hair; he was totally blind. He stood swaying at the top of the bank. Several men assisted Brockley out of the boat; in fact they lifted him bodily and carried him to the bank. He went up the few steps that had been cut into the soft earth of the bank. The crowd parted at the top and the two old allies stood in front of each other. Slowly they shook hands. Brockley said something—in Dayak, of course—and the Penghara replied with high, cackling laughter. The onlookers sighed with pleasure, and then, the spell having been broken, everybody was suddenly jostling to shake hands with Brockley. Those who could not get into position to shake hands touched him, and those who had shaken hands but wanted to do it again did so. Nobody would relinquish his hand until forced to do so. The women were in this with the men, even those with babies tugging at their breasts, for among the Dayaks women enjoy complete equality with the men. The crowd parted as the Penghara made to touch Brockley again. He put his arm on Brockley's as though to guide him, but in reality to lean on him, and together they moved slowly off up to the long-house. It was an extraordinary sight—Brockley immaculate in his shirt and shorts, the tattooed, plucked chicken beside him. The Penghara's neck and chest were covered with tattoos, but the tattoos that held my eye were the mass of blue bars on the knuckles of his fingers and thumbs.
112

Each represented a head taken—either in his extreme youth, which would have been at the turn of the century, or, forty years later, when the Japanese had come. I wondered, as I watched him drag himself up the notched log that was the long-house's staircase, whether he had really understood what the Japanese war was all about. Could he have seen it as the last brief fling allowed by a benevolent King-Emperor, mediated by his agent Brockley, when the Japanese were let loose in the land for three years, and there was one last, glorious season in heads?

Brockley went off to wash in the river with a large audience of children—and Briok. Graham had been in no time commandeered by the young men of the long-house, and had gone off we knew not where. Nasir and Mohammed sat holding hands with the old men of the long-house. Law Kiat How and I, the two people nobody could be prevailed on to amuse, found ourselves alone with our sponge-bags by the side of the river.

But Kiat How did not seem to mind. It gave him opportunity to exercise his lust for knowledge.

'Doctor is acquainted with the Marquess of Salisbury?'

'Well, I couldn't say I was acquainted with him, Kiat How, but I know of him.'

'Yes. Very wicked man! Want to place Chinese peoples in slave labour camps—all mixed in with blacks. This is true, Doctor?'

It was a question, but a statement at the same time.

'Well, I don't think that's absolutely right, Kiat How ...'

'Not right! Not British! Very un-British! Excuse me, Doctor, when will His Lordship and Mr Powell make a fascist bid for power? This year, next year?'

'Where did you hear all this, Kiat How?'

'Ah! So is well known!'

'Well, no, Kiat How,' I faltered. 'I don't think there is any likelihood of revolution in England at present.'

'Mr Powell and His Eminence will not be arrested, tried by people's court, and shot?'

113

'No! Actually, Kiat How, there are one or two things I ought to explain—'

'Not necessary, Doctor. Perhaps Mr Powell arrested and shot, but not possible in England arresting lord. Mr Beaverbrook and General Mountbatten will never allow.'

I grasped at something on which I could be definite. 'No, Kiat How, it *is* possible to arrest a lord in England.'

'Excuse me, sir, Mr Graham has informed is not so possible. Please inform last lord arrested?'

I looked down at the soap in my hands, becoming painfully aware that I could not think of one. 'Well, as it happens ...' I grinned ruefully.

He leaned over and put his hand on my arm—a thing Chinese seldom do. 'Thank you, Doctor, your information is invaluable. But please do not be afraid—the British authorities will never learn of our conversations.'

After we had eaten dinner—boiled rice and chicken again— fresh tuak was brought up and everybody was given a mug. Tuak is the rice wine the Dayaks make themselves. At its best it tastes like very sweet champagne. At its worst it is indescribable. Brockley lit his pipe, and the big medicine-chest was dragged into the circle of the light from the oil-lamp under which he was sitting, still on the floor, still cross-legged. Of course we had had a large number of spectators while we ate our dinner. Now the rest of the long-house started to shuffle along towards us.

The clasp of the medicine-chest was undone and the lid creaked slowly upwards. Kiat How, unblinking, lifted out the auroscope and placed it on a cushion in front of Brockley. He brought out the ophthalmoscope and placed it on another cushion, then the spatulae, the patella hammer and the tuning-fork, and last, the ultimate instrument, Brockley's old, worn, heavy rubber-and-steel stethoscope. He passed it to Domeng, who presented it to Brockley gravely with both hands. Brockley took it slowly and fitted it around his neck. Now he was ready for his first patient. Kiat How sat cross-legged beside him in the lee of the medicine-chest, ready to get out the medicines as they were required; the Panghara sat opposite him. The rest of the long-house crowded behind the Penghara, the lucky ones at the front sitting, the rest standing, pressing back against those who pressed forward from behind.

This was the nearest they ever came up-river to a theatre show. But savages have more inhibitions than we do. Everybody wanted to watch; nobody was inclined to provide the entertainment—and certainly not the sick. The Chinese medicine man who unrolled his mat on the padang in Bukit Kota warmed up himself and his audience with a display of snakes; it was up-river logic that Brockley would want to do something similar. It would be impertinent and foolhardy to present the really sick until he had got into his stride.

Brockley sat there serenely, chatting to the Penghara, allowing them to waste his time, smiling benignly on them like an indulgent father. Then he looked up absent-mindedly and made a remark in Dayak. They all giggled and a lot of pushing and shoving followed, and finally a girl of about sixteen with a cheeky face allowed herself to be pushed forward. She had, she said, a pain in her head.

A pain in her head? A serious one, or not so serious?

Very serious, she giggled.

Was it more here, or more over here?

It was here but also here: it was everywhere.

Brockley reached for his tuning-fork. He banged it against the floor, and then, as it vibrated, placed it against her forehead. Did that make it better?

'Yes, that made it much better.

He banged her gently on the bridge of the nose with his patella hammer. And that?

Yes, that was very soothing too.

He said he had just the medicine for her.

She pointed at his stethoscope. A stethoscope, of course, is for listening to chests and hearts and nothing else. But she wanted her head listened to. Without a word Brockley obliged.

One dose of his special medicine, he told her, and she would be cured.

Kiat How handed her a worm-powder, she shook hands gravely with Brockley and returned to the crowd.

The next man had ghosts in his liver, and the one after that whispering joints. Brockley treated them with the same cordiality and gave them each, with utmost gravity, a worm-powder. Every now and then he made a little joke, and everybody laughed happily, not because what he had said was funny, but because he had gone to the trouble. It was all very paternalistic, but they obviously adored him.

At last the sick were brought on—the old women with tuberculosis, the hunters with septic wounds, the children with vitamin deficiencies. His method did not change at all; he examined them, as he had examined the others, with the same grave courtesy, the same little joke; the only difference was that they did not get worm-powders.

When all the sick had been seen (and many of those who were not sick came round for a second go) the Penghara brought out his oldest wine, some of which had been in bottles for over a month, and announced that there would be dancing. A couple of drums were brought out, made of animal hide stretched over a circular frame taken from the trunk of a slim jonking tree, and an instrument that looked like a flute but blew only one note. Everybody gathered around the Penghara's living space, except for one or two old people who were sulking for one reason or another, the mugs were filled, and into the light of the oil-lamp jumped one of Graham's young cronies wearing the native bangsal with an ornamental belt of bark, ornamental soft-iron bands wound around his calves and a bark cap with two sheaves of hornbill feathers streaming from it. He was holding a native sword, the parang.

The Dayaks have only one dance, which they call the najat, but it never seems to weary them. It is supposed to tell the story of a hunt, but since hunting is the central activity of life to the Dayaks they can include in it more or less what they please. There is little interest among the Dayaks in orthodoxy, and this

116

applies to their dance steps too. The first performer was obviously the best in the long-house, and he clearly knew it. He stepped into the light and stood absolutely still, knees bent, parang pointing downwards and forwards, then very slowly he raised his free hand to his ear and started to walk with a mincing tread round the circle of light. He was listening for wild animals. Suddenly he stopped. Almost everybody in the long-house caught their breath. He leaned forward slightly. He had picked up the sound of a wild boar, say, browsing through the undergrowth. He raised his sword and started to creep up on it. The boar raised its muzzle. He jumped back. The boar resumed its feeding, and he started to advance again, with a queer sideways motion, stepping high, placing his feet with infinite gentleness, his whole body flowing into each step. The boar moved again; he went as still as a statue, his body bent back at nearly forty-five degrees. After ten seconds his muscles flickered, and he started to go forward again. The audience followed, rapt. It was the sort of attention interpretive dancers in the West must dream of. But it was not for the dance; it was for what it depicted. And it did not spring from artistic sensibility, but from the mystical preoccupation of a hunting race with an activity that did not stop at getting food but was a prime purpose of life itself. As I studied those rapt faces I thought of the row of heads I had seen curing over the Penghara's fire, and I understood for the first time how such a good-humoured and easy-going people could have become known all over the world for their horrifying practices (and struck terror into the heart of one small boy in particular, growing up in England, 12,000 miles away, just before the war).

He went forward, then back, forward and back again, his body sinking lower and lower, parang raised higher and higher, muscles tensed, legs bent. He was on the boar, thrusting his sword deep into him, drawing it out and thrusting it in again, the crowd—women and children as well—baying as though it were all happening just three feet from them. The boar fought back. With desperate but still graceful movements he slashed at it with his parang, dodging its charges, taunting it, eyes rolling

117

in a transport of passion which I knew I could never follow. At last, with six slow, powerful stabbing movements, muscles absolutely rigid, blood vessels bulging on his head and neck, he finished the animal and it lay dead. He collapsed on the floor beside Graham and everybody burst into feverish applause.

What could follow that performance? The answer was, another exactly the same but not quite as good. Mugs were filled and another boy was pushed on to the floor. When he had finished a girl got up, then another girl. They all did the same dance, though most of them did not go through to the killing at the end, but the audience applauded just as enthusiastically. Brockley and the Penghara formed the focus of the whole group, and as each dancer finished Brockley gave him an odd little ceremonial bow and clapped his hands formally.

At last somebody pulled Domeng to his feet, and Domeng did at least as well as some of the others for five minutes before falling back into his place. Then it was Nasir's turn, and after that Mohammed. They were wildly applauded, presumably for the same reason Brockley's jokes were—because they had tried. I noticed that Graham was rolling around on the floor with half a dozen of his new friends on top of him. Three of them got him by the feet and pulled him out under the light.

'I can't. I'm too drunk,' he giggled.

'Ga-Gong! Ga-Gong! Ga-Gong!' they chanted. That was their representation of his name.

'I can't. I can't get up.'

They jumped from his feet to his head, and put their arms under his shoulders. 'I don't know what to do,' he cried. 'I'll only make a fool of myself.'

They dragged him to his feet, all of them laughing, including him. They all stepped back and he was alone under the light. He tottered a couple of steps to one side. He looked bewildered and deserted. Then suddenly he was inspired: he fell over. Everybody held their breath, then he pulled himself up on to his hands, looked round with an expression that was a caricature of drunkenness, and everybody burst into delighted laughter. He pulled himself to his feet, took another few shuffling steps, and
118

then, no doubt concluding that, since his first effort had been such a success, he would repeat it, he fell over again. This time they all laughed immediately. He jumped up quickly with his lips compressed as though he were angry with himself for being incapacitated, and with everybody else for laughing at him. The audience held each other as he did two, three, four, a dozen, drunken steps, then howled with delight as he crashed ignominiously to the floor. He varied his routine, pretending to bang his head against the floor as he fell, and each time it seemed more painful for him to get up, his face registering a more ludicrous blend of bewilderment and torpor. It had never occurred to me that he could be such a good mimic. The long-house was in an uproar. I looked across at the Penghara, and there were tears streaming down his cheeks; even Brockley was laughing, his long yellow teeth gleaming unaccustomedly in the light of the oil-lamp. Only one person was not amused—little Briok had fallen asleep against Brockley. Even Law Kiat How's frown of concentration was relieved from time to time by an involuntary flicker of amusement. Graham held the house in his hand; and finally, judging his audience perfectly, at the very peak of their hilarity, he crumpled to his knees and sank slowly to the floor for what was obviously the last time.

The laughter and applause went on for fully five minutes, and Brockley himself, smiling broadly, clapped as heartily as anyone. There was no doubt that Graham was the celebrity of the evening. For an hour or so he even displaced his father. Everybody wanted him to sit with them, but his young cronies claimed him greedily, and dragged him back to where he had been before. The Penghara congratulated Brockley on having such a talented son, and Brockley accepted his compliments modestly but with obvious pleasure. One old man asked if Graham were a district officer cadet or a junior doctor, and when Brockley replied that he was 'just visiting' he was advised to solicit an appointment for his son in the provincial administration.

In the space of an hour the completely unexpected had happened : Graham had done something that Brockley could not

119

do and brought credit on his father. The old man beamed at the compliments heaped on him; he beamed—it was not a verb I could have applied to any of the expressions I had ever seen on his face before—and father and son went to bed in a state of complete concord for the first time since the day we had arrived in Bukit Kota.

The next day it was shattered, and this time never restored.

16

The whole long-house was up to see us off next morning. The volume of hand-shaking Graham had to endure was hardly less than his father had to face. The last to let go of him were the high-spirited teenagers with whom he had got on so well. I saw them passing a palm-wrapped package among themselves surreptitiously, and it ended thrust into the bottom of Graham's bag. It was obviously a present. I wondered idly what it was for a moment, then forgot about it.

That evening Graham had a fever of 104 degrees. It turned out that he had not been taking malaria pills, although he had been repeatedly told to, because the taste of chloroquin was too unpleasant for him and made him sick. Brockley took a blood film, and found that, as he had expected, it was full of parasites. I had never seen him in such a state of rage. To me he said over and over again, 'This sets us back ten years. When they see the tuans don't take their medicine they decide it's unimportant.' And to Graham he said, 'I'll give you treatment, and you can damned well soldier on. I'm not going to have this expedition ruined because you don't like the taste of your pills.' And into the jungle he growled, 'Don't you realize half the white man's job is always to be fit and show them how they could be if they paid more attention to the doctor?'

Graham did soldier on, but malaria is a terrible thing for somebody who has never had it before. A man who lives in an endemic area can be back at work the day after his treatment starts, because he has built up a certain amount of immunity over the years. But after the first attack a man is completely without strength for three weeks. He tried to sit up in the boat, but he gradually slipped down so that he was lying, and as soon as we got to our evening's destination he got into his bedding and turned his face to the jungle.

Law Kiat How took a certain malicious satisfaction in Graham's humiliation. It had, after all, rankled that when Graham had been taken up by the long-house youths he had been abandoned. But it had not interfered with his craving for knowledge. As we sat in the river washing ourselves, and the aroma of sassafras and cooking-oil drifted out of the jungle towards us, he said, 'I should like to ask some questions on the sexual topic, sir.'

'Oh ...' I said doubtfully, and then, essaying humour: 'But I should think you know more about that sort of thing than I do, Kiat How.'

His lids blinked slowly; his frown of concentration did not change one iota. I did not even get credit for trying. 'On question of taking lady out to dinner—'

'Yes?'

'At what point in the evening will you propose the sexual intercourse?'

I was breathing in. It turned into a gulp. 'Is this a lady you know well, Kiat How?'

'Unspecified, sir.'

'I see. In that case I think it is probably better not to mention sexual relations unless there is some pressing reason for doing so.'

'Thank you, sir.' I had expected disappointment, but if anything there was a note of satisfaction in his voice. 'That is what I have read in my Book of English Etiquette.' He pointed to a brown-paper-covered book lying tidily on the bank beside his notebook and toothbrush.

'They told you not to mention sexual intercourse?'

'Did not discuss sexual intercourse at all, Doctor. But Mr Graham is saying all English ladies will expect the sexual intercourse performance after theatre visit.'

122

'I think perhaps he is a little advanced in his views.'

'It is not necessary to place hands on ladies' chests during second act?'

'I don't think so.'

'Or unzipping ladies' trouser-suit on car drive back from said theatre?'

'Hardly ever.'

'I see.' Kiat How nodded slowly and blinked twice. Normally he only blinked about once every four minutes. 'Mr Graham has given me misinformations. He is not so informed.... One last question, Doctor: why do British immigration officers carry firearms?'

Now the river was getting so shallow that we could not use our motor for fear of damaging the propeller. We had to pole ourselves up-stream with staves that we cut out at the river side. When we came to the rapids we all had to get out and pull the two boats up over them. Graham lay on the bank while we did this. I mentioned the fact that we were not using our motor because that explained why at a very quiet period, when none of us were speaking, and the only sound was the splashing of the water over the rocks and the din of the insects in the jungle, it was possible for us to surprise a wild boar standing by the water drinking. Domeng, in the first boat, saw it immediately, and made violent but silent gestures to Brockley in the second boat. Brockley reached for his shotgun, rapidly inserted a cartridge and aimed. But at the last minute Briok saw it too and gave a whoop. The boar sensed danger, and as Brockley fired he was already turning. Both boats broke into uproar. Before we could even get into the bank Nasir and Domeng and the couple of Dayaks we had brought with us to help us over the rapids had plunged out of the boat and into the jungle. Parangs miraculously appeared in the Dayaks' hands as they were running up the bank. Brockley and I and Briok followed at a more leisurely pace. Guided by their shouts, we followed them on the animal tracks, and about two hundred yards from the river we came upon them, the boar bleeding, at bay, but still dangerous,

123

they in a circle around him at a distance of about ten yards each, waiting to see what he would do. Briok had his blowpipe. Presumably he realized that the boar was meant to be killed, and that blowpipes were used for killing. He dashed away from Brockley, raising the blowpipe to his lips. Brockley saw the danger and shouted. The boar turned, and with fantastic speed Brockley was across the clearing and rammed the muzzle of the gun down the boar's throat. The others immediately jumped on him and hacked him to death. It was only when it was all over that we saw the blood pouring down Brockley's leg. There was a large hole on the outer side of his thigh.

'I seem to have been injured,' he said urbanely. 'I'd better get back to the boat. I wonder if you'd dress it for me?'

By the side of the river I sat him down, got out the primus stove and boiled up some water. I cleaned the wound out. It was deeper than I thought. As he moved slightly in pain I could see the intact muscles contract, and the ones that had been severed hanging slack.

'You know this ought to be done in a proper operating theatre under general anaesthetic,' I said.

'Oh! Just slap a bit of spirit and a dressing on it.'

'It's not so simple as that. You've got severed muscles here. They're going to die. You could get gangrene.'

He waved away my objections. 'You don't know my constitution, old thing.'

'Well, I wouldn't take responsibility for leaving this in its present condition. I would think you ought to go straight back down-river.'

'Leave it to me. I've looked after myself for the last thirty-five years without any mishap.' His voice was still urbane, but hints of testiness were creeping in. I did not know how he could even manage to talk at all considering the pain he must be in.

'Very well. It's your responsibility.' I trimmed away as much of the torn muscle as I could and cleaned it thoroughly with hydrogen peroxide. It was clearly going to be impossible to stitch it. Tomorrow such a huge wound would be grossly swollen and any stitches that had been put in would burst.

124

'I'm afraid I can't give you any tetanus toxoid,' I said. 'There hasn't been any in the country for a month.'

'Never use the stuff anyway. We don't get tetanus up here.'

I wanted to give him some morphia, but he refused it. He went through the whole thing with no relief from his pain whatsoever. He must have been in excruciating pain but he did not make a sound. In a way I admired him. If I had been cutting off his leg it could hardly have been more painful. But it was useless, unnecessary courage. Why could he not just take a shot of morphia and go under the canopy in the boat with Graham? But he wouldn't. It was his expedition, and he wouldn't lose control of it for a moment.

Near the end of my dressing, Graham's head appeared over the side of the boat. 'Anything the matter?' he queried weakly.

Before I could speak Brockley said tersely, 'I grazed myself.'

'Oh, sorry! Nothing too serious, I hope.' He rolled wearily back into the bottom of the boat. Graham relied on his father's tone of voice rather than the air of strain in the faces of everybody who was standing in a circle watching me at my task.

The old man's tone changed as he seemed to realize for the first time that they were there. 'Get out of it! Rot off! Get that animal cut up. Stop breathing on me.'

It was the only time I ever heard him swear, the only time I ever heard him angry with his boys.

He sat upright in the boat for the rest of that day's journey, but now he did not help to pull it up over the rapids. When Graham got out and sat on the bank he did the same. Of course this slowed us up considerably because we had to use what was left of both crews to pull up both boats, instead of each crew pulling up their own boat.

'Better tomorrow. Better tomorrow,' he kept saying. 'Both of us better tomorrow....' The others, through the habit of believing him for as long as they could remember, probably believed him this time, but I, as a doctor, knew he would be worse tomorrow.

We were now far up in the Interior, beyond the most inland

125

Dayak long-house. Between here and the mountain range that runs along the western spine of the island there were no permanent habitations, and only about five hundred people—his beloved Nayans. From where we stood to the mountains was a distance of about fifty miles—from London to Brighton, say, but in that roadless and riverless jungle at least four days' journey with pack on back. Tomorrow we would come to the point where the river was completely unnavigable, even between the rapids, even to our flat-bottomed craft. The Nayans were another day's journey inland where they would cross whatever water there was without taking their feet off the ground. But to get to them we were going to have to walk. And Brockley was just not going to be able to.

He always took a whisky before his dinner and another after. But this evening, when we pitched camp on a gravel bed by the river, before Domeng had even assembled his pots, he had the bottle out. After dinner he went to rummage in the medicine-chest, and then dragged himself away into the jungle. When he came back ten minutes later his eyes were glassy, and when I looked at his pupils I saw that they were reduced to a tiny dot. He must have given himself a stiff doze of opium. He crawled into his bedding on the far side of the camp and turned his face to the jungle. Briok, the cause of it all, sat mournfully on a log, unhappy because Brockley was ill, but unaware, of course, why.

An hour later, when I was rummaging in my haversack for something and I had thought he must be well asleep, he turned painfully over and said: 'I'm sorry I was a little abrupt earlier, Reed. Appreciate your concern. But—' his lips tightened involuntarily with pain— 'I couldn't turn back now. I've got to see my boys. I've got to explain to them.'

The next day was terrible. As I had expected, and as he must have anticipated too, his leg was terribly swollen, hot and excruciatingly painful. I changed the dressing after we had boiled some water.

126

'It looks as though it might get infected,' I said. 'I'd better give you some penicillin.'

'All right, all right,' Brockley whispered, breathless with the pain from my changing of the dressing. 'Whatever you think.'

'And a shot of morphia.'

But there he drew the line. 'No! I wouldn't be able to walk.'

'But you can't walk on this.'

'Of course. Movement, exercise, that's what it wants, that's why half these things go so bad; leave them there motionless, suppurating.'

'I simply won't allow you to—' I got no further.

'Please allow me to make my own decision,' he said curtly.

I nodded coldly and withdrew. It hardly mattered. He would collapse anyway in a few hours and beg to be carried, or be unconscious so that he couldn't even beg.

'How are you feeling this morning?' he called across at Graham in an artificially jocular manner. 'Better?'

'Yes, thanks.'

'Good! We do a little walking today. We should be with the Nayans by nightfall.'

'Oh! Good!' Graham's effort at enthusiasm was not convincing.

The boats were dragged up out of the river-bed and lashed to trees twenty feet above the waterline.

'If the floods come,' said Law Kiat How, 'water rises very quickly and boats in the river are broken. Even big boats,' he added with a gleam of apprehension in his eye, the first hint of emotion I had seen from him.

Everything was divided between us into packs weighing about fifty pounds. Graham's contained only his own clothes, and although Brockley insisted on carrying his usual share he did not pay too much attention to what was packed into his rucksack, and what he carried had more volume than weight. Briok, of course, carried nothing but his blowpipe. We set off to trudge up the river-bed.

The river was ankle-deep in parts, thigh-deep in others. Where possible we walked on the banks, but now the terrain was getting hilly, and much of the ground sloped directly into the water. Where there were banks the soft earth was often water-logged, and we had to progress by jumping from stone to stone. This was wearying for Graham, but for Brockley, with one leg almost useless, it must have been agonizing. We stopped for a rest about every hour. Soon the temperature was in the nineties; the sweat was running off us. Soon we were so wet with sweat that when we stopped we rolled in the river with our clothes on. It made us hardly any wetter than we were already, and a lot cooler.

The halt periods were signalled by Brockley who was in front. But at eleven-thirty when we had been marching about three hours, Graham seemed to stumble on the bank and fell. He lay in surprise for a moment, like a tortoise with his pack on his back, struggling to get up. Then, as I watched, a spasm of sensual pleasure passed over his body, a beatific smile came on to his face for an instant; he stopped struggling. He closed his eyes and lay still, his head draped back over his haversack, one leg straight, one leg bent under him just as he had fallen.

'*Tuan* Blo Ko Lee,' Domeng, who was immediately behind Brockley, said in a low voice.

Brockley stopped. He turned. His face was shining with sweat, and though he was the only one of us who did not roll in the river his clothes were completely drenched. He stood there, pant-ing, his mouth open, then he put his hands up to his eyes and brushed away the sweat. His breath jerked again. He looked at Graham. There was nothing on his face but pain and weariness. For a dreadful second I thought he did not know where he was. Then he mumbled, 'All right. Let's have lunch.'

Afterwards we rested in the shade for half an hour. Even Brockley lay back—on the naked stones—his hat over his face. I had not seen him do that during the day before; usually he sat against a boulder drawing contentedly on his pipe, and perhaps gently despising those inferior races and inferior mem-bers of his own race who had to sleep after four or five hours' gentle walking or paddling. Now I was the only one who was awake. His face was blotched and swollen, his neck was a pattern of rills and crevasses down which the sweat poured. He was deeply asleep. He started to snore. He looked very, very old.

I had to wake him after half an hour. It took a long time, but as soon as he sat up and moved his leg an automatic spasm of agony passed across his face, and he rolled on to one side breathing rapidly, so that I could not see his face.

'How is the leg?' I asked as casually as I could.

'Not so bad,' he answered, just as casually. 'Perhaps I will be able to dress it myself this evening.'

'I don't think so,' was all I said.

The others were getting up. Only Graham had not moved. I shook his shoulder. 'Hey! Graham! Time to get on.' He shook my hand off; he was still more or less asleep. I shook him again.

'Graham! Wake up! Time to go!'

This time he did not shake me off. 'I hear you,' he whispered. 'I hear you.'

I started to stow my gear and helped Brockley with his. The boys cleared up the site, packed away the pots and pans, threw the burnable rubbish on the fire and left it smouldering—no need to worry about fire risks in Banianok where the average rainfall is two hundred inches a year, or over half an inch a day. We were almost ready to go, but Graham was still stretched out.

'Come on, snap into it, Graham,' the old man said. 'We're waiting for you.'

He raised his head a little. 'I'm sorry.'

'Come on. We're in a hurry.'

'I'm sorry, I don't think I can.'

I felt his face. It was sunburned all over, but his cheeks stood out a deep hot red. To the touch it was burning hot. It was obviously part of his malaria. I moved his head. It rolled with the pressure of my fingers. Every muscle was completely at rest; he was exhausted.

By now everybody was watching us. I picked up his wrist as though I were feeling his pulse. The public always think this

129

a most essential diagnostic procedure. It gave me time to think what was to be done.

'Look, Graham,' I whispered urgently, 'you've got to pull yourself together.'

'But I can't. I told you. I'm finished.'

'You can't do it this way. It'll kill your father. Just get up. Just start. If you collapse after that we'll carry you.'

He opened his eyes again. They were wide and earnest like a child's. 'But I don't want to be carried. I don't want to be any trouble to anyone.'

'But we can't just leave you, can we, Graham?' I began reasonably, then I cried, 'For God's sake, man—'

'You're angry with me now, aren't you, James? I'm sorry, I really am.'

It had been going on too long. Brockley limped over. 'What's the matter?' he grunted.

Graham's eyes flickered. 'I'm sorry, Dad, I just can't go on any longer.'

The old man looked him up and down as he lay on the ground. 'Why?'

'I'm finished. I just can't go on any more.'

Brockley's eyeballs bulged. 'Get up, you damned fool.'

'I'm sorry, Father, it's no longer possible.'

'You will if you get my boot up your backside.'

But Graham did not move.

Brockley looked at me, then he looked round at the boys who were standing together curiously in an unwonted group—the Chinese, the three Malays, and the two Dayaks. He looked back at me. There was something in his eyes that I had never seen there before—fear.

'Listen!' he started to whisper to Graham. 'You've got to get up. Please get up.'

'Father, I want to—'

'Get up and go on a bit. Just a bit, then we'll stop. I'm pretty fagged myself.'

'What am I lying on?' Graham patted the ground feebly beside him.

130

'Gravel,' I said.

'It feels so soft ...'

'For God's sake!' cried Brockley. 'Look, just get up, old chap. Just ... get up.... That's right,' he said, 'that's right,' though Graham had not moved. 'Look, if you don't get up they'll think you're no good.'

'But it's true. I *am* no good—no good for the jungle.'

'But then they'll think *we're* no good.' He was pleading now.

'We?'

'We—the provincial administration ... the colonial office ... England. We can't have them thinking that, now, can we?'

Graham did not answer.

'Please, old chap, make an effort. Make a big effort. I'm sick too, but I've got to keep going. I've got a lump torn out of my leg, but I've got to keep going. If I fall down whining what are they going to say? They're going to say, "Ah! look at the Englishman with the little graze on his leg, expecting to be carried. He's no better than we are: he shirks, he panics, he gives in." We can't have them thinking that, old chap, can we?'

Graham's hand travelled, apparently of its own volition, to his trousers. The zip had come undone. He pulled back his hand and glanced idly at it. It was dripping with blood. He gave a deep-throated, strangled cry, and was scrabbling at his trousers, trying to tear them off. He lurched to his feet; the pack was still on his back. Blood was running down his legs. He dashed for the river and wallowed into it, haversack and all.

Brockley, himself barely conscious, stared after him in bewilderment, and Law Kiat How murmured, his lips curled in loathing, 'Leeches!'

But of course the water would not get rid of the leeches. They had to be burned off—by Mohammed with a lighted cigarette. Graham stood knee-deep in the water while Mohammed touched his cigarette to the back of each leech and it contracted and dropped off. There were about a dozen in all.

The leeches had proved that Graham could stand. We did not let him sit down again.

17

We had reached a point now where probably not more than a score of white men had ever been before. This whole area had remained completely unexplored by white men (except Brockley) until after the Second World War, and the existence of the Nayans had not been officially recognized until the Census of 1949, though Brockley had learned their language ten years earlier. All the races of the island respected him—the Malays, the Chinese, and the indigenous races—and he them, and by his reputation during the Japanese war he was associated with the Dayaks who had been his myrmidons, but I think the only ones he really loved were the Nayans. He had discovered them, introduced them to the world in his anthropological writings, shown them off as it were, and then withdrawn them again. He had loved them as children, and perhaps that was not entirely good. There was something ambivalent in his attitude, as there is in most parents. He had wanted them to have Western medicine, but not Western clothes. He had expected them to submit to operations and X-rays—Western technology—but not to absorb any Western customs. He had wanted them to be always as they were, and never to grow up and get married. Ultimately, even if the road did not come next year, or the year after, they would have to mingle with the rest of the population, as the Chinese and Malays and Dayaks would have to mingle. He must have realized that and thought, like a possessive father, 'Yes, but not yet.'

Small hills were starting to rise up around us and we were well into the evergreen rain forest proper. We had left the mangrove swamps far behind, and now there were no more nipah palms either. But the jungle looked just as mysterious as we peered into it from the river. Everything was green in one way or another; as Graham had said: 'So many colours, but all green.' There was a terrible monotony about it. Here the trees were huge. The largest of them, the belians, soared one hundred feet before they even gave off a branch. Their foliage interlocked at the top to shut out light and sun. When you clambered out of the river into the jungle you had the impression of being at the bottom of an aquarium.

'Did the Abang and his troops get this far?' I shouted forward to Brockley.

'Just about to here,' he grunted. 'But they got away from the river. They went into the jungle. Big mistake!'

I could understand how many of them had deserted.

'Would there be any Nayans in there now?'

'No, of course not,' he said curtly. 'If there were they'd come out and see us.'

At five o'clock we stopped on another gravel bed by the river. When we stopped Brockley usually changed his shoes, took out his gun and went to look for game; or occasionally he went for a walk down by the side of the river with his washing-tackle. Today, of course, he was able to do neither. He sat on a rock, and even fifteen minutes after we had arrived he was still panting. I went and sat beside him.

'There's something wrong,' he said. 'They've always met me here or lower down the river.'

'It's a big area,' I said. 'They could have moved off for better hunting.'

He was silent. His breath came in deep ten-second gasps.

I said, 'You'd better let me dress that wound and get you into your bed-roll.'

'Thank you,' he said in a monotone. 'Can we have a drink first?'

He called for the whisky. Domeng brought the bottle and two enamel mugs; then he went back and brought a pan with water in it from the river. He poured two double doubles. I

refused mine. Brockley jerked his head at the two mugs and
Domeng poured one into the other. He added an equal amount
of water and gave it to the old man.

'Give the boys a drink,' Brockley grunted in Malay, and
Domeng went away smiling with the bottle held tightly in both
hands.

Brockley took a couple of gulps, then turned and stared into
the jungle. 'They're in there,' he muttered. 'They know I'm here
and they won't come out.' He reached for his whisky without
looking at the mug, and seeing he was about to knock it off the
rock I put it into his hand. He did not even notice. It was as
though there was just him at the side of the river, and nobody
else within two days' journey but his boys staring out of the
jungle at him, silent, invisible, unforgiving.

When we had had dinner we all sat in silence for a few
minutes, then he said, with an effort at brightness, 'Well, must
just go and check the supplies before I turn in.'

I saw him go over to where the medicine-chest was standing
covered by a tarpaulin in case of rain. Domeng watched him too
as he pulled off the tarpaulin, but obviously he knew not to
interfere. Brockley stumbled away into the jungle with some
things wrapped in a cloth. Opium again.

We were all bedded down when he came back—in a long row
under a shelter of tarpaulins and careom leaves. As he got into
his bedding Brockley was drowsy—from the opium, presumably.
I hoped he would sleep. The last thing he said was, 'It is just
possible that they're waiting till dawn. It *is* possible. . . .'

But at dawn they had not come. Briok was awake first, and
he woke everybody else—everybody except the old man. I found
him sitting by the river with his cold pipe in his mouth.

'I thought they might come out and see me if I were alone,'
he said, looking up at me. Then he shook his head. They hadn't.

I turned away. As though he thought I was on my way back
to Banianok he called, 'Let's give them another six hours.' He
dropped his pipe on the ground. 'That would be all right,
wouldn't it?'

134

I nodded.

Domeng made tea, then started to boil fish from the river and rice for breakfast. We ate our breakfast. Graham had some and said he felt better. Afterwards, in the absence of any instructions from Brockley, everybody loafed around the camp. But the two Dayak porters were soon off fishing with their circular throwing-nets draped over their shoulders. Law studied his Book of British Etiquette. Nasir, Domeng and Mohammed wandered off into the jungle with Briok trotting behind them. Brockley sat on his rock on his own at the edge of the river, and I sat in camp writing up some notes of the journey. Graham had a bath in the river and then came back and persuaded Law to go for a walk with him. As they passed I heard, 'Perhaps Bobby Kennedy could have done it—now there's nobody. . . .'

About an hour later, when only Brockley and I were still in camp, there came the unmistakable sound of shrieking and shouting from the jungle. The shrieking was from a woman. Brockley jumped to his feet, but immediately fell over again because he could not take the pain of his weight suddenly being thrown on his injured leg. He pulled himself up again, and into the camp came Domeng and Nasir dragging a Nayan woman between them. Briok ran along, looking puzzled, in front of them. The woman was shrieking in terror, and her feet dragged along the ground.

'What are you doing?' Brockley shouted angrily in Malay to Nasir and Domeng.

'Trying to escape, *tuan.*'

'Let go of her immediately!'

Reluctantly they let go of her, watching her carefully, with hands still ready to grab her if she should try and make a bolt for it. She looked at Brockley and shrank back in fear. There was no mistaking it. He did not mistake it. His face went pale. He started talking in a guttural language none of us could understand. The woman looked down at the ground. She was the first Nayan woman I had ever seen. She looked savage in a way the Dayaks had not. She was very thin, with grey hair tied at the back with rotan, but loosened from it, probably in her struggle

135

with Domeng and Nasir. I could see one front tooth in her upper jaw and four in the lower jaw. She wore a rough apron of bark and nothing else. Her breasts hung slack and empty. She was very dirty. She looked about sixty. Brockley talked away in his guttural language. She continued to look down into the ground. There was a wildness in her eyes like those of a hare in a trap. This is what the wild men of Borneo must have looked like before Brockley and his predecessors tamed them. He talked on. There was a pause. He talked again. Again a pause, then the same words again. He was asking something. He was pleading. She stared at the ground. Brockley's voice lowered. It was softer and even gentler than before; there was none of the abruptness with which he habitually addressed his fellow-Europeans. She seemed to relax a little. She reached out a hand and touched Briok on the shoulder. Her hand went round his shoulder to his breast and she pulled him to her. Brockley repeated his question. It looked as though again she would not answer, then, suddenly grasping Briok convulsively to her, she shrieked at the old man, and went on shrieking, words that were meaningless to us, but the same words over and over, till she broke down and Briok pushed himself out of her convulsive grasp.

We did not know the words. We were open-mouthed spectators. But it was clear that Brockley did. His face had looked awful when I changed his dressing and he had to control everything in him to stop himself crying out. But this was worse. It was more frightening because he was so impassive. The colour left his face; it went a grey-yellow and he looked as though he certainly ought to faint. But instead he seemed to draw himself up even more firmly; his lips clamped tight; there was not the slightest expression on his face. Then he started to speak again, in that soft murmur, and it was obvious from his intonation that he was pleading. It was extraordinary to see the master of the whole Interior pleading in a language I could not understand with a woman who must surely have been as wild as it is possible for a human being to be.

Suddenly she turned and dashed away. Domeng and Nasir

started after her, but he shouted to them and they came back. His face composed as though he were a sidesman walking up the aisle with the Sunday offering, he dragged himself, erect as he could maintain, to the river.

'What happened?' I said to Nasir and Domeng in Malay. But they only said the same thing to me. Briok trotted off down to join Brockley at the river, and there, after fifteen minutes, I went too. He was sitting on the same rock, his back to the jungle. Briok sat beside and slightly behind him about five yards away, looking up at him mournfully.

Brockley stood as I shuffled hesitantly to him. 'Galag did not get back,' he said curtly. 'I knew he wouldn't. I knew it was impossible. He must have died in the jungle of course. Not far from Bananiok ... I don't blame them.' His self-possession was frightening. 'You must understand that the logic of the primitive mind is not our logic. I've been trying for twenty-five years to get them to come down-river for treatment. I had a notion it might suddenly happen, that some brave soul might decide to come when I was not up here. That was why I asked the Mission if they'd bring them if ever it became necessary. Of course I told them, repeatedly, that they must never, ever, take a Nayan anywhere but direct to me in Bukit Kota. It's my own damned fault. You can never rely on the Mission. I've known it for the last thirty-five years. ... I've no excuse.

'So now my boys believe I've been waiting twenty-five years to take one of them away; my plan finally came to fruition and I sent Bones to carry it through. Now, emboldened by his success, I have come for another. It is logical, isn't it?' he tried to smile quizzically, but his lip trembled.

'It's like their counting, you see, Reed. They count as follows: one, two, many. That is all.' He did not want to stop talking. Perhaps if he did he would break down completely. 'I've tried to get them to count higher. I tried one, two, three, many. They said one, two, and when they got to three they just shrugged and said many. Any differentiation above three was quite unnecessary and quite illogical. It's like their policy with mentally subnormal children like Briok. They believe they have been

137

punished for something wrong they have done when they bear a child like that. Bearing the child is the punishment, and then, perhaps, the further punishment for the mother of having to abandon it in the jungle knowing that it will probably be taken by a python. But given the basic premise that it is a punishment, what they do is quite logical, is it not? And works to the benefit of the tribe, too, because in the nomadic life they lead they can't be carrying around an unproductive member of the family who has to be cared for all the time.'

He dried up for the moment. But if talking helped to take the pain away he must go on talking. 'But what about that old woman we just saw?' I asked. 'She must be a burden on the tribe. Are there many of them at that age?'

He looked up at me and smiled, that bleak, weary smile. 'How old would you say she was?'

'Well, it's difficult to say, of course. Sixty? Between sixty and seventy?'

'She's only thirty, Reed.'

'Thirty? But she looks twice that age.'

'It's a hard life, the nomad life.'

I thought back carefully. Had I made a mistake? Had I not taken her in properly? But I knew I had not been mistaken. I remembered that single tooth that seemed to be buried on its own in upper lip, the grey hair, those long, papery dugs. And she was only thirty! But how, I wanted to shout at him, can you want to keep a system going which produces women of thirty who look sixty? How can you write papers on it and glorify it? But of course I couldn't. I was silent, we were both silent, for a few moments. I could think of nothing to say to comfort him. Then I thought of the woman. Where had she come from? How had she been caught by Nasir and Domeng?

'But how—how did she come to be the only member of the tribe who came near us? Why was she caught?'

Brockley essayed a smile; he tried to sound urbane. It was more nerve-racking than if he had broken down completely.

'I forgot you didn't know, you thought she looked sixty, didn't you? But she isn't. She's only thirty. She's Briok's mother!'

138

He told the boys curtly to strike camp.

He sat on the same rock, his back to the jungle, staring out, unseeing, across the river. When I told him we were almost ready to leave, he said:

'I'd be grateful if you'd give me half an hour.' He started to stump into the jungle, and I took a few hesitant steps after him. He stopped. 'I shall be quite all right, thank you,' he said pointedly.

He pulled himself stiffly away along the animal track leading up from the river, and a minute later we could not see him any more. The boys finished stowing the gear, then sat down on the gravel to wait. Mohammed took out his pipe; Graham and Law put their heads together; Domeng and Nasir, both grandfathers, sat silently holding hands. To pass the time, and in anticipation of hours with a pack on my back, I strolled up-river to the cataract which was almost two hundred yards away. When I had got there I turned into the jungle to walk back to camp. The track led in, but I knew that as long as I could hear the water I was all right.

But the sound of the water grew dimmer. I was beginning to think I should have to turn back when I heard a shout from somewhere to my left. In a second I was running, and I had plunged off the animal track before I had realized what I was doing. I stopped. The forest receded before me, every tree different but not a landmark among them. The track was fifty yards away by this time. I knew I must get back on to it. The shout came again. I plunged on deeper into the forest.

There, thirty yards in front of me, stood Brockley. He was holding his boater with the Trinity ribbon in one hand, and with the other he was mopping his bald and shining scalp with a white handkerchief. The bandages round his left leg looked thick and soggy. He was shouting in a language I had heard only once before—in his interrogation of the woman—the language that he, of course, was the only non-Nayan in the country, and in the world, to speak. He was holding his last conversation with his boys.

Though I did not know the words I understood the tone. He

was not pleading: it was the voice of authority that spoke, repeating certain guttural syllables over and over again. His face was firm and inscrutable. The voice did not tremble. He was telling them what damned fools they were. I had to keep myself hidden. It was only when I looked very closely that I could see tears running freely down the groove between his cheek and his nose, and into either corner of his mouth.

18

In the early afternoon of the second day we reached our boats. They were still lashed twenty feet above the waterline; nobody had touched them; nobody had been that way. When Brockley had fallen for the third time I told the boys to cut some staves and gather rotan to make a litter. This time he had not demurred; he was finished. Now my first concern was to get him back to a hospital, which meant Banianok. We pulled down the boats and loaded them. We laid the old man in as we had laid Graham on the way up. We set off down-stream as quickly as we could, paddling between rapids, stopping to let the boats down gently when we came to them. We managed three hours' travel before the light failed and we were forced to camp for the night. Tomorrow we would be back in Dayak country and we could stay at a long-house. The night after that we would be in Bukit Kota, and if the radio was working we could send a message to the Abang asking him to send one of his two new helicopters for Brockley.

Brockley was fully conscious, but hardly spoke. He seemed to have given over the leadership of the expedition to me without question. I gave all the orders and everybody obeyed. His leg was now black and swollen around the wound, and the blackness was spreading. Briok stayed close to him, though he seemed hardly to notice the boy. Domeng had made him a crude crutch; he still refused to let anybody help him once they had lifted him out of the boat on to dry land. The second night on the journey down he took his gun and dragged himself off down the bank. For a moment the thought crossed my mind that

141

he should not be allowed a gun in his condition, and in his misery. But then I saw Briok trotting after him, and after that Graham strolled off in the same direction. I started to arrange the dressings for Brockley's wound.

Domeng said to me in Malay, 'Doctor, we are about a mile above where a large tributary joins the river. Up that tributary is the up-river headquarters of the Banianok Evangelical Mission. We could take Doctor Blo Ko Lee there for treatment.'

'It might have been an idea,' I said wistfully, 'But Blo Ko Lee wouldn't go near the missionaries now.'

'Because of how they killed the Nayan in Banianok. Very bad!'

'Well they didn't exactly kill him, Domeng,' I said hastily. 'You know what happened. They took him down to Banianok by mistake and there—' But it was too late. I could see from his eyes looking through my left shoulder that he wasn't listening. Another myth was born.

'We'll get him to Bukit Kota, and probably we can get on the radio from there.'

I strolled off in the same direction the old man had taken, to tell him we had better do his dressing before the light went altogether. He was sitting on the ground, against a tree, his gun beside him, his leg stretched out in front of him—it was impossible now for him to bend it. Graham sat beside him about five feet away. Briok splashed in the shallow water ten yards away.

Brockley looked up and grunted as I came along. Graham nodded.

'Time for your dressing,' I said. 'It'll be dark soon.'

He grunted again, and looked at me ironically, as though to say, 'Is it worth the trouble?'

He looked up sharply, and our eyes followed his. Briok was no longer splashing around.

'What is it, Briok?' he called.

Briok stood in the river, motionless on one foot, the other against his calf just below the knee, his blowpipe dug into the gravel beside him. He cried out something in a shrill, unintelligible voice.

142

'Pass me the gun,' Brockley said tersely.

He pulled himself up and held out his hand for the gun.

'What's the matter?'

'Take cover,' he grunted. 'Stay out of sight. Keep absolutely quiet. Wild boar.'

Thirty yards below, the river curved away to the left and out of sight. The bank rose steeply on either side, so steeply that a few naked faces of black rock stood out like ragged holes in the mottled green back-cloth of the jungle. It was a perfect place for an ambush.

But opposite I could see, from the raggedness of the vegetation and the new mud for a stretch of about twelve yards of the bank, that we were at a watering-spot.

'Briok always hears them first,' Brockley whispered. 'They come down to drink at about this time of night.'

We lay in absolute silence, Brockley, with the thrill of the hunt animating his face almost like those Dayaks at Penghara Ngang's, looking almost well again. The jungle rustled across the river, then from somewhere beyond where the river curved out of sight below us came the sound of singing. The tune was 'Onward Christian Soldiers'.

It came nearer, and louder. The tune was 'Onward Christian Soldiers' but the words were in a language I had never heard before. 'Damn!' Brockley whispered hoarsely. 'Damn it, it's those missionaries! They'll drive the animals away.'

But just as he spoke a mouse-deer appeared through the bushes. He sidled unconcernedly to the water and stood there motionless before drinking. It seemed more wrong for a beautiful animal to die than an ugly one, but Brockley grunted and shot it anyway. The Dayaks needed the meat. Briok, shrieking with excitement, promptly fell over into the water, and the Dayaks plunged across with blood-curdling yells. Behind them, Domeng waded silently through the current, his huge gutting-knife in his hand. From down-river the whole scene must have looked terrifying, but Domeng only wanted to cut the animal's throat and satisfy his exiguous Muslim conscience that that was how it had died. He would then be eligible to join in eating it.

143

I pulled Brockley's arm. The singing had stopped, but there were two boats visible in the gorge. There was a white man in each, and four Kelwans, big fat fellows, not like our wiry Dayaks. They turned, the paddles working furiously. Obviously they had not seen us, but just the two Dayaks. One of the boats turned too fast and was swamped in the wash of the other. It slipped away, upside down, gathering speed as it entered the gorge, its former occupants clinging on around it. The other, outboard motor whining at full power, was after it, past it and soon far ahead of it.

Brockley sat on his rock shaking with laughter. 'Give them a shout,' he cried. 'They think it's an ambush.' But it was too late. They were well out of sight by this time and going for their lives.

He shook his head as though he were trying to stop himself laughing. Briok danced around him, hunching himself up into the same position as the old man, parodying every shake of the shoulders, every wipe of the hand across streaming eyes, every incredulous shake of his head. 'Oh dear! The expressions on those faces! No time for communing with the Almighty! The rate they were going they could have taken every cup at Henley.' He wiped the tears from his eyes.

'They may have gone for reinforcements,' Graham said sharply.

'Not them. They'll be paddling for dear life till dark. Then they'll probably hide in the jungle for the night.'

'We'll look a bit stupid if they get the police up here.'

'My dear fellow, the police won't come up here. They won't go more than an hour outside Bukit Kota. I'm the only law they have this far up-river.' I remembered that. He did not say it boastfully, but as a matter of commonly accepted fact. 'Oh dear! I haven't laughed so much for years.... No, there won't be any police. The missionaries will have this story pretty much to themselves. And I dare say you'll find they succumb to the temptation of exaggerating as easily as lesser mortals.'

19

Now we were on our last thirty-six hours before reaching Bukit Kota. We were not going back the way we had come. Then we had taken a wide sweep into a tributary of the Banianok to visit Penghara Ngang's long-house and two others. On the way back we would go direct, by-passing them completely and getting to Bukit Kota more quickly. Of course I had never seen any war surgery, and what I knew of traffic accidents was derived from experience in England, where any accident case can be on the operating table two hours after the accident. But I had dealt with many snake-bites since I had come to Banianok, so I had seen what can happen to limbs when their blood supply is cut off—I was familiar with gangrene. That was what Brockley's wound was turning into. The area around the wound was now black and lifeless. I could stick pins in it and he felt nothing. Each day the area over which he felt nothing increased; each day the black area extended. Now his leg was lifeless almost from his knee to his hip. Miraculously the blood supply still got through to his foot and his leg below the knee, but I knew that could stop in a matter of hours. It almost certainly would stop before we got to Bukit Kota. Everything depended on whether we could get a helicopter up to take him from Bukit Kota to the capital. If we could, perhaps his leg could be saved. But it was not certain that we could; in fact it was unlikely, with the state of chronic inefficiency in the capital, that a helicopter would arrive within two days of our asking for it. The only chance of that happening would be if I could talk to the Abang directly on the radio-telephone.

We camped at six in the evening by the river. It was the latest we could stay on the river. After that it would be too dark to pitch camp. We selected our gravel bed, and pulled up the boats. We started to unload the gear and set up awnings of tarpaulin furbished out with meyim leaves against the rain. Domeng got the fire going, and the rice water boiling.

Then we noticed, about two hundred yards down-river, another fire on another gravel bed. As we strained our eyes we saw shadows moving around it, and at the same time they saw us. Domeng shouted in Malay, and back over the breeze came the question, 'Who are you?'

It was a female voice, a Wolverhampton accent.

'Doreen!' Graham gasped.

'Stay where you are,' I shouted. It was almost completely night now. 'We're coming.'

'What's happened?' Brockley grunted.

'You remember Doreen Trimmer, the English nurse who came up with the Abang,' I said.

'Good God! What's she doing?'

'Don't know. We're just going to find out.'

'Ask her for a drink,' he called after me.

I started off walking, but after thirty yards Graham overtook me and we finished running, jumping from rock to rock.

She came out to meet us. We saw her standing against the fire, with three Dayak porters behind her, but she was easily the biggest of the four. She was wearing tennis-shoes, brown dungarees and a grey sweat-shirt with Ohio State printed across the back of it in red. Her boys were obviously in awe of her.

'Thought I might bump into you,' she shouted. 'How's it been?'

'What on earth are you doing up here—and alone?' I searched beyond the circle of the fire for signs of any other Europeans.

'It's a long story. But what about you?' She dug Graham in the ribs familiarly but continued addressing herself to me. 'What have you been up to? Where's the old man?'

'He's up there.' I jerked my head in the direction of our camp.

'I'll come up and say hallo to him.'

146

'He's pretty sick, I ought to warn you.'

She did not ask what was wrong with him. She just said, 'I'd go a long way to shake the hand of the man who made a mug of that little nigger Yusuf.' It seemed that she and the Abang had fallen out again.

When we reached camp all the boys were staring open-mouthed at Doreen in her extraordinary clothes. Brockley made an effort to get up, maintaining the proprieties even in the middle of the jungle, but he had not stood up for two days. He fell back.

Doreen strode forward and grasped his hand. 'That's a hand I've been wanting to shake for a long time—the man who gave Abang Yusuf the run-around. Salutations!'

'Please forgive me,' Brockley gasped. 'My leg, I'm afraid.... We're all delighted to see you again.'

'Sure you are. How've you been keeping anyway, you old crook?'

'Oh! very well, thank you,' he said, his lips tight with pain. 'And you?'

'Just doing a little exploring up here to pass the time.'

'I take it you are accompanied?'

'I've got three tame slaves.'

'Three ... er ...?'

'Natives, Dayaks, picked 'em up down-river.'

'You mean you have no European with you?'

'No. Nobody else wanted to come to this God-forsaken hole. So I had to come on my own.' She looked round at the trees rising out of the night. 'Can't say I blame them.'

'But my dear Miss Trimmer, this is most extraordinary, in fact, unheard of—that a young lady should set off into the Interior completely alone. The consequences for you could be dangerous. I'm surprised they allowed it in Banianok.'

'Allow it? Of course they didn't allow it. I didn't tell them I was going. That silly little shit—'

'She's talking about the Commander-in-Chief of the Armed Forces,' Graham put in.

But Doreen did not detect the irony. 'Anyway, my contract finished, and we had a row over something or other, I forget

147

now, but he tells me I'm on the next plane out to London. You know?' She turned to Brockley. 'Playing the big shot?'

Brockley nodded. He was mesmerized. He had probably never heard a woman use language like that before.

'So I said, "Uh-huh! no shiny little nigger tells this girl what to do; you can get stuffed." So here I am.'

'You mean ... excuse me ... that you came up here just to ... embarrass the Abang?' It was a long time since Brockley had dealt with a lady, and it was clear he was not sure he was dealing with one now. But whatever she was, he was clearly enjoying it.

'To spite the little bastard, yes, that's right.'

Brockley chuckled. 'I'm sure he's not often ... er ... thwarted by members of the opposite sex.' It interested and saddened me to see that he referred to sex with an archness that placed him firmly as a pre-war product. He was of his generation.

'And you have come up here, entirely on your own—exploring?'

'Oh, not exactly. I really just came up here to show that little twat he couldn't push me around. Then I thought I'd better do something while I was here, so I thought I'd come along and work for you a bit.'

'Very kind!' he said with extravagant and unconvincing sincerity.

'But you weren't there. They told me you'd gone up-river with the two boy scouts.' She jerked her head at Graham and me. I was not pleased to be classified with Graham. 'So I thought I'd come up and work for Eric Bones, the missionary, for a bit. But listen—'

'Yes?' said Brockley eagerly.

'Now about all this business six months ago when Yusuf brought his boys up here?'

'Yes?'

'Now, I want you to promise to tell me the truth, you old crook!'

Brockley almost giggled with rapture.

'We knew your Nayans were getting into the camp and changing things around, which really sent our boys berserk. But one thing they couldn't have done was change all the pills in the malaria tin. That would take somebody with medical knowledge. Now did you or did you *not* change those pills for aspirins?'

He pealed off into laughter like a girl asked a faintly improper question outside the palais on a Saturday night. 'Oh! My dear girl ... you *are* sharp!'

'Come on, you old bugger, don't mess about! Yes or no?'

'Well ... I must confess I thought it would be best if we could get rid of the Abang's forces without bloodshed. Bloodshed only leads to more bloodshed, whereas sickness—'

'Just as I thought! Just as I thought! You know I was blamed for that?'

Brockley's face was immediately serious. 'Oh, my dear, I'm most awfully—'

But she cut him short with a mighty slap on the shoulder. 'Shake, you old bugger! My God, I've got to hand it to you. If you could only have seen that little twat's face when he realized it had been you all the time. We'd been looking all over the Interior for you, and you were right there in our camp. You old crook! You've got a thing or two to teach these youngsters.'

Brockley laughed self-consciously. Then he said, 'Well, my dear, I hope you don't mind me saying it's very refreshing to have you with us this evening.'

She waved her hand vaguely in acknowledgement.

Our boys sat on their heels in a semicircle just outside the light of the fire. Usually Law sat on his own, Domeng and Nasir messed together, and the Dayaks sat forever polishing their parangs, also on their own. But at times of great emergency they drew together, and now they squatted in a tight row staring, awed, at Doreen. In the darkness I saw the shadows of Doreen's Dayaks creeping up to join their fellows of their own race.

She sat there, the centre of an astonished circle, occasionally scratching at her ringworm. 'Well, you are a cheerful lot,' she said. 'When you meet a woman alone in the jungle you're

149

supposed to start stabbing each other in the back and slipping cobras in each other's sleeping-bags. You never been to the pictures?'

Brockley laughed delightedly, but vaguely.

Doreen leaned forward almost menacingly. 'You wouldn't have a drink, would you?'

'Oh dear! Hasn't anybody offered you a drink? I'm so sorry, I'm afraid we haven't any sherry; but we could offer you some whisky.'

'What makes you think I drink sherry? There's an enamel mug right in front of me. Cover the first three inches of brown stain with scotch, and the next inch with water.'

'Domeng, Domeng, whisky, quickly!'

Domeng brought the whisky and some more mugs, and a billy-can of water. Brockley insisted on pouring himself. When we all had mugs in our hands (mine, of course, containing just water) he raised his and said, 'Welcome to our young lady visitor. And let us hope ...' But he was not eloquent after thirty-five years in the jungle. He could think of no more to say than, 'Welcome, Miss Trimmer.' He lifted his mug to his lips.

'But how did you manage to hire the boys and the boats?' I asked.

Brockley nodded. 'I must tell you this is a most unprecedented achievement for a lady to come up here alone! Quite without parallel.'

She shrugged. 'Nothing to it! Just came up to Bukit Kota on the Chinese launch. Realized you weren't there, so hired myself three Dayaks who had come round to town selling mats and monkey gall-stones.'

'But they must be expensive,' I said. The boat would cost about five rupiahs a day, and each boy would have to be paid three rupiahs. That came to nearly two pounds a day, and Doreen's honorarium as a volunteer had been four pounds a week.

'I won't go short of a shilling for a while,' she said. 'You remember that ring I had?'

'The one the Abang gave you?'

'That's right. Silly sod asked for it back. Not a very bright

150

move. I went straight out and sold it. Got five hundred for it.'

'Five hundred rupiahs?' Brockley asked breathlessly.

'Rupiahs nothing! Pounds! Five hundred pounds!'

'The Abang won't be pleased,' Graham put in.

'He can take a running jump!'

Brockley laughed, a little shrilly. 'Well, my dear, I don't know about the propriety of you accepting presents of such value from the Abang, but I ... I can certainly understand him wanting to make them to you.'

Then he suddenly looked at me aghast. Had he gone too far with his compliment-paying? 'Oh! I assure you I wasn't meaning to imply that you ... that he and you ... Oh dear!'

He was horrified lest it should seem that he had been suggesting Doreen's relationship with the Abang had been in any way improper.

'Don't you worry, Fred, he got what he deserved.'

'Oh! I'm sure!' he cried, very relieved. 'Very silly of him to give out such presents in the first place. I'm sure he got what he deserved.'

It was an extraordinary revelation to see the old man simpering and posturing and ingratiating himself with this far from lovely girl. The monolith crumbled, the inscrutability disappeared. He was like an awkward youth meeting his first beautiful and sophisticated woman. He knew how to handle natives superbly well, but with women he was lost. It was like seeing one's own adolescent efforts again, twenty years on. Having paid elaborate compliments and created arch excitement, he now proceeded to showing off.

'I think the Abang saw quite a lot during his last tour up here,' he essayed. 'I don't think he'll need to come back for some time. I don't think so.'

'Don't you be so sure, mate! You humiliated him and he's got a long memory. He'll be back—if only to get his picture in a few more papers. He was hoping for big things from the world press over the last trip. He was going to come home having saved the country from being taken over by a crew of savages. But you put pay to that.'

151

'Oh, my dear, I really don't know what you mean. The Abang and I had a very pleasant chat when we finally met at Penghara Ngang's house. Some of the Penghara's men were a little boisterous perhaps with the Abang's troops. They *are* so high-spirited!'

'You had 'em crapping in their pants and you know it, you old bugger,' she gurgled. 'Well—' she started to get up—'better get back down to my camp. Haven't had any feed yet.'

'No food yet!' He held up his hand in front of his chest. 'She's had no food yet,' he said in a direction somewhere between Domeng and myself. 'Oh, you must have some with us.'

'No, no, don't sweat. The boys will be cooking up some rice down there.'

'Your boys are here.' Graham pointed to the three Dayaks sitting with our Dayaks just outside the circle of the fire.

'What the hell are you doing up here?' she shouted in English. 'You're supposed to be down there getting the food ready. Food, scoff, chop—*comprenez*?'

They bolted away all together. Doreen had proved the age-old contention of white women in the tropics, that it is quite unnecessary to speak the language provided you speak whatever you do speak loudly enough.

'Cheeky bastards!' she shouted after them. And then to Brockley she said in a more normal voice, 'What about that? Cheeky bastards!'

What happened next I could not have believed unless I had seen it myself. Brockley laughed. Somebody, an interloper in his jungle, had shouted at his Dayaks, and he laughed. If Graham or I had done it we should have been frozen with half a dozen words. But with Doreen he just laughed.

'Look, boys, I'll see you in the morning. O.K.?'

'Oh, do let us give you some supper. It wouldn't take Domeng five minutes. Besides, we can't possibly allow you to sleep down there all on your own.'

'What do you mean you can't possibly allow me to sleep on my own? I've been doing it for the past week.'

'But aren't you ever frightened—in the night?'

152

She raised her left eyebrow. 'Frightened? Of this lot? You must be joking!'

'But do allow one of us to escort you back. Unfortunately I can't do it myself. As you see, my leg ...'

I stood up. 'I'll walk down with you,' I said.

She shrugged. 'Please yourself. Well, goodnight, boys. See you in the morning.'

We set off down the bank of the river, she in the lead, me training my torch just in front of her so that she could see where she was going. But she gave the impression, as she jumped from one patch of firm ground to another, that she would have managed just as well without it, or me.

'The old boy's not looking so well,' she said casually.

'He's very sick. He's got a gangrenous leg. I think he's going to have to have it off.'

'Oh yes?' she said. She did not ask how his leg had got into that condition.

'It's sad, though,' she mused. 'He was a bit of an anticlimax all round. Before I met him I imagined him as a big tough fellow in a bush-shirt telling everybody what to do.'

'You mean a white hunter out of Ernest Hemingway?'

She responded with a perfunctory jerk of her head. 'Nobody's ever the way you think they're going to be.'

'The funny thing is,' I said, 'he may not really look the part, but he always *has* been the strong, silent white-hunter type. I've never seen him eating out of anybody's hand the way he was with you just now. You've made a conquest, Doreen.'

'Oh! God, no! Not that poor old bugger! He wouldn't be interested in anything but the Sunday papers and his afternoon kip. Not that I couldn't do with a conquest or two right now. But when they're that old it doesn't do a girl's ego much good. The two bachelors up this river certainly aren't the world's most eligible men.'

'Who's the other?'

'Eric Bones the missionary, of course. He is—or was. Good God! I knew there was something I had to tell you. You know he's dead?'

'Dead? Bones? How?'

'Trouble up-river. I met his sparring partner, Snavely. They were on their way up-river to their Mission, and they ran slap into a shoot-up between some warring Dayaks. Anyway they had to run the gauntlet of all this apparently, and in avoiding bullets Bones went overboard and was drowned.'

'Where was this?' I said quickly. But I knew before she spoke.

'Close to where their branch of the river joins the Banianok.'

So it was Bones and Snavely who had been in those two boats! The man who had been indirectly responsible for Galag's death in Banianok and Brockley's estrangement from the rest of the Nayans was now dead, and Brockley was indirectly responsible!

'And you mean to say you carried on up-river, even after a report like that, Doreen?' One could not help admiring her sheer blundering courage. She had not known that the 'warring Dayaks' were just Brockley and his shotgun.

She jerked her upper lip sardonically. 'These Abos don't bother me!' Then she mused on unconcernedly, 'I wonder what the trouble was they ran into. I suppose it was to do with this stolen head.'

'What stolen head?'

'Don't say you haven't heard about that? It's the talk of the whole river.'

'We've been right up the Interior for the last ten days.'

'Well, there's a hell of a row going on. Everybody's accusing everybody else and they've had some fighting between the long-houses. There've been about half a dozen people killed.'

'What happened?' I said urgently.

'Penghara Ngang's favourite head is missing. It was a special one with a pair of gold-rimmed glasses attached to it. It was a Japanese timber expert apparently, who came up to look into their hardwood during the occupation. It's the glasses that make it special. It was the only head they had with its own glasses. Now I come to think of it, of course you wouldn't have heard about it. It disappeared just after you were there. There's a hell of a lot of trouble about it. All the Dayaks are turning against each other—not the Dayaks versus the rest, but the Dayaks against each other. I tell you everybody in the Interior is suspected—except you lot, you'll be glad to know. Apparently it's a well-known fact that Brockley hates heads. Sometimes they get them out to show visitors, but never when he's there. But it's certainly causing a hell of a lot of trouble for everybody else. I've heard them saying if the old man didn't get down-river soon the whole Interior would be in a state of civil war. They reckon he's the only bloke who can stop it.'

'But he can't,' I cried.

'What do you mean—he can't?'

'He mustn't be allowed to. He mustn't be told. We've got to get him down to Banianok. I told you he's going to lose that leg—that's almost certain. But if there's any more delay the poison could spread to the rest of his body and kill him.'

'It's not that bad, is it?'

'Yes! The poisons in his leg will start to spread to the rest of his body very soon. They've probably started already.'

'All right—you needn't put it in baby language. Don't forget I'm a nurse. I know a *little* bit about it.'

'Of course. I'm sorry! But then you know how vital it is that we don't lose an hour. He can't stay for any conciliation. It would take days. By that time he would be dead.'

'But he'll insist.'

'He mustn't be told.'

'But they'll be out to stop him.'

'We won't stop. If I can induce him to have some morphia tomorrow morning we can take him more or less hidden under blankets straight to Banianok. If they want to stop us we'll just keep going. He won't object because he'll hardly know what's happening. Then I'll get straight on to the Abang on the radio-telephone and get a helicopter up for him.'

'There's just one thing—' We were standing in her camp now. 'What happens after he's had his leg amputated in Banianok? You know he won't be allowed back into the Interior by Yusuf and his boys?'

155

'Yes, yes of course. But none of that matters a damn. I'm not thinking about his future career, I'm trying to save his life.'

'All right, keep your hair on!' What she said next surprised me. 'Well—is there anything I can do?'

My astonishment must have been apparent. 'Don't look so bloody flabbergasted! Do you want me or don't you? I could help with nursing him.'

'We don't need you for nursing,' I said. 'Law and I can handle that side of things if we have to. But I'll tell you how you could be very useful: the old man does seem to have taken a fancy to you. If you came along I'm sure it would have a good effect on his spirits, and he'd probably prefer you doing his bandages and the rest, to us.'

'All right, I'll come. This bloody jungle's beginning to get on my nerves anyway. I'll come down with you, then I'll get the first bloody plane out of the whole bloody country and never bloody well come back again.'

'Thanks, Doreen,' I said. For a moment I almost felt intimate with her. But it was only a moment.

'Don't thank me,' she said. 'I'm going your bloody way.'

20

I walked slowly back to our camp. Doreen and I had talked for over half an hour. I hoped that everybody would be in their beds and on their way to sleep, and I would not have to talk to them. But they were still up. Brockley was smoking his pipe for the first time in several days. Did that mean he felt better?

'Well, how did you get on?' he asked, as though I were Doreen's boy-friend.

'She asked if she could come down-river with us tomorrow,' I said.

'Of course, of course! Delighted!' he said eagerly. 'I knew she didn't really want to be up here all on her own. Really the Abang must be an awful fellow in his approach to women if the poor girl had to go to such lengths to get away from him.'

Graham sniggered. Whether Brockley heard him or not, he gave no sign of it. He leaned farther over towards me. 'But what a refreshing girl!'

I did not agree, but I did not disagree either.

'I must say her language is a little ... racy. But so direct, so informal; I can quite understand the Abang being taken with her.'

'He sure was,' Graham sniggered.

'Did you say she was a volunteer? Now *that's* the sort of young person we need out here. Of course I must say her attitude to the natives is a little superior, but you'd never have found women of my generation coming up-river all on their own like that. She must have been a very useful nurse down in Banianok.'

'When she wasn't busy with the Abang,' Graham said.

Brockley was obviously trying to decide whether he should acknowledge that remark or not. His curiosity got the better of him; he turned to Graham. 'Was she friendly with the Abang at one time, then?'

'You could say friendly if you wanted to put it mildly. Friendly would be putting it mildly.'

There was a significant pause. 'I'm afraid I don't follow you,' Brockley said at last.

'Well, surely you can put two and two together, Dad?'

Oh, no! I thought. He's not going to tell him! He's not going to tell him and ruin his harmless little illusion!

'Doreen was quite friendly with the Abang at one time,' I said hastily. 'He cultivates young expatriates. He invited Graham and myself a number of times.'

'I've been there more than a few times. Bill and I are personal friends,' Graham said a little huffily. Then he recovered his good humour and leaned over his father with a 'have you heard this one?' look on his face: 'The difference is I don't sleep with him.'

The inference was obvious, but Brockley did not make it. 'I should think not,' was all he said in a rather bewildered voice.

'Well, somebody not too many hundred yards from here did.'

'I don't follow you.'

'Come on, Dad!' Graham's tone was jocular, a little patronizing. 'I don't have to spell it out to you. You're a man of the world. Why do you think she hates him so much? Because he chucked her over.'

Brockley said deliberately, 'You are a blackguard.'

It was obviously a complete surprise to Graham. 'Dad—what's the matter?'

'That is a blackguardly thing to say about a lady.'

'Dad, I'm sorry,' Graham said earnestly. 'I didn't know you felt—'

'It is a blackguardly thing to say of any lady, but particularly is it so of a lady who is our guest.'

'Dad, she's not our guest. She's camping two hundred yards down the river.'

158

'She is under our protection.'

Now Graham became huffed. He was, after all, only speaking the truth. 'All right, Dad. All right! Sorry I spoke. Maybe I dreamed the whole thing.'

'Do you really expect me to believe a girl of Doreen's calibre would give herself to a native?'

It was a ludicrous statement. It was sheer East of Suez. It made Graham do the worst thing he could have done in the circumstances. He sniggered. 'I'm sorry, Dad,' he gulped, trying to swallow his amusement.

Brockley suddenly dashed out his pipe with great violence against a stone beside him. 'Ugh! it tastes like earth.'

He dragged himself away to his bedding. He shouted to the boys in Iban to go to bed as well. I took Graham by the arm.

'I want to talk to you.'

'What about?'

'Over here.' I pulled him down to a clear space by the river.

'Let go. You're hurting me.'

Something had happened to me that had not happened for eight or nine years. I was feeling. I was no longer the automaton, doing everything to order, guided only by efficiency, bereft of love or hate, the need for love or vengeance. I was feeling again, which meant that I was breaking at last. But for the moment it did not feel like that. It was like a long-remembered brew coursing through my veins again. I knew it was going to reach a summation in a few moments: I was going to hit him; and I was going to enjoy it.

I took a good grip on his shirt, a good handful six inches below the neck. 'You know your father is very sick, and could be dead in a week?'

'What's the matter with you? Let go of me!'

'He has no pleasures left in the world. But he develops a schoolboy crush on Doreen, and you have to destroy it.'

He struggled. 'I don't know what you're talking about. Let go of me!' He was weak, of course, from his malaria, and I was strong. His very weakness made the anticipation of hitting him all the more pleasant.

159

'You've done nothing but get in the way and gum up the works ever since you arrived in this country.'

'Look, I didn't know he fancied her.'

'He doesn't. You still don't see it, do you, you little half-wit. He's got some sort of harmless illusion about her. She's young, she's English, she's a woman. It's silly, isn't it?'

'Yes, it is. Look, if you don't let go of me I'll shout.'

'Yes, it is,' I hissed. I pulled his face towards me till I could feel his breath. 'It's stupid, but it's all he's got now. But you just can't see it, can you? You snivelling little worm! You're so obsessed with your fancy bloody ideas, with your *New Statesman* and your *New Society* and your racialist claptrap—you haven't got time to see what's three inches in front of your nose.'

But it was no good. The moment of passion had passed. It had passed when I called him a snivelling little worm. *That* was sheer prep school. I had tried to keep it going by swearing, but that was no good either. I let go of him.

He jerked his shoulders a couple of times and put his left hand up to where I had been holding his shirt. 'You're going mad. I've never seen you like that before.'

I was completely emotionless once again. There was no more reason to be angry with Graham than there was to be angry with Brockley, the Abang, the Director, the Nayans or the Army.

Later, when we got into our bedding, I was able to talk to him more freely. 'We are going to have to extend ourselves to get to Bukit Kota by nightfall tomorrow,' I said.

'Will I be glad to see Bukit Kota!'

'We may run into some trouble, but we'll have to keep going. I'm telling you this so that you'll be prepared. We may be stopped because they may want Brockley to mediate. But if he does he will certainly die. So we must keep going.'

'I see,' he said evenly. 'What's the trouble about?'

In a few sentences I told him about the head that had disappeared, and the repercussions of its disappearance.

He nodded gravely. 'I see. Thank you very much.'

We rolled into our bedding.

I was awoken when it was still dark. Graham's face was about six inches from mine. He held his hand ready to clamp over my mouth if I should utter a sound.

His voice was a harsh whisper. 'James! That head—it's in my rucksack. They gave it to me—the long-house boys. I didn't take it, James. They gave it to me.'

21

Everything went according to plan in the morning. I told the boys about the Dayak trouble and its cause, but I did not say its cause was in Graham's haversack. It was still there. In his first terror he had wanted to go out into the jungle and bury it; but I knew it must be returned. How that was to be accomplished I had not worked out yet, but I knew it must be. It would not be till after we had got Brockley to Bukit Kota and then out to Banianok. I could not leave it with anybody else. So it remained at the bottom of Graham's haversack.

Doreen bustled into camp at six o'clock. We went away by the river with boiling water and gauzes to change Brockley's dressing. I no longer did it for any benefit he might receive from the powerful antiseptic solution we still soaked the wound in, but to modify the stench of dead tissue that came from it. Doreen did not blanch or flinch an instant as she assisted me, though she could have seen and smelt few wounds so bad. She keep up a jocular flow of conversation which seemed to keep the old man's spirits buoyant.

'I'm awfully sorry to expose you to this sort of thing,' he said as she sponged away the dressings with warm antiseptic solution.

'Don't worry about that, chief; all in the job.'

He smiled up at her timidly, pathetically.

'All right, lift up a bit.' She tapped his knee gently as she proceeded with the dressing.

He tried. 'I'm sorry, I can't.' He put both hands under the upper part of his thigh and lifted.

162

She smacked his hands away. 'Get those dirty maulers away from my clean dressing.'

'I'm sorry,' he said contritely.

She lifted the leg herself. 'Bit of a mess, isn't it?'

'It is, it is. I'm awfully sorry.' He was ashamed of his wound, as people always are of really horrible wounds.

'Few more shots of penicillin and a trim-up in operating theatre'll work wonders.'

'Do you really think so?' He had known for several days how bad it was, but he talked as though he had forgotten—just as he had told himself that Galag had got back to the Interior.

'Of course. What do you say, Doctor?'

'Absolutely,' I mumbled uncomfortably.

But he was not interested in what I had to say.

'I must say you're very gentle,' he said to Doreen.

'Practice, squire!'

'What was that—squire?' He laughed vacantly. 'I'm not quite that. Maybe I should call you matron.'

'I've been trying to get people to call me matron for years.'

'I will then. I'll be the first.'

'Keep still!' The fresh dressing became dislodged and fell on to the dressing-towel. 'You're a very naughty boy, moving around all the time. Know what we do to patients who give us trouble?'

'No.'

'We give 'em an injection.'

'Oh, no!'

She finished the bandaging, and then patted him gently on the knee. 'There we are.'

'That was the most pain-free dressing I've had yet,' he said earnestly.

'You can't beat the woman's touch. Right! Now for the injection!'

'Oh, no. I don't deserve it. I didn't move after you told me not to.'

He was, pathetically, trying to keep the game going. But Doreen was not. 'I want to give you some morphia to make your journey more comfortable.'

163

'Oh, no. I don't have to do that, do I? I'm quite comfortable really.'

She started to draw up the injection. 'Now come on! Don't argue. Roll over.'

'You're not going to—Oh, no! ... Oh, really!'

'Well, where else do you expect to have it—in your elbow?'

'I really don't think I can allow—'

'Push off!' she said roughly, with a wink, to me. 'Can't you see you're embarrassing the boy?'

I walked away. A minute later she called, 'O.K. All finished.'

I came back and looked at her interrogatively. She nodded, grinning. Brockley blushed. 'Really, I didn't feel a thing.'

'Experience, squire, I told you. You ought to have me on the payroll.'

'I think we should,' he said fervently.

Something in his voice made her turn. She looked down at him dispassionately for a second or two. Then she said, quite softly, in as tender a voice as anybody was ever likely to hear from her, 'You poor old bugger! What have they done to you?' It was a tone that I had never heard from her before.

Brockley discerned it too. A flush spread slowly up from his neck to his cheeks and then to his forehead. For a second or so nobody moved. Then Doreen slapped the bark of the tree she was standing against. 'Come on, then. Let's get those lazy buggers moving, or we'll still be here tomorrow.'

We lifted him into one of the boats and loaded the gear in around him. We agreed that the only two other occupants of the boat would be Nasir and Doreen, and if the luggage was carefully arranged and Brockley lying down he would be invisible from the bank. We were to pay off our Dayaks after negotiating the last set of rapids. Then the other boat would contain myself, Briok, Domeng and Graham, and Mohammed my driver from Banianok. Both Nasir and Mohammed had strict instructions not to stop for anything unless given direct orders from me. I was now completely in control. Although everybody still treated Brockley with the greatest respect, as

164

far as the expedition was concerned he was just cargo. It struck me for a moment, as I saw how automatically they all obeyed me, how incongruous it was five years after Independence. But that was perhaps one thing Graham had been right about; up-river they did not feel independent. They knew they were independent, but the feeling had not penetrated yet. In Banianok everything was changing; up here everything was just the same.

We were on the water and moving at seven o'clock—an hour later than I had intended. An hour down the river—we were travelling in front—Mohammed turned the boat in a curve to avoid something in the water. It happened all the time. After heavy rains you could sometimes see whole trees floating serenely down-stream; and very occasionally what you thought was log turned out to be a crocodile. I paid no attention until Mohammed slowed the boat and took a wide turn back up-stream without consulting me, as though he had all the time in the world. He brought the boat drifting to a halt, the engine still running, and the mass in the water slowly drifted the dozen yards down-stream to bump against our bows. It was more of a slap than a bump. It was an unpleasant sound. The thing had an unpleasant smell. Mohammed turned it over impassively in the water with his boat-hook. It was a headless body. To judge by the smell and the bloated appearance it had been in the water three days or more. 'My God! It's true,' Graham whispered.

There was nothing for Mohammed to do but push the body away with his boat-hook and put his engine back into gear.

I looked at everybody else in the boat. There was fear on their faces, except for little Briok; he was just bewildered. 'Bukit Kota,' I said to Mohammed. 'Don't stop!'

'Please, sir,' Law Kiat How pleaded, 'do not waste any time.'

'Oh, my God!' Graham breathed in my ear. 'What shall I do?'

'Just keep your mouth shut,' I grunted back at him. 'We'll sort out that side of things when we get to Bukit Kota.'

'But to think of them dying—because of me. And I didn't know. If I'd known I'd never have—'

165

'If these people knew you had that head,' I said through my teeth, 'they'd drop you straight overboard with it. So don't say any more.'

'Sir!' said Law. 'Respectfully suggest you load Dr Brockley's shotgun. Then if we see any Dayaks we can shoot first.'

'We're not frightened of Dayaks,' I said calmly. 'They're not after us.'

'Excuse me, sir—I—*I* am frightened of the Dayaks.'

'Well, you've no reason to be.'

'Excuse me, sir, they are only safe when under control of Dr Blo Ko Lee.'

'Well, we've got Blo Ko Lee with us.'

'But he is weak now. Perhaps now they will no longer respect him, and instead they will cut off our heads. Excuse me, sir, for private conversation—' He turned his back to Graham and lowered his voice. 'Best plan will be to put everybody else into the other boat and for you and me and Mohammed, to be our driver, to go immediately to Bukit Kota for help. Very faster. I think you agree.'

'No, I don't agree. Law, you're a coward,' I said trying to sound jocular. But of course Law had no sense of humour.

'Yes, sir, that is correct,' he said. 'I think you agree my plan is best plan, sir.'

The boat lurched wildly. 'Dayaks!' Graham cried hoarsely, attempting to stand.

'Get down! You'll have us all in the water.'

'There they are—this side of the rapids. They know we'll have to stop at the rapids.'

'We don't have to stop,' I grunted.

'We can't get through that. That was the worst one when we were coming up-river, and the river's swollen now.'

I shouted to Mohammed in Malay. He knew every inch of the river. I asked him if he could get us through. He raised his chin and momentarily closed his eyes. It was his equivalent of a nod. I shouted the same question to Nasir. He cut his engine and shouted back at Mohammed. The two boats were about thirty yards apart. Mohammed cut his engine and shouted back

166

his reassurance. Without hesitation Nasir shouted in English, 'O.K.'

'Can we do it?' Graham was crouching, his face over my shoulder, as though I could see something he could not.

'Mohammed says it's all right.'

'Please don't consider stopping, sir,' Law piped up. 'Suggest we proceed over rapids to ignore danger, in view of alternative.'

'We're going over,' I said. 'Hold on! Are you all right, Doreen?' I shouted across.

'What the hell's going on?'

'See those Dayaks down by the falls? They'll try and stop us. We'll pretend we're going to stop, but carry on over at the last moment. O.K.?'

'O.K.'

'How's the old man?'

'He's fine. He's asleep.'

'Hang on to Briok in case he does anything silly.'

'I've got him. You'd better tell Nasir to watch what he's doing. If he turns this bloody thing over Brockley's had it.'

'He'll be all right. He's as steady as a rock.'

She moved so that she was exactly beside Brockley lying flat in the boat and she could put a protective arm round Briok as well. There was something in her expression I had to admire. She would not let a short-arsed nigger like the Abang bother her; she became the first white woman to travel alone in the Interior with a nonchalance that even Brockley could not duplicate; she seemed all set to make it clear to the rapids and the Dayaks that they were no sort of challenge either.

'There's something about that awful girl ...' I muttered.

But Graham was not listening. 'Can we do it. Are you sure?'

'Sit down. The lower you are in the boat the less likely it will be to capsize.'

We were now three hundred yards from the rapids.

'Don't you think perhaps we should stop and explain? They wouldn't mind. If I gave it back and explained it was a present. Then maybe they'd help us pull the boats down round the rapids and—'

167

'Shut up!' I said. 'And *get down in the boat!*'

'You think Mohammed can do it? You sure?'

Law's teeth were chattering now. '1952 Governor Grenville's boat capsizes over these rapids.'

'What happened?' Graham cried harshly.

'Very kind man. Rest in peace ... Doctor, please sir, boat is going too fast, perhaps?'

'You heard what he said,' Graham cried. 'We're going too fast.'

Mohammed's face was expressionless. Now, two hundred yards from the rapids, he pulled his engine up out of the water and over the support lug, so that it would not be ground to bits as we went over the rocks. Nasir was doing the same.

Law, the yellowness of fear imposed on the ordinary yellow pigment of his skin, began to chant to himself over and over again. But it was not any recondite spell brought by his ancestors from the vastnesses of China. It was, 'Oh dear! Oh dear! Oh dear! Oh deary me ... Oh dear! Oh dear! Oh deary me ...'

We had one Dayak in our boat. He was at the front holding a stout stave to ward the boat away from the rocks. 'Get hold of one of these!' I thrust a stave into Law's hands and then I crawled up to the front of the boat with the other. I should have put it, not into Law's hands, but into Graham's. Now we were less than a hundred yards away from the rapids. The formation of the boats was changing. As we got closer we were being sucked from the slow-moving water at the side of the stream to the racing flow in the middle, and now our boat was directly in front of Brockley's. We could see the line of rocks in the river clearly now, and the Dayaks on them waving us down with stern expressions on their faces. I waved back casually.

'We are going too fast, aren't we? Law was right,' Graham cried.

Brockley's two men dug their paddles into the water. Their boat slowed. 'We should do the same.'

'No! We need a good distance between the boats as we go over.'

168

A sudden sheet of spray covered Law. 'Oh dear! Oh deary me!'

'But it wouldn't hurt to slow down. Look at that barricade of rocks. How can he possibly know he's not going to hit one of them and smash us all to smithereens?'

'He's aiming for the gap in the middle.'

'But if he misses?'

'He can't miss. Eighty per cent of the water crossing these rapids is being sucked through that channel, because it's the only one of any depth. We're going to be sucked in too.'

He stood up. 'No! I'd rather stop and tell them the truth.' He turned to Mohammed at the back of the boat. 'Stop!' He shouted. 'Paddle for the bank.'

'For God's sake sit down,' I shouted. 'You'll have us all killed.' Now we were almost on top of the rapids and the roar of the water breaking on the rocks drowned almost every noise.

'Father!' he shouted. 'Father! Brockley!'

Briok took up the chant. 'Blo Ko Lee!' But Brockley did not even wake.

We were thirty yards from the fall. Graham was still shouting desperately to his father. The boat rolled wildly. Law's lips twisted with fear and he threw himself on to Graham to pull him down. Graham moved back. One moment he was on both feet, legs bent at the knee, shrieking at his father, the next he was falling. It looked as though he would fall into the boat, but the current seized it and pulled it from under him. Mohammed reached out his hand instinctively as he went past, but at thirty miles an hour he did not even touch him. The prow of our boat sliced into the roaring water, then we were over the edge, exactly midway between the two ramparts of rocks with a clearance of a yard on either side, with our astonished interceptors running up and down the bank in rage.

The first cataract was the biggest. We fell about ten feet in as many yards. We were all completely soaked with spray, and at the bottom of the cataract the level of the water was within

169

inches of the gunwale at the bow of the boat. They seemed absolutely level; another couple of inches and the water would pour in, the prow would sink a little lower, more water would pour in, and the boat would be swamped and drift helplessly broadside to the inevitable crash against the rocks. For perhaps a tenth of a second, which was like a minute, it seemed as though that was what must happen. Then the prow was bouncing up out of the water and Mohammed was being soaked at the back. The river curved. Directly ahead, forty yards down-river, the water dashed over flat, almost invisible rock; the only evidence that it was there was the water leaping up over it. Over it and round it the current thrashed. We were part of the current now; we could not get out of it; but we could get as near to one side of it as possible. But not too far to one side, for then the stern of the boat might be grasped by the current while the front was in comparatively calm water, and we would be in the most terrible position of all for going over cataract water—broadside on. Leaning far over the side, his paddle dragging in the water, Mohammed squeezed the boat foot by foot to the edge of the current. I had my stave ready to fend us off the rocks as we went by; we were clear by a foot or more. The current curved again. There was a second cataract. With a grinding lurch of the boat against the rocks we were over it. Mohammed leaned out over the side; we were at an angle of about thirty degrees to the current and drifting without control. The next gap was about ten feet wide; we had thirty yards to straighten ourselves. Now I knew how Graham must feel not knowing how to do anything. I watched, helpless, as Mohammed slammed his paddle blade into the water and held it there. The blood-vessels bulged in his old neck as he went down to meet the water. The Dayak did the same thing at the front on the opposite side of the boat—my side. Their blades held. The current tried to tear the boat one way, the forces created by the paddles pulled it the other. Each of them crouched with his head inches from the water, one at the front, one at the back. They did not move, the paddles did not move, but in front of me I could see the muscles of the Dayak's neck bunched under his skin abso-

170

lutely rigid. As we went into the cataract we were at an angle of about five degrees to the current. The Dayak came up in a racing crouch and leaned far out over the water to plant his paddle among the rocks, and then again, and again, as we crashed down over the whirling water, each time pulling back a fraction of a second after it seemed he had left it too late and that he must share Graham's fate.

Suddenly we were into smooth water. Mohammed was sitting back, grinning, his paddle dragging in the water, and below us, as far as we could see, was clear water, gunmetal-grey without a ripple. Domeng and Nasir and Doreen were laughing forty yards behind us and to starboard, their boat drifting broadside, but now out of danger. Now the river would slide, deep and broad, between the brown banks clothed with evergreen rain forests. The nearest Dayak was three hundred yards away. We had a clear run to Bukit Kota. There was nothing to stop us now—only Graham.

I half expected to see his mangled body come shooting over the last cataract. It did not. Slowly, unwillingly, we paddled into the bank. Now we were in the really deep water we could push the boats in under the shade of a belian tree. That was what we did. Doreen hung on to Briok and held the shade over Brockley as the rest of us got out. Slowly we went up the rough path that we should have been walking *down* carrying everything from the boats, while the boats were manoeuvred down the subsidiary channels of the rapids. It would have taken about two hours altogether. We had done it in forty-five seconds. It had been a complete waste of time. We had risked the old man's life for nothing.

Law saw him about four hundred yards up-stream, which was also about four hundred yards below the first cataract. Law always saw everything first. The Dayaks spotted him at the same time—as Law was in the act of pointing. Four of them ran down the bank. He was lying half in and half out of the water on his front. The stream washed over his legs and buttocks, but the rest of him was on gravel. I never saw anybody who looked more dead.

171

'Graham!' I shouted, just as the Dayaks got to him. We were still fifty yards away. He did not move. They reached him all four together. Two of them bent down, put their hands under his shoulders and pulled him completely out of the water. He screamed with pain.

'My arm! Oh God!' It was a terrible scream, deep-throated but only a second and a half in duration. Involuntarily I started to run. The Dayaks were not trying to hurt him; they were trying to help. They started to roll him over. Again he screamed; they pulled back.

'My arm! My God, it's smashed.'

'Graham!' I was there. 'It's all right. We're all here.'

'Don't let them touch me.'

'We won't. They were trying to help.'

One of the Dayaks, his face frightened at having been the cause of so much pain, came towards Graham again.

'Don't let them touch me,' he shrieked. 'Give them the head! It's in my haversack. For God's sake give it to them ... and then give me something for this pain....' He started to sob. 'Please ... please ... please ...'

Law looked at me, and then at Graham. His almost lashless eyes blinked, but his face was completely expressionless. Without a moment's warning he sheered away, and he was dashing down the bank, jumping from pathway to rocks and back to pathway. Four hundred yards down the river I could see him arriving at the boats. He was rummaging through the baggage. Then he was dashing back again. He arrived breathless with the head under one arm and the glasses in the other hand. He thrust them into the hands of one of the astonished Dayaks and gasped in Malay, 'It was the white people who took it. No good people. I got it back for you, remember. You've got to let me go.' Perhaps he forgot I understood Malay. But probably he was so terror-stricken he was not thinking of anything but survival.

I did not know exactly what I expected to happen then. What did happen was that the Dayaks stood there, one with the head under his arm like a cabbage, looking as astonished as Nasir,

172

Domeng and the rest of our boys, while Graham sobbed softly into the water.

I splinted Graham's arm after giving him a third of a grain of morphia into the buttock, over which the trousers were torn. I discovered a gash over his left temple—the one on which he had been lying—about five inches, and a fracture of the skull beneath it. But a fracture of the skull is not necessarily dangerous unless the broken pieces of bone have been pushed inwards into the brain. We had no time for stitching; I put a pressure-dressing on to stop the bleeding; I could stitch it up properly at Bukit Kota. After the morphia he was unable to walk; we carried him back to the boat.

I had been expecting Dayaks to begin pouring out of the forest at any moment. As I worked on Graham, and then as we carried him down the bank, I expected every moment a whooping noise in the jungle, or a poisoned dart plunged in my neck. (But then I remembered the Dayaks did not use blowpipes now—they had shotguns. It would be a hundred pellets of shot.) But nothing happened. The Dayaks stood looking on with great interest as I bound up Graham's splint, every now and then one of the others stealing up to touch the head that remained tucked under the leader's arm, and passing the glasses from hand to hand. Then we were ready to go. They came forward eagerly to help lift Graham—except the one holding the head. As always when there are eight people carrying somebody, they managed to drop him. The second time they dropped him was when they were nearing the boat. Brockley was awake and sitting up. They looked at him (he hadn't seen them) and at each other. Then they looked lovingly at the head.

'Blo Ko Lee gets angry when he sees heads,' the one who was holding it said to me in Malay. 'We'd better not come any farther.'

That suited us perfectly. I nodded understandingly. Suddenly they sheered away into the jungle. We who were left picked up Graham. We got him to the boat without dropping him. We put him in the other boat, lying flat as Brockley was in his.

173

'What happened?' Brockley murmured.

'Graham fell into the water,' I said. 'He's got a grazed arm.'

'Oh!' He was hardly comprehending what I was saying. He had let himself down again so that his head was resting on Doreen's lap. When she moved her knees slightly he realized; he had obviously thought his head was on a pillow. He started up. 'I'm awfully sorry ...'

'That's all right,' she said gently. 'It's quite comfortable, old feller.'

'Are you sure?'

'You just go to sleep.'

He looked up at her gratefully, like a child, and she smiled down on him like a mother; he slept again.

As we cut our way through the smooth, deep, slow-flowing water that separated us from Bukit Kota I wondered why we had got away with returning the head with so few questions asked, and so little anger. I could only think that Brockley's prestige was such that nobody could believe that anybody under his command could do such a terrible thing as Graham had in fact done. As it had been so often in my five years in Banianok, I did not consider the perfectly sensible explanation that should have occurred to me long before we got to Bukit Kota. I did not find out until several weeks later, when the Abang and his troops were back in the Interior: we had given the head to the wrong people.

The men who had borne it away, whooping, into the jungle, had been not from Penghara Ngang's long-house, but from that of his hereditary enemy Penghulu Jugah.

So the killing went on.

22

We got back to Bukit Kota at six-thirty. It was nearly night.
There was no point in carrying Brockley all the way up the hill
to his house; I told them to prepare a bed for him in the hospital,
then I went off to find the radio-telephone. It was kept in the
police station. There was one man sitting there in a sarong, bare
feet, no shirt, chewing betel and dandling a baby on his knees.
'Where is the duty officer?' I said in Malay.
'I am the duty officer, lord,' he replied politely.
'Where is the radio-telephone? I want to use it.'
'The lord will be disappointed. The telephone broke down
many days ago and the engineer has voices in his head.'
'Can't anybody else mend it?'
'The lord will appreciate that we poor people have no skill
for such things. Will the lord honour me and take a cup of
coffee?'
'Look, this telephone must be got working.'
'If it were only possible ...'
'Blo Ko Lee is lying in the hospital very sick. His leg must
be cut off.' I made a sudden, brutal chopping movement with
my hand, suggesting a leg being cut off with a sword. The baby
began to cry.
'Blo Ko Lee! The greatest friend to all people!'
'We must get a helicopter up from Banianok to take him down
first thing tomorrow morning for operation. If we do not he will
die.'
He made a sound as though the breath had been suddenly
punched from his chest. 'In half an hour we can be ready, lord.

175

But I must go to my house for my screwdriver.'

He thrust the baby into my arms and dashed away. He came puffing back a minute later, dropped the screwdriver, took the baby, and dashed off again. He came back without it.

The radio-telephone was standing in the corner covered by a large cloth. He pulled the cloth away and started work with his screwdriver. 'Forgive me, lord—on Blo Ko Lee's direct instructions we keep the telephone out of order. I could not go against his orders except for something so serious.'

'Blo Ko Lee's orders? You mean all the times the telephone has been out of order it's been on his orders?'

'No, sir,' he said seriously. 'Sometimes it breaks down on its own.'

'But why? Why keep it out of order?'

'Too much talking with Banianok only causes difficulties for everybody, lord. Blo Ko Lee has said it. It is true.'

'But you don't work for Blo Ko Lee. You work for the government.'

He stood up and smiled at me. 'But the government, lord, is Blo Ko Lee.'

He motioned me towards the machine with exquisite Malay politeness. In Banianok there would have been surliness and an air of 'Don't think you're any better than me, mate'. Here it was deference and respect. I felt what it must have been like in the old days to have power. Suddenly something snapped in me. I shouted, 'Come along! Quickly! This is a very serious matter.'

'I am such a poor mechanic, lord. If only the engineer—'

I walked away from him to the door. I strode up and down outside a turn or two. When I entered again he had the front of the machine off and he was peering uncertainly into it.

'Well?'

'Does the lord know anything about electricity?'

'No, I do not. Look, this is an extremely serious matter. We have got to get to Banianok soon. If you can't repair the telephone we will go by river. We'll start tonight. Now, can you do it or not?'

176

The skin round his eyes wrinkled; he ducked his head. 'I can do it.'

'Are you sure?'

'I'll try.'

'Do you or do you not know how to repair this machine?'

I walked up and down for two minutes. 'What happens when Banianok wants to tell you something serious—a murderer has escaped and is coming up-river?'

'For that we will always answer them.' He rolled his head from side to side to emphasize his sincerity.

'But how can you answer them if the machine's broken down?'

He stood there, his lips pursed, considering the question; his screwdriver was still in his right hand.

'Well, have you finished?'

'No, lord.' He bent back hurriedly over the machine.

If only he hadn't been so deferential! In Banianok I would have been silenced by now with a rough retort. Mechanics being such rare men in Banianok where everybody was either a servant, a beggar or a fine arts graduate, I would probably not have got a civil word in the first place. The mechanic might have been just as bad, but I would have been reasonable and calm, aware that he was working under the stress of knowing that he was half-trained, knowing that he had been only recently liberated from colonial bondage, knowing that he had a chip on his shoulder.

I knew what I should do, but for once I could not. He stuck his screwdriver hopefully into the works here and there, like a cook seeing if the potatoes were done, and that enraged me even more.

At last, after nearly nine years without a drink, of abstinence from every emotion, I was feeling again; it had happened momentarily two days before up-river with Graham, but now it was far stronger; it did not abate, it intensified with each futile effort he made to convince me that he might find the right screw to turn any minute. As when I had got angry with Graham, it was not wickedness that had achieved what had been for

177

nine years impossible; it was not cruelty, or greed, or spite that finally did it, but stupidity.

I remember thinking that this must be what it was like to run amok. 'Amok'—a Malay word, a Malay disease; but perhaps it was a product of this jungle, this climate, the sun, the clouds, the humidity, the jungle always pressing in, hemming you in wherever you went on the island.

I was thinking it while my hands were doing something else, as though another brain had their control. One hand was around his thin neck. I had my fingers deep in the cleft between the two columns of muscle on either side of his spine. My thumb was on his larynx. I was squeezing, and rasping over and over, 'You can't do it, can you? You don't know how to do it. You don't know how to do it! Don't know how to do it!' The other hand moved convulsively at my side. I flexed it up to my shoulder and down again to my thigh. He could have escaped; I was only using one hand. But he just looked at me, faintly surprised, faintly hurt, his eyes bulging and his tongue coming out between his teeth, looking as though it had filled his mouth and more. Was it Malay passivity, or was it astonishment, or was it a conviction, deep-rooted in colonial days, that you couldn't win if your opponent was white?

I would have strangled him to death, without meaning to, and without knowing that that was really what I wanted to do. But suddenly his neck became heavy in my hand; he crumpled to the floor unconscious. I was still gasping, 'Don't know how to do it! Don't know how to do it!' I had been taking my breath in deep, choking draughts. I had over-breathed. Now I stood there light-headed, giddy, just about to pass out, and I did not take a breath for half a minute. At the end of that time he stirred. He pulled himself on to his hands and knees. I felt exhausted, drained of emotion.

I bent to help him up. He shrank away, still on his hands and knees. He pulled himself up and half lay against the wall as far away from me as he could get.

'Don't be frightened,' I said. 'I'm your friend.'

He did not move.

178

'You see, you shouldn't say you can do it if you can't,' I pleaded. 'It wastes so much time.'

I waited for a change of expression—for a sign that he did not hate me. It did not come.

'I know it's not your fault really. The police should be properly organized. It's *their* fault.' I jerked my head in the direction of Banianok, two days' travel away, indicating not just the Chief of Police, but the whole home-grown élite who were now his masters.

'The whole Interior should be properly organized. It's been ignored ever since Independence. Money should be allocated for development. Why haven't you got a proper hospital here? Why haven't you got a proper police station? Why hasn't there been a district commissioner since Independence? Because nobody in the capital cares about the Interior.'

I knew I should shut up; I was talking just like a volunteer. I felt more tired than I had ever done in my life; but it was not just the lethargy of physical exhaustion—the chief part was the enervating weariness that comes when you have done something shameful that can never be undone or wiped away.

I heard my voice and it sounded far off, belonging to someone I had never known.

I took his hand in mine. 'You see, I want to help you. But *they* don't. They just want to drive round in fancy American cars. The Chief of Police—on his salary how can he afford a Cadillac? How can anybody in this poor country afford a Cadillac? Have you got a car? No—you ought to have one. Not a big one, but you ought to have the chance to own one some time in your life. They've got mohair suits from Hong Kong. You should have the chance of an ordinary suit from Singapore. Every snotty youth in Banianok is walking around with a transistor radio on his wrist. Why haven't you got one?'

He blinked; and as he did so I remembered Brockley's summary of Western civilization: blue jeans, transistor radios and V.D. I had just offered my new friend two out of the three.

'You don't understand. You just don't understand, do you?' The anger seethed back again. Brockley had wanted everything

179

to remain just as it had always been. Graham and his friends
came out in search of a direction they had missed in London and
would not find again until they got back there. But I had
worked, silently and dispassionately, to try and modernize the
country. I had done what Graham and his friends only talked
about. But I had done it silently. Some instinct, inherited from
a time when the English were a more taciturn race, had warned
me against giving expression to all the good I thought I was
doing.

The instinct had been right: in the act of betraying what I
had worked for, I had started talking. There was nothing more
to say. I mumbled, 'I'll go back to the hospital. Send a message
when the radio's ready.'

He ducked his head and dashed from the room. I walked to
where the radio-telephone stood, kicked it dully, and followed
him more slowly from the police station.

When I got back to the hospital there seemed less activity
than there should have been. When Brockley was there, there
were always more people around. As I walked in the door I
saw the old Malay wash-amah leaning up against the wall with
a friend. I went through the wards to Brockley's office. He was
not there. I came back and asked the amah what had become of
him. We spoke Malay.

'He has gone to his house, lord,' and she raised her chin so
that it was in line with the top of the hill.

No wonder the hospital was so empty! Everybody would have
to go up to help to carry him and his gear. And then tomorrow
they would have to carry him down again. No doubt they had
dropped him a couple of times going up, and they would drop
him a couple of times more coming down in the morning. All
that time and effort wasted when he should be resting quietly!

'Why has he gone up the hill?'

'I don't know, lord. He wanted to go to his house.'

'Weren't they able to put up a bed in his office?'

'Oh yes, lord. Very nice beds down here.'

'Well ... Oh! it doesn't matter!' I turned away. I had been

180

starting to get angry with her, just as I had with the policeman, and she was even less blameworthy of anything than the policeman.

'Has everybody gone up?'

'Everybody, lord. They took a stretcher, and mem was walking beside him to give comfort.' She shook her head dreamily. 'Very kind mem; she was holding Blo Ko Lee's hand.'

'Holding his hand?'

'Yes.' She took a step closer, then, realizing her impertinence, stepped back again. She bent forward confidentially. 'They say she is Blo Ko Lee's wife come back to Bukit Kota after so many years, to save him.'

'His wife? But she's thirty years younger than he is.'

'She's not his wife?' There was disappointment in her voice; it had obviously passed over her completely that there was thirty years' difference in their ages, and that when Brockley's wife left Banianok for ever Doreen would have been only about two. Europeans often used to say how difficult it was to tell the age of a native between twenty and fifty. It had never occurred to me that the natives should have the same difficulty with us.

'Perhaps she will be his wife—soon?'

'No! She's a nurse. She's going back to England.'

'She'll get married in England?'

'I don't know. I shouldn't think so.'

'Then Blo Ko Lee can marry her?'

'I haven't got time.... Did they take my luggage up to Blo Ko Lee's house?'

'They did, lord.'

'Very well. I'm going to the police station, then I shall be going up the hill, if anybody wants me.'

'Yes, lord. I hope Blo Ko Lee is not too sick. I hope he will get better soon. I think he will.'

'He is very sick. And it is unlikely that he will get better ever.' I probably sounded grief-stricken, but that was not the way I felt at the moment. I said it in that particular way to shock, and therefore to hurt her. Why? Partly it was because she had the same deferential politeness as the policeman, which

181

seemed to bring out something in me I had not known existed; I turned away and strode out of the hospital. I walked back to the police station. When I was in thirty-yard range I could hear the clatter of static and the whine of shortwave signals. When I got into the room there was a Chinese sitting in front of the machine with headphones on, manipulating the knobs with an air of concentration. The little fat Malay policeman was nowhere to be seen. The Chinese turned round as I came in.

'Good evening, Doctor. How is Blo Ko Lee?'

'Bad, I'm afraid. I want to get a helicopter up here to take him to Banianok tomorrow morning.'

'I was through to Banianok a little while ago. But there is a lot of cloud—perhaps a storm between here and there.'

I sat down to wait. 'I'm glad you could come,' I said.

He shrugged. 'I have the contract.' None of the Malay's charm about him!

'You mean you have a contract to repair this machine? From the government?'

He nodded absently, concentrating on his knobs and dials.

'The policeman—the man who came to get you—it's not his job? He doesn't know anything about it?'

He raised one corner of his mouth and lowered the eyebrow on the same side. 'Not a thing.'

'And yet he spent half an hour playing around with it, pretending, wasting time while the old man lay there ...' But I did not say it; I only thought it. Even in the depths of my rage I still remembered the cardinal rule of never criticizing one subordinate in front of another.

'We're through,' the Chinese said suddenly. 'Who do you want to speak to?'

'Abang Yusuf.'

His eyes opened wide and his lips pursed in involuntary acknowledgement of the importance of the call. He told the operator. They spoke in English.

'They're getting him.'

He sat drumming his fingers on the ledge in front of him, beneath the dials. 'When we get through you can speak.

182

Remember to press this knob when you speak and to release it when you finish. When you finish you say "Over" and he will speak to you.' He turned another switch and removed the headphones and the Abang's voice filled the room saying, 'Hi there, Doc! Where you been? Long time—'

'I've been up-river from Bukit Kota with Graham and Dr Brockley. I'm afraid the old man got gored by a wild boar. The leg's gone gangrenous. I'm afraid he'll have to have it off. We must get him to Banianok as soon as possible. Can you send a helicopter? Over.'

'You say he's got to have his leg off? You mean cut off? Over.'

'Yes. But if we delay much longer the poisons will have spread to the rest of his body and he'll die. When could you send a helicopter up here? Over.'

'We're very tight with 'copters, just now, Doc'—three months before they had not had any helicopters at all—'but I think we can do it. When do you want it? Over.'

'Tomorrow morning as soon as you can. Over.'

'O.K. We'll probably have to work through the night on the maintenance boys but we'll do it. You know we had a lot of trouble with our 'copters lately, Doc. My maintenance boys are no good. I talked to the fellows in California, and they're going to send a couple, three fellows over to really get my boys in trim. Hey! You know I told you we were getting four new Gook-Busters? I talked to Merlin Wilkins trans-Pacific today, and they'll be here next month. How about that? ... You there, Doc? Over.'

'That's good news, General. So we'll expect the helicopter as early in the morning as you can make it? What time do you think it'll be here? Over.'

'It's about a two-hour run up there from here. If you're standing on the padang at eight o'clock my boys shouldn't be along much after that. You want me to alert the hospital? Over.'

'It's all right. I'll talk to the surgeon myself when I've finished talking to you. We'll see you some time tomorrow, I hope. Over and out.'

'O.K. Doc. Nice to hear you. Nice to be able to help a grand old guy like Doc Brockley. See you tomorrow. Over and out.'

I then spoke to the hospital and told them to prepare a bed for Brockley and to get the instruments packed and sterilized for an amputation. They should be packed and sterilized ready for an emergency at any time, and perhaps they were. It was not a waste of time to check. When I had done that I thanked the Chinese who had mended the radio. The policeman was still nowhere to be seen.

I walked out, and along the path to the hospital. By now it was completely dark and a cool breeze was coming up off the river. It was only when I felt it against my cheeks that I realized how hot they were. I thought of the harmless little man I had almost strangled to death, and then of the Abang, whom Brockley had humiliated so terribly only six months before, saying, 'Nice to be able to help a grand old guy like Doc Brockley.' I thought of the wash-amah in the hospital dreaming of marriage for Brockley, of Law Kiat How suggesting in his precise, rational way that he and I should abandon everybody else up-river to make good our escape. Everything was gradually getting more and more confused. I had built up 'correction' for adjusting what everything seemed to what it really was, but the correction seemed to have disintegrated. There were no longer any fixed points in my mind. I looked at my watch. It had taken me two and a half hours to get my call through to the Abang. All I wanted was to sleep.

23

I woke up feeling sick and weary, as though I had been battered all night. But I must have slept because it was six-thirty and everybody else was up before me. I could hear the sound of a row going on in the next room—Brockley's room. All the doors and windows were wide open. Outside, in the covered space that ran between the house and the servants' quarters, I could see Doreen scrubbing Briok in an old tin bath. In the next room I could hear Graham and Brockley.

'I did not go down to town. I did not go near the police station. I never moved from here last night.'

'Do you think he made it all up?'

'I don't know. I never know what these slimy natives are going to do next. You come out without any preconceived notions, and try to help them, and what thanks do you get for it?'

'Look, I know very well that Ahmed is not the brightest of chaps, but he does not tell lies.'

'All right—he doesn't tell lies. Very good. But I never laid a finger on him. I never left the house last night. You can ask Doreen or Wee.'

'Could there be other white people in town? They do get up here sometimes. You remember those two Americans just before we set off up-river?' He gave a bellow of frustration. 'Here I am lying here like a cripple and I should be down there sorting this out. They rely on me. I'm the only person they have who *can* sort these things out.'

'Well, the only other person it could be is James Reed,' Graham said.

'But it couldn't be Reed. He knows far too much to do a thing like that. Are you sure it wasn't you, Graham? Tell me the truth, man.'

'Oh, my God! If you won't believe me what can I do?' I heard the thump of his bare feet across the floor, then the door of Brockley's room slammed behind him. I should go in straight away and tell him that I was the culprit. It was obvious whom they had been talking about: the policeman. He must have brought his trouble to Brockley.

But was that the best thing to do? I was ashamed of what I had done; but if everything went according to plan we would be out of Bukit Kota within two hours, and then Brockley need never know. What would be the point of disillusioning him about me? 'It couldn't be Reed,' he had said. 'He knows far too much to do a thing like that.' I had done a very stupid thing, but I would never do it again. I kept on telling myself that I did not want Brockley to suffer any more disillusionment about his own people. But it was more than that; I did not want him to know; I did not want him to know that even I had failed in the etiquette of the jungle. He was the only man on the island whose opinion I cared for; I wanted him to go on thinking well of me. It was odd that all the time I had been doing the right thing in Banianok I had never cared what anybody said of me or even what lies they made up about me. Now that I had done wrong I did care—I did not want anybody telling the truth about me. If we could just get out of Bukit Kota in the next couple of hours, in the flurry of our going everything else would be forgotten and I would never do it again.

I washed, shaved, dressed and brushed my hair. My body felt heavy as I performed the familiar movements. My mind moved with only one thought—to get Brockley out of Bukit Kota and into hospital. I walked through to his room. I knocked on the door and entered.

'Good morning,' he said. 'A message came. I didn't wake you. The plane won't be here till this afternoon.'

At two o'clock another telephone message arrived to say the

186

helicopter would arrive at four, and if we were ready to leave immediately it would get us back to Banianok before nightfall.

At four came the final message of the day; the helicopter had just left. It would arrive by nightfall, stay overnight in Bukit Kota and leave at dawn for Banianok.

Before five everybody in town was gathered around the padang, or village green. I watched them from Brockley's verandah through his binoculars. By five o'clock I neither expected the helicopter to arrive, nor did I expect it not to arrive. I had regained my old state of composure. This was what I was used to. Against such inefficiency anger was useless; besides, whoever it was on the other end of the telephone would certainly not think of apologizing; he doubtless thought he was doing a tremendous job getting a helicopter off the ground at all at such short notice.

I kept out of Brockley's way as much as I could, taking special care not to be alone with him, in case he brought up the subject of Ahmed, the policeman. I still did not know whether I would own up, or deny it. I did not want to find out. Luckily he did not seem particularly keen to talk to me; he had Doreen and Briok with him. I heard them talking on and off, though I could not hear what they said, and when she left him for a while, to do some washing, or to pack up some gear for Banianok, he seemed to find some reason to call her back. His voice was becoming thin and piping, and peevish.

It was the voice of an old man now.

About five o'clock—I was pointing out the crowd round the padang to Doreen—Briok ran out of Brockley's room with a terrified scream. Doreen and I dashed in. She was ahead of me. Brockley was lying half in bed and half out. His legs were on the bed, his head on the floor. His hand was outstretched to a bowl she had been using to wash him, and there was vomit on the floor. She helped me lift him back up on to the bed and roll him over on his front. He gasped and coughed, and gradually his breathing settled down.

'You silly boy!' Doreen scolded gently.

'I was trying to reach the bowl.'

'You know you're not supposed to do things like that. You're supposed to call for me. You could have fallen on the floor and really done yourself a damage.'

'I'm sorry!'

'I don't know what we're going to do with you. You give me more trouble than a ward full of ordinary patients, you bad boy!'

He was all right. I tip-toed out of the room. He did not need me. At the door I heard him say after a long sigh, 'You must have known lots of bad boys.'

'But none as bad as you.'

He gave a funny, sickly little giggle. 'It's funny you should say that. I suppose I was a bad boy at one time. But not any more.'

'Don't tell me that. I know when there's life in an old dog.'

He snuffled again. 'You should have known me in my undergraduate days.'

'I'm glad I didn't, thank you very much!'

'I was quite a lad then. You wouldn't think so to look at me now, would you?'

'Don't try and pull the wool over my eyes. It's you quiet old buggers are always the most dangerous.'

All the time they were talking she was doing things for him; wiping the vomit off his face, pulling his sheets smooth, plumping his pillows.

A discreet cough turned me from his bedroom door to the verandah. There stood Chumley at the bottom of the steps, waiting permission to ascend.

'Ah! Mr Chumley. You're just in time for tea. Will you have a cup?' He was the very next native I had had to deal with since the little Malay policeman. I wanted to make up for my behaviour by being especially affable.

He came up a couple of steps. 'Ah! Yes, sir. Or rather, no, sir ... Ah! I wouldn't mind. Thank you very much, sir.'

'Good!' I called for Wee and asked him to serve tea.

'And how have things been at the hospital? I meant to come down and see you today.'

188

'Oh no, Doctor. You must be far too busy.'

'No. I meant to come down, but ... time slipped away from me,' I ended lamely. I should not have replied at all. His remark was only a formality.

'And how is everything going down there?' I went on quickly.

'Oh! Very well, thank you, Doctor, very well.'

'I'm so glad. It must be a great strain on you having to take charge when Dr Brockley goes up-river and now to remain in charge while he goes to Banianok.'

He flapped his hands. 'Not at all, Doctor, not at all. It is a great pleasure.'

'Have you finished for the day now?' It was difficult to think of things to say.

'Yes, thank you, sir. Now finished for the day. Except in case of emergency, of course.'

I could think of no more questions.

'How is Doctor?' he asked.

'About the same. A helicopter is coming later. He'll leave for Banianok in the morning.'

'Thank God! And let us pray that he recovers!'

The tea came. Wee put the tray down on the table, bowed and withdrew. Normally he stayed to pour and pass it around. But normally we were all white. I took up the pot myself. It was a light, scented China tea. I poured two cups.

'Do you take lime, Mr Chumley?' I said.

'No milk, thank you, sir. But sugar ... I can get myself.' He jumped up as I reached for the sugar. He got there before me. Bent over from the waist, he dipped his spoon four times into the sugar bowl. He withdrew to his seat, stirring vigorously.

'Do have a biscuit.' I proffered the biscuit tin.

'Oh no, thank you, sir.' He shook his head. I took off the lid. He took two custard creams.

We sat in silence.

'So ... Doctor will go to Banianok. And then he will go on leave?'

I smiled. 'I gather he hasn't been on leave for seven years. I don't know what he'll do.' I had not thought that far ahead.

'And you will go back to your job at Medical Headquarters? Such a vital post!'

'I suppose so.'

'And Mr Graham, Doctor's son?'

'His year will soon be done. He'll go back to England.'

'Very nice!' He nodded omnisciently. 'Very nice!' as though he had nothing more to say, but felt it impolite to allow silence.

But that was not the case. Suddenly he leaned forward and put his hand on my knee. 'Doctor, what will happen to me?'

I looked up at him. His eyes were staring, his lips parted. Then I looked down at his hand on my knee. Embarrassedly he withdrew it.

'Won't you carry on up here as before?'

He sat back in his chair, as though that simple reply answered all his fears. Then his head and hands darted forward again. '*He* won't come back, will he? Doctor won't come back?'

It must have seemed to him that I was considering my answer carefully. It took me a long time to get it out. I said quietly, 'I don't think so.'

'Then what will happen to me?'

'I should think you'll be even more necessary up here than before,' I said.

'But without Doctor nobody will pay me any attention. You don't know what they were like this morning, sir. That is always the way when Doctor goes up-river. But they know he's coming back, so they can't go too far. But now, today, they know he is going away and not coming back. They'll drive me mad. They will.'

'I'll see what can be done when I get back to H.Q.,' I said glibly.

'Nobody will come up here. I know, sir. Doctor used to laugh when they told him they would retire him and send another doctor. He knew no other doctor would come.'

'I know. It *is* difficult. But perhaps ... we have some more Koreans arriving soon.'

'No, sir! We must have another Britisher. These people don't want to be treated by a foreigner. Down the coast perhaps, they
190

are more used to foreigners. But our people are conservative. They don't like change. They want us British. Doctor—would you consider coming to be our doctor?'

I was astonished. He must have taken the silence of the next few seconds for hesitation. 'You wouldn't have to eat the stuff Mr Wee makes, sir. None of these natives can cook. My wife could cook you roast lamb with Yorkshire pudding, Irish stew and dumplings, guava pie. . . .'

'But my job at headquarters ... Honestly, I would love to come up here,' I said untruthfully, 'but I can't just abandon my job down there. They wouldn't let me.'

He stood up. 'You and Doctor and I, sir, were the last Britishers in the medical service. I have the honour to submit my resignation.'

'But you can't!'

'I must, sir. They always said in the old days that we Britishers must stick together. The time has come when we must do so even in leaving.'

'But they need you up here. Now you're the only man they've got.'

'When I joined the service in 1920 we were promised a pension at fifty-five. Now, sir, I am sixty-eight. I am tired. I want to rest, and I want to go and visit my daughter who married a very nice British soldier—not a warrant officer, but very gentlemanly. She lives in Bootle, England.'

I knew that was untrue. Brockley had told me. Her soldier had knocked her about, she had suffered depressions in England and been under the psychiatrists; she had had a baby, killed it four weeks after it was born and then killed herself.

I said, 'Mr Chumley, these people needed you and Dr Brockley, and over the last thirty years you have done tremendous work together. Everybody in Banianok knows that. But now they are going to need you even more.'

'I think you know Bootle, sir. Historic and traditional place?'

'Without you the medical service in the Interior will collapse, Mr Chumley.'

'You know, sir, the time has come for us to lay down our

191

burdens. Let us admit that these natives don't want us and don't appreciate us; they'd rather be savages in the jungle, Doctor, let us admit it at last. You, I am sure, a man of such good breeding, must have a nice town house in London, and a place in the country. Perhaps I will go home and settle too.'

Of course he wouldn't. His passport was Banianokese.

'Doctor and I have given the best part of our lives to these natives, sir. Now we will retire. Please don't make same mistake, sir.'

'But you can't desert them without giving us the chance to find a substitute.'

He stood up. He held out his hand, like a well-bred governor saying goodbye to a retiring resident, looking the epitome of relaxation. I stood up to take his hand. His mouth opened. He sucked in his lips in a spasm as though he had just had a whiff of ammonia. A little squeak came from his throat. Without shaking hands he walked rapidly to the verandah. He stopped and came back. He stood in front of me, bent forward from the waist, one hand out in front of him at eye-level as though I were about to hit him. Tears ran silently down his cheeks.

'They won't listen to me; they won't do what I say; they laugh at me. Without him there behind me I can do nothing. They say ... they say I'm a half-caste.'

I put my hand up to my cheek and realized my face was burning hot. It was not his words I remembered most clearly as his footsteps disappeared down the path. It was his expression as he had groaned, 'They say I'm a half-caste.' It was hurt, but more than that it was incredulous. As though he had never realized it before.

At 6.00 p.m. when it was almost dark we heard the pulsating noise of the helicopter blades. We had two white sheets spread in the middle of the padang to guide the pilot and, with every pair of eyes in Bukit Kota on him, he landed exactly between them. It was a big Wessex transport. The cargo bay contained half a dozen soldiers. When the door of the cockpit opened and the pilot jumped out I noticed something about him that was unaccustomedly athletic for Banianok. He shouted, 'Hey, Doc! How about that? We just made it in time. Impress you? Think I deserve a Jack Daniels!' It was the Abang.

His troops released themselves from their belts and swarmed out of the side of the helicopter. They were all from his personal bodyguard. I recognized the two who had accompanied him to Doreen's quarters in Banianok. There were eight altogether. The children of the town—chiefly Chinese—were dashing, whooping, on to the padang, to surround the helicopter. The troops pulled long truncheons from leather holsters on their left side—the other side from their guns—took a few menacing steps, and the children ran back. One of them, older and cheekier than the others, got whacked across the knees and limped back yelping with pain like a puppy.

'Doc! It's great to see you. Sorry we didn't make it earlier. But how's the old guy? Is it bad?'

'I'm afraid it is. It looks as though he'll have to have his leg off.'

'As bad as that?' He whistled. 'That's too bad! How'd it happen?'

I recounted the story of how Briok had dashed forward on to the boar and Brockley had had to pull him off.

'Stupid little bastard!' he sighed. 'How'd it go all round? You find any trouble up there?'

'No! Everything seemed to be reasonably all right. But there may be trouble now Brockley isn't going to be there to keep an eye on things.'

'Why? Anything brewing up?'

'We stayed at Penghara Ngang's long-house a couple of nights and Graham got himself a head as a souvenir—'

'Hey! What about that? Good for the kid!'

'The Penghara didn't know he'd been given it. They missed it and there's been some trouble between a few of the long-houses. There have been a few people killed. As far as I can make out it's just been the Dayaks killing each other; they haven't attacked anybody else, but you know how these things can spread.'

193

'Too right, Doc ... That stupid little bastard Graham!'

I saw Graham fifteen yards away. He was close enough to have heard, but obviously he had not. He walked towards the Abang with arm outstretched. It was the broken one of course.

'Gra-ham! Well, nice to see you, boy, but what happened to the arm?'

'Fight with a waterfall. I lost,' Graham said modestly.

'No kid? You went over the rapids?'

'Never stand up in a boat going over the rapids, Bill. Take it from somebody who did.'

'Hey! You stupid limey bastard!' The Abang punched Graham playfully in the chest. 'But you're looking good apart from that.'

'You mean in spite of having had malaria?'

'You had malaria? You too? Hey, they didn't change *your* tablets, did they?'

'No. I forgot to take them.'

'Hey! You stupid goddam ... take a limey to forget his pills in the first place and then soldier on with malaria. Hey! You are a character, boy! You are a character. That right, Doc?'

'That's right,' I said stolidly.

He was in high humour. 'You know, seems to me you guys didn't have any more luck in the Interior than I did. The old guy got himself gored, Graham got malaria and a broken arm— what happened to you, Doc?'

'I lost a lot of weight with worry,' I said, making an ineffectual effort to join in the general gaiety.

'Doreen was the only one who took everything in her stride.' Graham gave the Abang a malicious smile.

'Doreen with you? Here? How long?' His voice was eager.

'A week, eight days—'

'I was wondering what happened to her. You know, one day she was there, and the next she was gone. What was she doing up here? It'll be great to see her.'

'I thought you two had fallen out,' Graham said, sounding slightly disappointed.

'Uh! We had a spat—it was nothing. I had to go over to

194

Singapore anyway. I forgot all about it. When I got back she was gone. So she was up here? How the hell did she get up here?' He shook his head. 'It'll be great to see her. Well, let's get up to the house. You still in the house on top of the hill? Maybe I can get my boys billeted in town. The police station's the place. Where's the policeman anyway? He should be here to meet me. He knows that.'

The skin between his eyebrows tightened, and his mouth puckered up—not angry, but hurt. For the first time I noticed his swagger-stick. He snapped it twice or thrice against the outside of his thigh. He called to one of his men who had three stripes on his arm. He was the one who most usually lounged against his car when it was parked outside Doreen's quarters in Banianok. He asked him in Malay where he and the rest of the men would stay for the night. 'Don't worry about us,' the man leered back.

'My boys are bastards,' the Abang chuckled in an aside to me. 'They got any nice little chicks in this town, they better get them out of sight tonight.'

Then the skin between his eyebrows tightened again and his forehead wrinkled. 'But look, where's the policeman, where's the Kapitan China, where's the Tuai Rumah? I don't get enough respect in this town. Never have done!' The next logical step was to consider that the chief reason he did not get enough respect in Bukit Kota was that it was Brockley's town, and everybody followed his lead. Brockley was to be blamed, if anybody. But he did not take that step.

'Nobody knew you were coming,' I said in a conciliatory tone.

'But what about whoever was on the other end of the radio? I spoke to him personally. He didn't tell you?' That would be the unfortunate policeman. 'Anyway, people should turn out to greet the Army, whoever comes. We had a bit more co-operation we wouldn't be in the state we're in now. You came, didn't you, Doc? Foreigner co-operates with the Army and the local people won't. How about that?' Now his lower lip was trembling; he was very hurt.

The old Chinese shopkeepers, always happy to shake hands with anybody in power, or anybody who might be in power one day, were lining up to greet him. I pointed them out. 'Aah! Chinks! I get sick of them,' he muttered.

Across the padang, from the direction of the police station, the policeman came running. He was out of breath when he arrived. He came to a halt a foot away from the Abang and pulled himself to attention. His salute overshot and his hand slid over his right eye.

'Nice of you to come. What kept you?' The concept of a man being able to sound like a sergeant-major and an American while speaking Malay is a difficult one to grasp. But that is what the Abang managed to do.

'I was watching the helicopter, Your Highness.'

'Where from? The other side of the river?'

'My child is sick, Highness. I was at home.'

'That's better—the truth. You know you're supposed to be here to meet the helicopter. Is the police part of the Army or isn't it?'

'It is, Highness.'

'Don't keep calling me Highness. General!'

'General! Yes, General!'

'You're a real credit to the force. A real credit, if you don't mind me saying so.' The Abang walked round the man once. He was wearing his uniform—his proper uniform. Obviously he never wore it ordinarily. Police uniforms were one of the few things that had not been changed since Independence. The police still wore blue shirts, coarse grey flannel shorts, a serge beret with badge, long, thick grey woollen socks with garter tabs, and standard-issue black boots that would have been just right for the Cairngorms or the Pennines. He had got into his uniform and looked quite presentable; he had forgotten only one thing—his socks. His spindly brown legs ended in those huge, black, laced-up boots, but no socks.

'They tell you at police college it's correct to go around with your buttons undone?' The two top buttons of the man's shirt were undone. Regulations only allowed one to be undone.

196

The man looked from the Abang to me, and back to the Abang. I was standing closest to the Abang. He could have thought the Abang was doing all this for my benefit.

'You wear your hat on top of your head like you were carrying a kati of rice. That's smart?' The man reached up, trembling, to pull down his hat.

'Why do it now? It's too late. But the main thing is—you the man I was talking to on the telephone this morning?'

'Yes, General.'

'Why didn't you tell the doctor I was coming?' He jerked his hand at me.

'I did, Highness.'

'You did? The doctor says you didn't; he's a liar?'

'I mean I told Blo Ko Lee the plane was coming.'

'It's not a plane, it's a helicopter. You know the difference. Helicopter, the wings move.' He jerked his head round to me. 'You like that, Doc? The wings move....'

By now the crowd was tittering, reading permission in the Abang's jaunty, humorous style of interrogation. They were chiefly Chinese. As I said before, they do not take other people's misfortunes with our lugubrious indifference: they enjoy them to the full. It must have seemed more than they could ever have dreamed—one Malay publicly humiliating another. I noticed that the few Malays in the crowd did not laugh, and the few Dayaks, just down-river for the day to buy ammunition, clothes and sugar, obviously did not know what was going on.

'You told Blo Ko Lee the helicopter was coming?'

'Yes, Highness. The very first time the radio spoke at dawn.'

'And then you thought you'd done enough. So when I told you to tell him I was coming personally you thought you wouldn't bother?'

'No! No, Highness. I went up again, up the hill; it is a big hill. But Blo Ko Lee was sleeping and nobody else was there except—'

'Except?'

'Except the *tuan* doctor.' He raised his chin at me.

'So why didn't you tell him?'

197

The tittering had died down. The attention of the audience was beginning to wander. 'So why didn't you tell him?' the Abang roared. The policeman jerked to attention as though he had been given an electric shock with a cattle-prodder. His beret, precariously balanced on his head, slid gradually over the left side of his head so that it completely covered his left ear. He put up his hand to replace it and the Abang roared, 'Hands by your side!' Now he looked ridiculous. The laughter of the crowd swelled back.

The Abang scowled at them momentarily, then he laughed too. 'Now where were we? Yes! Why didn't you tell the *tuan* doctor?'

'I didn't want to disturb him.'

'You didn't want to disturb him? What was he doing that was so important?' The Abang winked at me.

'I didn't want to disturb him. I told the house-boy. Maybe the house-boy did not tell Blo Ko Lee.'

'Is that the way you deliver messages from the Commander-in-Chief of the Armed Forces to the Provincial Medical Officer—you tell the house-boy?'

'Highness, the *tuan* doctor was writing on the verandah. I was afraid. I was afraid he would be angry.'

'You were afraid?'

The man did not answer.

'Tell me that again?' He bent forward in parody of deafness, bending from the waist, one hand cupped behind his ear. The crowd laughed aloud. 'Are you a policeman or aren't you? You go up to see a highly respected, law-abiding headquarters doctor, and you're afraid. What do you feel like when you go to see a criminal?'

The crowd roared. A fat, jolly-looking Chinese woman with a child on her hip detached herself from the crowd momentarily and cried ingratiatingly, 'Take him away for punishment, General-Highness. Sleeping all the time, never arrest anyone.'

His hat finally slid from over his ear on to his shoulder and then to the ground. Quick as a flash he bent down and in a second he had it back on his head and pulled down roughly as it should be worn. 'I told you to stay as you were,' the Abang shouted. 'You come here half dressed; why bother about a little detail like no hat?'

'No socks either, Highness,' a happy voice came from the crowd.

'That's right! You never heard of—'

But that was as far as the Abang got. 'He tried to strangle me, Highness.'

'Oh! no! Don't let this get too ridiculous,' the Abang pleaded with mock-humility.

'I was afraid he would do it again. I was afraid, Highness.'

'Do it again? Where did he do it the first time?'

'Last night, at the police station.'

'So you arrested him?'

The policeman's narrow shoulders came forward and he flattened his palm towards the Abang. 'How can I fight with a white man?'

The crowd sensed that something had gone a little wrong. Up till now they had laughed at everything the man had said. But the sigh of anticipation as he finished the sentence died away, and everybody looked at the Abang.

Till now it had all been a little bit of fun for him, but now he was angry. 'What was that you said?'

'How could I, Highness ... how could anybody ... try to arrest a white man?'

'You arrest whoever you have got to arrest. It doesn't matter if he's white, Malay, Chinese, or native. And you are not scared of anybody because everybody is just the same before the law now. Do you understand that?'

The man did not speak.

'Do you understand that?'

Tears started to run down the man's cheeks.

'Do you understand that?'

'But Highness, how could I, a poor policeman, do what your whole Army could not do?'

'What?'

'When the Army came—five hundred men—to take Blo Ko

199

Lee away, and they could not do it. How could I arrest Blo Ko Lee's friend?'

The crowd was silent now. They would not laugh aloud at the Abang: he represented Force; he had his half-dozen body-guards with him, and if that was not enough he could always come back another time and wreak vengeance on them. So they were silent. But every one of them knew that what the little man said was true. If they had wanted to spare the Abang's feelings they would have withdrawn, disappeared, melted away. But they did not want to.

'You're a liar and you don't know what you're talking about,' the Abang shouted. 'You're suspended from duty.'

'Yes, General. Thank you, General.'

The Abang realized too late that that was exactly what the man would like. 'Just a minute—before I suspend you. Did the doctor strangle you and did you fail to arrest him?'

The man looked up into the Abang's face. Then he looked at me. I stared back at him unblinking. I knew I ought to say, unemotionally and straightforwardly, 'Yes, I did almost strangle him.' I knew I ought to, and in England I would have done. (At least that is what I told myself.) But here everything was so relative; the law was relative, truth was relative, justice was relative, but especially truth. If I stepped forward and said I had tried to strangle him nobody would believe me, as plainly nobody believed him when he said it. There would be no im-partial justice, whatever either of us said; far better reach some approximation of the truth, that would cause everybody the least trouble.

So I remained silent.

'Did he strangle you or didn't he? If he did, arrest him now. He won't get away.'

The policeman itched one huge boot up the inside of the other naked leg. He looked from the Abang to me. I just stared straight ahead as though I had never seen him before.

'Well?' the Abang shrieked.

The little man spread his hands. 'I was mistaken, Highness.'

'You were mistaken! You're a troublemaker. You'll never

work again for this government. Now get out of my sight.'

The little man turned and started to walk away.

'And the rest of you—standing there gawking. What do you think this is—the movies? Get moving! Get going! Go on, go on!'

The little policeman half turned his head to the Abang, then he started to run. His gait looked funny because his boots were so heavy; he looked as though he were running through a swamp with a thirty-pound weight attached to each foot. The crowd laughed. A brave boy dashed out and tripped him up. One of the Abang's bodyguard hit them both on the head with his truncheon. The rest were busy unsheathing theirs. The crowd scattered. A minute later there was nobody on the padang. But the Abang was still shaking his head. 'You see what I mean, Doc? How can we ever hope to pacify this country with people like that in our ancillary forces?'

That was the first sentence he had said in English for the last ten minutes. 'What happened?' Graham said breathlessly.

'Aagh! Just a goddam stupid policeman!' the Abang muttered. 'Not much worse than the rest of the police in this goddam country. What, do they expect me to keep the country pacified single-handed, me and my boys? Jesus, this place depresses me. Come on, fellows, let's go up to the house and see Doreen and the Doc ...' He took a couple of steps, then stopped. He looked round at the little padang, and the rickety shop-houses on three sides of it; 'I'll never know how the old guy put up with this place for thirty-five years. I'll never know!'

24

The Abang seemed to be looking forward to seeing Doreen. I was apprehensive about what her attitude would be to him.

Graham was clearly thinking along the same lines. 'This is going to be interesting,' he murmured, with a sigh of satisfaction, as Doreen, eyes bulging with astonishment, caught sight of us nearing the top of the track with the Abang beside us. She was shaking Brockley's blanket from the verandah outside his room. The Abang shouted as we reached the top of the path:

'Doreen!'

'Good God!'

'How you doing, Dor?'

'Never get rid of you for long, do we?'

She stood at the top of the verandah steps. He bounded up them in two steps and grabbed her by the waist. 'Hey! what you say, what you say?'

'Get *off*, you uncouth bugger, there's a sick man in there.' Then she shrieked once, involuntarily, as his fingers found a bit of her waist where she was susceptible to tickling.

He desisted. 'How is the Doc?'

'I've just got him off to sleep, which is a bloody difficult thing to do, so I won't be very pleased if you wake him up again.'

'Doc says he's not in any too good shape.' He indicated me.

'That's the understatement of the decade.'

'Well?'

'Go into the sitting-room. I'll be with you in a minute when I've finished with the old man.'

We went up the verandah steps into the sitting-room, and

202

called for cold drinks. Wee came in, his mouth strained so wide open in his smile of welcome for the Abang that it seemed his gold-spattered false teeth must pop out on to the floor at any moment. He had not been keen to serve old Chumley, but the most powerful member of the race the Chinese regarded as their enemies came in for different treatment. When he was taking my order he merely leaned forward respectfully, but with the Abang's he seemed to lean over him diagonally, both forwards and sideways, so that he gave the impression he was just managing to hold himself back from embracing him.

'Got any bourbon, Doc?'

I knew now that giving the Abang spirits was a waste of time because, though he always asked for bourbon or whisky, he never drank it.

'You want a long drink, General,' I said. 'Let's have some long lime fizzes and we'll have a scotch later.'

'Great idea! Great idea!' he said gratefully.

A moment later Doreen stepped from her bedroom. In five minutes she had made herself look very different.

'Hey! Hey! Hey!' The Abang raised himself to his feet.

'Sit down you silly bugger—making an exhibition of yourself,' she hissed. 'Got a cigarette?'

He pulled out a packet of Camels.

'You still smoking those filthy things?' she said as she sucked in flame from his gold lighter.

She was wearing a short white blouse which she had tied at the waist. She had no brassière, and the sarong she had put on she had managed to secure with a belt so that it looked as though it were about to slip off her hips. Doreen was not one to bother much with make-up, but she had put on some lipstick, and her hair had been put up, so quickly that a couple of her hairpins were still sticking out. She was not a beautiful creature, and her hasty toilette had exposed two of her least attractive features, her thick waist and her muscular neck, but there was something undeniably attractive about her that had not been there this morning. It had nothing to do with her appearance; perhaps it was the fact of having tried—of *wanting* to look attractive. As I studied her now I was conscious of a tremor in my blood that had not been there in the previous few days. She had not cared how she looked for Brockley and Graham and me, but she clearly did for the Abang.

'So—you impressed? The C-in-C comes up personally in his own helicopter to take you back to town?' he said.

'You've come to take Brockley. You needn't think I'm going in that thing with you. Remember the last time you took me out in a helicopter?'

'So we crash-landed!' He roared with laughter and slapped Graham on the knee. 'Those stupid maintenance bastards! We got rid of them all.'

'So who's the pilot?'

'For you, baby—the best we've got!'

'Oh! God! I know who that is.'

'Right first time! You'll think you're in the Merc. Hey! Dor, you're looking lovely tonight.'

'Do you mind?' she said *sotto voce*, scowling with pleasure.

I got up and left them. I was going to the lavatory, in fact, but as I passed Brockley's door I heard his voice. It was weak. I went in.

'Is that you, Reed?' He pulled himself up a little on the pillows Doreen had arranged behind him. 'No, thank you, I can manage. Sit down a moment. Don't turn on the light.'

I sat down on the bed. Instinctively he moved away. I moved to a chair; he moved back.

'Is that man out there?' he said.

'The Abang? Yes. Would you like to see him?'

'I suppose I have to. But not now. Later.... Has Doreen seen him?'

I nodded, but he did not see it. He was looking straight in front of him with a look in his face that gave the impression he saw nothing. I said, 'Yes.'

'Is he—bothering her?'

'No,' I said. 'He's not—bothering her.'

'You know part of the reason she came up here was to get away from him and his advances?'
204

I did not answer, but murmured something that could be interpreted as assent.

'Yes ... that was why she came up here.... Blast him! Why couldn't he stay away?'

'I think he is really concerned about you.'

I got no further. 'No, he's not. He came for the girl, and also so that he could give the impression he had captured me and brought me back to Banianok as he said he would.'

'I agree it could be interpreted like that, but I honestly believe that hasn't entered his head. He's genuinely fond of you. He admires you, Brockley.'

'No. He's come for Doreen.' A thought struck him. He rolled over towards me, although he could not see me by now. 'How did you know?'

'How did I know what?'

'About him bothering her with his attentions in Banianok. You weren't surprised when I told you.'

'If you remember, she told us both together the night we met her in the ulu.'

'My mind's going,' he groaned. 'I can't remember a thing. I can't think straight for more than two minutes at a stretch. Of course, of course!'

His tone changed again. 'You were in Banianok, of course, weren't you? Had you no notion he was making these insolent advances to her?'

'No,' I said, but I hesitated a fraction of a second too long.

Something very moving happened. He addressed me by my first name. He had never done it before; he did not do it again. He said in a keening, anguished voice, 'You must tell me, you know James, if you know anything.'

I did not speak.

'Well?'

'I know just as much as you do,' I said softly.

'You remember Graham, in that ungentlemanly way of his, was hinting that she had been his, well ... you know ... his mistress!'

I said nothing.

'But I know that could not be true.' But it was obvious that he suspected all too well that it could be true. 'Oh, God!' he cried, 'if only I wasn't lying here a cripple!' He leaned forward from his pillows, but just that slight tightening of his leg muscles necessary to balance his change of position made him grunt with pain, and he sank back again, breathing noisily for a moment or two.

When his breath came easier he whispered, 'Was she ... not too upset to see him?'

'He's behaving very politely.'

'And she?'

'She's chatting now with the Abang and Graham. She's taking it all in her stride.'

'I believe you ... believe you. She is a remarkable girl, isn't she, Reed?

'She is.'

'I don't mind telling you—'

The door opened and the light went on.

'So what's going on in here? And you supposed to be asleep, you bad old bugger,' she said to Brockley. 'You give me more trouble than a wardful of kids.'

Brockley was rubbing his eyes in the glare of the light.

'And I told you not to sit up. You know it only makes the blood run to your leg, and then you're complaining about the pain half an hour later. I don't know what I'll do with you. I think a good tanning on your BTM is what you need. And you'll get it too!'

He took his fists away from his eyes. 'But you look so pretty, Doreen, in that sarong. I didn't know you had a sarong. And your hair ... Why did you never—' He did not finish the question. I suppose it would have been, 'Why did you never do it before?'

But before he finished it he knew the answer.

The Abang crowded into the room behind Doreen. 'The Doc's awake? Hey! Doc! Nice to see you! Hear you been in a scrap.'

He pulled himself up straight in bed; or rather he tried to.

He looked pathetic lying stiffly in bed at an angle of forty-five degrees with the horizontal, his hand extended. 'Good evening,' he said coldly. 'I understand you've been put to some trouble on my account. I'm sorry.'

The Abang took his hand, then slapped his other hand across it. 'It's a pleasure, Doc. It's a privilege. It's a privilege to take a grand old campaigner on his last ride down the river. And after what you've done for this province and this country you deserve to go out in glory.'

Brockley trembled. It could have been pain but it was almost certainly not. Doreen saw what was wrong. 'What are you talking about, you silly bugger? Bit of treatment, couple of weeks' recuperation and this obstinate sod'll be back up here ruining his health again in no time.' The nudge she gave him almost sent him flying across the room.

'Yeah! Sure, sure!' he said hastily.

'That doesn't concern us tonight,' Brockley said formally. 'I am sure you must be ready for a cocktail—it's well past seven. Please go into the sitting-room and I'll join you directly.'

Doreen stepped forward as though he were getting out of bed that instant. 'You're not going out there.'

'My dear girl, what are you talking about?'

'You know you can't get up. You know it hurts like hell when you put your leg down.'

'My dear,' he said serenely, 'I always take a stengah on the verandah before dinner. Tonight even more so since we have a guest.'

Of course that was untrue. He had not been out of bed since we had arrived back.

Doreen stood between him and the Abang. She looked at him first, then at the Abang. She clenched her fist at the Abang and at the same time pursed her lips and narrowed her eyes at him.

'All right, get out—all of you!' She turned to Graham and me, including us.

'I'll see you in a moment,' Brockley called, almost playfully.

As she pushed us out Doreen gave the Abang a punch in the kidney.

'Why'd she do that?' he cried plaintively when we were outside and the bedroom door had slammed behind us.

'You wouldn't know why Doreen does anything,' Graham said.

'I know why,' I said slowly. 'You shouldn't have said that about his going on his last round-up, I'm afraid, General.'

'Well he is, isn't he?' Graham cried.

'Don't you see it, General?' I said.

'No I don't, Doc.' His voice was hurt. 'All I know is I go to a lot of trouble to get a helicopter and escort up here, and he treats me like some sort of playboy who doesn't know a thing.'

Doreen came out at last. 'You bloody fool!' she said angrily to the Abang. 'Now you've done it!'

'*I've* done it? What have *I* done?'

'We had it all set up. He was all ready to go on the helicopter first thing in the morning.' She smacked her fists into her palm.

'Well ...?'

She turned on the Abang. 'Now he refuses to go.'

'But why?'

'Why do you think?'

'Well, don't look at me,' he cried.

'You tried to get him out of here six months ago. You came up with five hundred men and you couldn't do it. Now he's down and out, he's down for the count and all ready to go—and you have to come up with all that patronizing shit. And now he's not going—at least, not with you.'

'Well, how the hell *is* he going?'

'By boat—two days. And by the time he gets there he'll probably be dead.'

'But I didn't mean him to think that—'

'Well, why couldn't you keep your mouth shut? Just once?'

'I could make him go.'

'Yes, that would be just like you, wouldn't it? Take an elephant-gun to a sick dog! You would just do that, wouldn't you? You go in there shooting orders from the hip; we'll watch.'

208

'Aagh! Shut up!' He flung himself out on to the verandah and thence down to the garden.

Doreen dropped her weight into a chair and spread her arms and legs. 'You go in and see him. He might pay attention to you.

'Go on,' she muttered. 'You have a go. He's got my head in a bloody whirl.'

I went back in. He was still in the same position in bed—his back at forty-five degrees to the horizontal, managing to look formal in bed. He raised himself even farther as I came in. 'Did she say anything?'

'She said you were being rather silly and refusing to go on the helicopter.'

'That's right,' he said eagerly.

'But you know that leg needs amputation now. It needed it days ago.'

'Oh, yes! I'm not going to stay here. I'm going to go down. Tomorrow morning. Early. I realize my time here is up. Perhaps they may let me come back when I'm better, just to say goodbye, just the one last trip right to the top of the river and down again. Then I'll be quite happy to go.'

'So the quicker you get down there and get your treatment the better.'

'Yes. Quite! Yes,' he whispered excitedly. He put his hand out. His skin was burning hot. 'But not with *him*.'

'The Abang?'

'Yes, the Abang. Oh! don't misunderstand me. It's not that I dislike him. He's a fool, of course, and he's caused a lot of trouble with his foolishness. He'll never be half the man his father was. But I don't hold that against him. It's something else. I know I can rely on your confidence, Reed?'

'Of course.' It was ludicrous but strangely moving to see this old man in a state of semi-delirium, but still retaining the punctilious locutions that must have been already old-fashioned when he was a young man.

'Doreen has told me that she did have a ... certain relationship with the Abang.'

'She told you? Good God! When?'

'Just now. I asked her. She told me. I think you knew already?'

I nodded.

'But it's all over. She assures me of that. It was just one of those inexplicable things that happened, and now she wants to forget about it. We must not judge, Reed.'

'Of course not.'

He hurried on. 'She finds his presence here extremely disturbing. She was astonished and disgusted to find that he had followed her. She never wishes to see him again. In the circumstances it is quite impossible for me to go back in his helicopter as his guest.'

'But that's ridiculous, Brockley.'

'Don't you see I have a duty to her?'

'No.'

'But, my dear Reed, you're a gentleman; you understand.'

'I only understand that you have to get to Banianok at the very earliest moment, and that Doreen is well able to look after herself.'

He tried to moisten his lips. 'Reed, you surprise me. Surely you realize that her care has been invaluable to me. It may even have saved my life. I would have a duty to her for that alone.'

'All right—you have a duty to thank her, to be grateful to her, perhaps to make her a present. But you don't have to fight her battles with her boy-friend. She doesn't need it.'

'Ah! But that's where you're wrong, Reed. She's only a woman. What can a woman know of such things as standing up to the Abang? When I think of how it must have been my blood boils, Reed. It boils.'

'Look, Brockley, what you're saying is ridiculous. She just came out now. She's furious with you; she's furious with you, not pleased. She's calling you every name under the sun.'

He smiled serenely. 'Perhaps she is. Perhaps she is. But she knows underneath that I had to do it.'

'She doesn't, Brockley. I've got to tell you; she doesn't. She

210

wants to go tomorrow on the helicopter, and she wants you to be on it, and that's that.'

But his eyes were glazed now. He was no longer listening to me. He was carrying on an imaginary conversation with himself. 'Imagine how it must have been, Reed; she was a lonely young nurse in Banianok; lonely, young, fresh, unspoiled, brought out by the British Government to she knew not what, thrown into a bustling Eastern metropolis without chaperone or tutelage—oh! this volunteer system is a wicked thing. Reed. And then along came a middle-aged voluptuary, sated with ordinary pleasures, a man notorious for sensual excess of every kind, who thought, Ah! I'll amuse myself by corrupting this innocent young thing whom Fortune has been so indulgent as to throw in my way. How did they meet? It doesn't matter. She was young, innocent, lonely, she fell for his charm, his *savoir faire*, his suavity....'

'Brockley, she's thirty if she's a day.'

'Is England so debased now that it should be a source of astonishment to find a girl of thirty who has not lost her character? Is it? He took her out, he showered her with compliments, and presents—oh! I know how well he would be able to do it. Perhaps he promised to marry her. It is not for us to ask how she sank to the ultimate degradation, Reed. It is *not* for us to judge, and it is *not* a final state. Nothing is ever final. Doreen can be redeemed. You do see that, don't you, Reed?'

There were flecks of foamy white saliva at the corners of his mouth. They moved in and out with each gasping breath. I was sweating freely; his skin was dry and hot, his eyes staring. 'Do you see, Reed?'

I saw what I should have seen days before, what even the amah down at the hospital had seen: the poor old fool had fallen in love with her. Suddenly I remembered the little bag of monkey gall-stones he had brought down to Banianok for her. Had it happened as long ago as that? I asked myself if she could have given him any encouragement. It was inconceivable; she was too honest, for all her other faults. The story of her seduction—she had not told him all that rubbish; he

211

had made it up. Not wilfully, knowing it to be untrue, but in the same way as the old scientists had accounted for the swarms of flies around dead meat by the theory of spontaneous generation—because it was the only explanation they could think of. He was incapable of seeing the relationships between the sexes in any other way. He was a man of his time. His Abang was a creature of the 1930s or even the '20s. Even his wording—charm, suavity, *savoir faire*—they were all '30s words, irresistibly evoking George Sanders with gold cigarette case, Charvet tie and co-respondent shoes. Even though his wife had been pregnant by another man she had divorced him, and not the other way round.

No, Doreen *couldn't* have given him this grotesque travesty of her relationship with the Abang. 'Has she talked to you about ... herself and Yusuf?' I asked, almost bullyingly.

He shook his head. 'She's a very proud girl, Reed. She reacted almost with bravado when I asked her.'

'Well, don't you think that's exactly how she feels?' I cried eagerly.

'I could see behind the bravado quite easily. What I saw was a longing for redemption.' His voice was very calm. 'You might say that redemption was impossible for a woman who had given herself to a native, Reed. But you are wrong.'

It was grotesque, ludicrous. Doreen had not 'fallen', and it did not matter a damn who she slept with. But given his premises —fifty-years-out-of-date premises—there was something very moving in his compassion for her.

But it was still ludicrous. 'Look, Brockley,' I said in desperation, 'I wasn't going to tell you this until later: there's big trouble up-river and everybody says you're the only man who can settle it. Now you've got to get down to Banianok immediately, get treated and get back up here.'

He looked at me coldly and said very clearly, 'Don't talk nonsense, Reed! You know they won't allow me back up here.'

'For this they will. This isn't a job for the Army. This is something only you can settle.'

'What is it?'

I paused. 'Heads!' I said dramatically. 'A head was taken from Penghara Ngang's house—a Japanese head.'

'A Japanese head?' he repeated listlessly.

'While we were in the Interior. On the way down we found out about it. The men from Penghara Ngang's house attacked the neighbouring house.'

'Penghulu Jugah's?'

'They thought they'd taken it. We found two bodies floating in the river.'

'Why didn't you tell me?' he slurred.

'You were drugged. We wanted to get you down here as soon as we could. That was our main objective—to get you down to the hospital for treatment so that you would be fit as soon as possible to get back up there and restore the peace.'

For a while his face was expressionless. Then his lips flickered into the faintest of smiles, and his face was expressionless again. After a long time he said: 'The Dayaks—you say they've started taking heads again. You're shocked and surprised. You shouldn't be, you know, Reed, you shouldn't be. They're savages. They've got no finer instincts.'

'But ...' He could not have said anything that would have flabbergasted me more. He had been the one man on the island who had seemed to stand out for his savages being more decent than so-called civilized men. For the moment I could think of absolutely nothing to say.

Then I must have spoken. I must have said, 'I thought you loved them,' for I heard him murmuring, 'I *did* love them. They were my boys. But I think I made the great mistake, Reed, of believing I was indispensable to them. The Nayans—I thought they needed me. They didn't. They'd rather be as they are. Thirty-five years it took me to gain their confidence, then one stupid act by one stupid missionary ... they wouldn't see me, they wouldn't let me talk to them. One mistake in thirty-five years, and they wouldn't even let me explain.... They didn't care what I had to tell them.'

'But the Dayaks! The heads!'

'I used to think I'd stopped it. I used to think they'd stopped

213

for my sake. Maybe they had ... but it's in the blood, Reed. You can't really change them. You know, in the old days they used to cut the heads off children and old women rather than wait for a man their own size. But you never hear about things like that, do you? I'll tell you something now that I have never told anyone—I have never told anyone, Reed. In the last days of the war, when everybody knew the Allies were coming, the word went round that the Australians would be paying bounty on heads—Japanese heads, of course. I don't know how it started. It was quite untrue, but off they dashed to greet the Australians, culling heads as they went, and the men of Penghara Ngang's house killed more of their fellow-countrymen in a week—Dayaks, Malays and Chinese—than they killed Japanese in three years. You'll not read that in the Official War History, and I've never told anyone. I've often wanted to, but I never have. That's the way it was. They're savages, Reed. You'll never change them.'

'Brockley, please don't ...' I faltered and stopped. I could not find the words for what I wanted to say. It would have been something like 'Don't incriminate yourself, don't go out sounding like all the others—the others who had kowtowed, invariably resentful but always obedient to the Colonial Government, and then, still more resentful, but even more obedient, to the Independent Government, that nothing might endanger their pension. But Brockley had not been like that.

'I've got a devilish thirst,' he croaked. 'I'd be grateful if you'd pour me a glass of water.'

I got up and walked over to the table by the window. Inside it was quite dark now, but outside for once there was no cloud, and the garden was brilliantly illuminated by the tropical moon. I looked at the little square of grass he had tried to cultivate on that rocky ground, and the ramin seat like a park bench beside it.

The water was about blood heat. 'The ice has all melted,' I said. 'I'll get some more.'

'No, give it to me.' He took the glass in both hands and drank noisily. It welled out of the side of his mouth and dribbled down on to his pyjama jacket. When it was empty he put it down.

'I made a very great mistake. I knew they were savages. I tried to delude myself they could develop into something better. But I was wrong. They don't want to be any different. They were like naughty children you can't help loving because they are your own. But they grow older; and you grow more tired; and the time comes when you cannot be bothered any more. And you also realize that ... they didn't really need you at all. It was all an illusion....'

'Brockley, don't say these things!' He *had* loved his boys, and they had loved him. He could only have existed in the Interior, where nobody was interested in representative government, but just wanted to be left to get on with things as they always had; and he could only have been allowed to exist by a government that did not care what happened in the Interior as long as it did not get into the papers.

He stared at me, hot-eyed. His skin was as dry as a bone and his hands trembled, yellow against the white of the sheet. But his voice came calm and rational. 'They didn't need me. But there is someone who does.'

'Not—not Doreen?' I almost shouted.

'What is that poor girl's future now, Reed?'

'Well, she'll go back to England, of course.'

'Yes, of course she couldn't remain in the Colony after having given herself to a native. But even in England the scandal of it would follow her. It would be inescapable. No decent man would look at her.'

'Perhaps forty years ago, Brockley. But not now. Not now!'

But he was not listening. 'As you know, Reed, I am in my fifties and Doreen is only thirty—' I knew from his records at headquarters that he was sixty-three '—in other circumstances I would consider it an impertinence to offer my name and my protection to a girl such as she. But as things are ...'

'You can't mean that you're intending to—'

'I can give her the protection of my name and my honour, such as it is. I can protect her from the world and from herself.

215

I can give her some of the things she has been denied by her humble origins. I am not a poor man, Reed.'

'But ... what about Briok?' I blurted.

He was looking directly at me. The skin around his eyes tightened for a moment, then he said very calmly, 'Briok is dead.'

I thought he meant that Briok was dead to him, figuratively speaking, that he was no longer interested in him. But I knew that could not be. Before I could reply he said, 'He was killed by the Abang's soldiers.'

'But that's ridiculous! They've only been here about three hours.'

'Ahmed the policeman was here.'

'But he's a half-wit himself.'

'Briok was in the bazaar a couple of hours ago. He had his blowpipe to his mouth and he was pointing it at one of the soldiers. The soldier did not appreciate, of course, that Briok had no poison darts. He thought he was being attacked. He took out his gun and shot Briok dead.'

'But I don't believe that,' I cried. 'Who told you?'

'The policeman—Ahmed.'

'But he hasn't been here!'

Brockley nodded. 'He was here,' he said softly. 'People come very silently to see me and nobody knows. He was here while you were all on the verandah.'

'But I can't believe it.'

'He also told me who it was who had assaulted him.'

I held my breath.

'It was you, wasn't it, Reed?'

So it was true—only Ahmed could have told him that.

'Brockley, I am very ashamed—'

'No—please. I know how infuriating these people can be. Ahmed probably more than most.'

'It was inexcusable. I am terribly ashamed.'

'Not exactly inexcusable, Reed—but perhaps a mistake. It was a mistake to use violence because the whole mystique of the white man was that he did not use violence. If it were necessary

216

another native could always be employed to do it.'

His self-control was awful to see. He could not escape the habit of a lifetime: dressing up his deepest convictions with cynicism.

'So Briok is dead,' he went on. 'He was the only thing that might have held me here. But he's dead. Would it have been better to let him perish in the jungle near his own people than to bring him down here to die like a dog in the street?'

He was not asking me. He was really talking to himself. But I said, 'No! You gave him fourteen years of life. It was something.'

'One had so many notions, so many incompletely-thought-out ideas. I thought I understood them, you see, Reed. I thought I understood them. But I didn't understand them at all.'

Through the window a movement caught my eye. It was Doreen. She moved through the brilliant moonlight, across Brockley's pathetic little lawn, but not with her usual manly stride; now she seemed to drift rather than walk—across a carpet of silver. I saw her face quite clearly. It had the same look, almost beauty, as I had seen the very first evening at her quarters in Banianok when she had heard the klaxon of the Abang's Mercedes.

I must have started.

'What is it?' Brockley said.

'Nothing! I was just looking out at the garden. It's very brilliant tonight.'

At the far edge—about twenty yards from where I stood—she stopped, then the Abang grappled her into the shade of the ramin tree.

'You see, Reed, Doreen brought something into my life that I had not known for twenty-five years. I didn't intend to live alone all these years. It wasn't what I had intended at all.'

The Abang was tearing at Doreen's clothes, and she at his.

'I was never your solitary type of man. I was never a misogynist. Every man needs a woman's gentleness. But I'd forgotten. If it hadn't been for Doreen ... Doreen brought it all back to me after all these years.'

217

She stamped her sarong away from her. Her buttocks gleamed in the moonlight. The Abang's trousers were around his ankles. There was a sudden shriek as they crumpled to the ground. It was a shriek of pain, surprise, pleasure. It did not come from Doreen.

'What was that?' Brockley asked.

'What was what?'

'I thought I heard something.'

'I don't think so.'

He glanced vaguely in the direction of the window. Then he put his hands up to his neck to loosen an imaginary collar. 'It's so hot, isn't it? I'd be obliged if you'd pour me another glass of water, old fellow.' It was the first and only time he ever called me 'old fellow'.

When Doreen went in at eleven to settle him for the night he was dead. There was a little dark frothy blood on his pyjama jacket. Almost certainly a clot had been carried in the blood-stream from his gangrenous leg to his lung. Death would have been instantaneous.